THE EDGE OF PARADISE

Christmas Key Book Three

STEPHANIE TAYLOR

Stephanie Taylor

For Holland Elise:
Sweet potato,
Pumpkin pie,
Apple of her mother's eye.

"Why don't you tell me that 'if the girl had been worth having she'd have waited for you'? No, sir, the girl really worth having won't wait for anybody."

— —F. SCOTT FITZGERALD

DON'T MISS OUT ON NEW RELEASES...

Want to find out what happens next in the Christmas Key series? Love romance novels? Sign up for new release alerts from Stephanie Taylor so you don't miss a thing!

Sign me up!

CHAPTER 1

The ear-splitting sound of a cannon firing rocks the building. Holly reaches out and grabs the cup full of pens and pencils next to her laptop so that it won't rattle and fall off the edge of her desk.

"Oooh, that man better give his heart to Jesus, because his butt belongs to me!" Bonnie Lane says hotly, standing up on her side of the white wicker desk that she shares with her boss. "I'm about to go down there and give him a piece of my mind."

Holly lets go of the cup and resumes her typing. "Won't do any good, Bon," she says. "They warned us in advance that the cannon firing was part of the package."

Bonnie splutters and huffs, then tugs at the hem of her shirt a few times before she sits down again.

"We've gone above and beyond here, sugar. Can't we demand a little peace and quiet in the evening? It doesn't seem unreasonable." Bonnie pats her bright red hair.

"It's just for a couple more days," Holly says soothingly. She hits 'send' on the email she's been typing and closes her laptop. "Listen, the sun is setting and we've put in a full day. Why don't we wrap it up here and head to the Ho Ho?"

"I suppose a drink might calm my nerves."

The women shut down their computers and lock up the back office of the Christmas Key B&B for the day, stopping by the front counter on the way out. Holly normally forwards the phone to her cell for the evening, but because the B&B is busting at the seams with a group of men dressed as pirates, she's temporarily hired on several of the locals to make sure the inn is fully staffed and running day and night.

"Pirate coin?" Maggie Sutter offers Holly and Bonnie from behind the front desk. She holds up a bowl of Oreos that have been sprayed a shiny gold with edible food spray.

"These are really cute, Maggie." Holly picks up an Oreo and examines it.

"We have grog, too," Maggie says, pointing at a jug and a stack of mugs at the other end of the desk. "It's really just apple cider," she says in a stage whisper, one hand covering her mouth like she's giving away top-secret information.

Holly bites into the cookie. "This is actually good," she says. "Where did you come up with this idea?"

"Pinterest," Maggie shrugs. "Not much else for a body to do when she's retired and likes to sleep all day and stay up all night."

"I can think of a few other things to do with a body that's up all night," Bonnie interjects, popping a hip as she examines her make-up in the mirror behind the front desk.

"Yeah, yeah, yeah," Holly says, finishing her cookie and brushing the gold flecks from the front of her shirt. "Let's get you over to the Ho Ho and see if we can't find a pirate for you, you old wench."

"Now, I don't mind the wench part," Bonnie objects as she follows Holly out the front door. "But I'm not a big fan of this 'old' business."

Holly rolls her eyes and waves at Maggie as she pulls the door shut. The porch lights on the front of the B&B have been switched out for special light bulbs that flicker like candles, and their orange-yellow glow is partially obscured by the black netting that Holly's draped over the fixtures. She's put an incredible amount of work into turning Christmas Key into a pirate's paradise, and the special touches that her neighbors have added—like the gold Oreos made to look like coins —please her.

"The only pirate I'm looking for tonight is that dadgum Sinker McBludgeon—"

"Whose real name is probably Bob Kent or something. I bet he's an insurance agent who golfs on the weekends and likes to dress up as a pirate once a month," Holly adds, walking next to Bonnie on the sidewalk.

"Exactly. And when I find old Sinker at the Ho Ho, drinking his rum and telling everyone what a good cannon-shooter-person-guy he is," Bonnie says, getting amped up as she talks, "I'm going to give him a piece of my mind."

"As you should," Holly says indulgently, climbing in behind the steering wheel of her hot pink golf cart.

For the pirates' weekend, Holly has taken down the tinsel and lights that she keeps up on her cart almost year-round, instead decorating her ride with more of the black netting that she used on the B&B's porch lights. She's set up a few flickering electric candles on her dashboard that can be turned on with the flip of a switch, and strapped two fake swords to the back of her cart, crossing the plastic blades so they point down because she read online that pointing them up means she's ready for a fight. And inviting a brawl with Sinker McBludgeon or any of the other weekend pirates is not something she's keen on doing.

It's just before six o'clock and the sun is making its final descent as the women pull away from the curb on Main Street and drive west to the beach. Holly turns on her cart's headlamps and bounces off of Main and onto the unpaved, hard-packed road of Cinnamon Lane. It's the street that leads to her house. Just beyond the plot of land her grandparents had built their family homes on is the stretch of sand where the Ho Ho Hideaway—one of the island's two watering holes— stands under the palm trees.

"Do you think Jake and Bridget will be there?" Bonnie asks casually, looking into the blackened depths of the thick trees around them as they rumble over Cinnamon Lane.

Holly blows out a puff of breath. "Probably," she says. "I feel like they're everywhere."

Jake—Holly's ex-boyfriend and Christmas Key's only police officer —has been squiring his new love interest around the island like his life depends on it. It's been a confusing six months for Holly, with the arrival of River O'Leary, a former pro-baseball player from Oregon with whom she'd had a well-intentioned fling, to the reality show that filmed on the island at the end of the year.

Bridget had been one of the contestants on the show, and when the producers roped Jake into participating, the attraction between him and Bridget had bloomed. By Christmas, the show was over but Jake had asked Bridget to stay on the island with him. Had things worked out between Holly and River, she probably would be happier for them, but instead her feelings for Jake have grown more complicated.

"Let's just ignore them, sugar. Besides, we have Sinker to deal with, and from what I've gathered so far, that's going to be a two woman project."

Holly pulls into the sandy lot behind the Ho Ho Hideaway. Joe Sacamano—the bar's owner and a former traveling guitarist for some of the world's biggest rock bands—agreed to let Holly decorate the open-air shack, and she's gone a little crazy with it. As she and Bonnie walk up to the bar, she admires the fake guillotine that she asked her uncle to make from wood scraps, and she stops to examine the scarecrow from Halloween that Bonnie has repurposed and dressed like a pirate, his head and hands dangling from the wooden holes of the guillotine. Bonnie's covered his straw hair with a red bandana and tied a patch over one button eye, and she's dressed him in a striped boat shirt and knee-length black pants.

"This looks great, Bon," Holly says, touching the dry straw fingers of the scarecrow.

"Eh. I made do. It's not the *Pirates of the Caribbean* ride at Disney World or anything, but he looks alright." Bonnie walks past the scarecrow and up the stairs, her shoulders squared for battle. She parts the black netting that covers what is normally an open doorway and steps into the bar. "Now where is that donkey's behind?" she demands, hands on both hips. Holly is right on her heels.

Inside, the bar looks like a pirate's den of iniquity. Joe Sacamano has set his empty rum-making barrels around the bar, and Holly brought clusters of flickering electric candles to set on the barrels and the bistro tables. A giant ship's steering wheel hangs behind the bar with a skull at the center of it and bones acting as its spokes. Around the edge of the wheel the words 'Dead Men Tell No Tales' has been carved artlessly into the wood. Joe is moving around behind the bar, pouring shots and mixing drinks. He lifts his chin at Bonnie and Holly and keeps working.

"There he is," Bonnie says, homing in on her target. She pushes her way through the bar, bumping into swashbuckling faux pirates as she goes. "Excuse me," she huffs, pushing a man in a tattered black overcoat. He looks down at her from his considerable height with amusement in his eyes, holding his drink in one hand. His fingerless gloves reveal thick digits with moons of dirt under each nail, and his salt and pepper hair curls out from under a rakishly tied bandana.

"Oh, ho, ho," he chortles, taking in Bonnie's heaving chest. She's clearly gaining momentum, ready to dress him down in front of his group of pirate friends, but Holly can see that he's not going to give her the chance. "Ye shout into the wind that a wench is just what ye need, and the wind blows one in on the waves," he says, putting his highball glass to his cracked lips. "And a luscious wench she is," he adds with a glimmer in his eye as he looks Bonnie up and down.

"You know, the pirate talk is cute, but a little bit goes a very long way," Holly says to him. She puts a hand on Bonnie's back to show her support—and to remind her friend gently that punching a guest would be wrong. In response, Bonnie releases the deep breath she's been holding.

"Well, Jack Sparrow," Bonnie says, "this 'luscious wench' rode in on a wave to tell you that the cannon nonsense stops here. I did not agree to have a group of unwashed, middle-aged doctors and lawyers show up here on my island to mess with my zen."

Holly takes a step closer to Bonnie and wraps a hand around her elbow. She knows Bonnie well enough to know that she can get a little hot under the hood, and Holly isn't ready to watch her overheat in front of their guests.

"Cool your jets there, Red," Sinker McBludgeon says with a wicked smile. "I've got a thing for fiery women, so I won't make you walk the plank tonight." He clinks glasses with his laughing friends.

From across the bar, Wyatt Bender is watching this exchange carefully. He and Bonnie have a long-running history of antagonization and flirtation that lasts the extent of his annual October-April stay on Christmas Key, and at the heart of it is Wyatt's quiet longing for the feisty widow from Georgia. Holly keeps an eye on Wyatt's face as Sinker McBludgeon moves closer to Bonnie.

"Maybe we should give you a new name—after all, a pirate's wench needs a name." Holly prepares to grab Bonnie and pull her from the bar before she can take a swing at Sinker. "How about Bubbles Anchorbottom? Because I wouldn't mind dropping my anchor on *that* bottom!" The other pirates howl with laughter.

In an instant, Wyatt is across the bar and standing between Bonnie and Sinker. "Apologize to the lady," he says, his face set in a scowl.

"Who'll make me?" Sinker sneers at him. "A scrawny dude in a cowboy hat and Wranglers? I don't think so." Without a lick of concern, Sinker turns his back on Holly, Bonnie, and Wyatt, and steers his group of friends over to the beach side of the bar.

"These pirates aren't gentlemen," Wyatt observes, staring at their backs as they go. "But they're our guests on the island, so I'll behave myself—for now." Wyatt puts both hands in the air in surrender before backing away from the women.

"I don't know what to say." Holly watches the men reassemble near the stairs leading down to the sand. She turns to Bonnie, whose eyes are lingering on the sword that hangs from Sinker McBludgeon's belt. "Bon?" Holly snaps her fingers to break Bonnie's trance. "Hey—you in there?"

"Hmm?" Bonnie says, still watching the pirates. "Yeah, sugar. I'm here."

But she isn't. It's subtle, but Bonnie's attention has clearly shifted, and the banter she normally shares with Wyatt has been cranked up a notch and redirected towards Sinker. Holly can already tell that this isn't going to end well.

CHAPTER 2

"I'm confused," Holly says over the loud spray from the sink. She's leaning back in a chair at Scissors & Ribbons on Main Street the next morning while Millie Bradford rinses the shampoo out of her hair. Across the room, Bonnie is sitting under a dryer with an open magazine in her lap.

"What's to be confused about, sugar?" Bonnie flips a page. She and Holly have both scheduled Saturday morning appointments at the salon, and Holly is trying to understand how a man like Sinker McBludgeon could possibly hold Bonnie's interest.

"You went over to the Ho Ho with guns blazing, and you left with your tail between your legs. How could you even be attracted to a man who talks to you like that?" Holly closes her eyes as Millie works a thick conditioner through her long, chestnut hair.

"It's all part of the dance, doll—it's an act. Kind of like those married people who dress up and go to bars and pretend to be strangers so they can pick each other up and go home together."

"Um, role-playing?" Holly sits up, holding the towel around her shoulders to keep her wet hair from dripping onto her shirt. "Are you sure Sinker isn't just an *actual* jerk?"

Bonnie shrugs. "I don't know. But my hunch is that it's an act. It's all part of the pirates and wenches bit." She closes the magazine and tosses it onto the empty chair next to hers.

"But if all you want is some verbal sparring that barely conceals an unbridled desire to be naked with the other person, why don't you just break down and go out with Wyatt?"

"Wyatt Bender?" Bonnie guffaws. "Oh, lordy, girl. I've known Wyatt Bender *way* too long. There's no way I want to see that wrinkled old cowboy out of his Wranglers."

"Hmm." Holly purses her lips. She doesn't believe this for a second, but she plays along with Bonnie anyway.

"I need a change, sugar." Bonnie leans forward in her chair, talking loudly over the whir of the hair dryer. "I need a dark, sexy stranger with an unknowable heart. I need a hunk of a man with carnal desires who'll rip the laces out of my bustier and ravage me." She picks up the magazine again and starts to fan her face as she talks. "I think I need a *pirate.*"

"You need a cold shower, honey," Millie Bradford says sensibly. She points Holly to the chair next to Bonnie's and sets her under a dryer. "I'm going to put you under this with the conditioner still on your hair," she explains to Holly. "It's a leave-in that will soften this hair after all of your salt water swimming, and then I want to give you a trim."

"Sounds good," Holly says as Millie lowers the dryer over her head. She turns to Bonnie. "I honestly believe these guys are just weekend pirates—IRS employees with a swashbuckling fetish—but I still want you to be careful, okay? Promise me?"

"I promise, *Mom,*" Bonnie says in a sing-song voice, holding up one hand like she's being sworn in on the stand. "But nothing dangerous ever happens on Christmas Key. I'm ready for a little rough and tumble romance. I'm ready for some *excitement.*"

Holly peeks out from under the hood of the dryer. "Hey, Millie, how's the search for a masseuse going?"

"Not bad." Millie erases something from the planner on her front desk. "I've got a gal from Canada coming out here for an interview in a couple of days. Said she wants to bring her family and check out the island."

"Would she be full-time, or just seasonal?" Holly asks.

"Full-time. She says they're ready to leave the snowy winters behind."

"We haven't had any new full-time residents in a while," Bonnie says. "That would really shake things up."

"I wouldn't say we haven't had *any* new residents," Millie says, cutting an almost imperceptible glance in Holly's direction.

"Right. Bridget." Bonnie nods, holding one red-tipped finger in the air. "But we have yet to see whether she's going to be permanent or not."

Holly shifts around under the dryer.

"She comes in here once a week to get her nails done," Millie says, putting her pencil back in a cup next to the register. "Talks a lot about how much she loves it here. She says the people remind her of home. Not of L.A., but of some small town where she grew up."

"So she's staying?" Bonnie asks.

"For the time being, I think." Millie steps out from behind the desk and comes to check on Holly's hair. "Looks like we can comb this out and shape up those split ends a little bit, Mayor." She switches off the dryer and lifts it from Holly's head. "For what it's worth," Millie says gently, looking down at Holly in the chair, "I always thought you and Jake made a cute couple."

Holly smiles weakly. Loyalty runs deep on Christmas Key, and she's grateful every day for the friendship and support from the other islanders. It's not her intention to see them tiptoe around her when it comes to Jake and Bridget, and it's certainly not her desire to see people be unwelcoming to Bridget. But even though Bridget's been on the island for a full month, Holly has done her best to avoid running into her on Main Street, and she's gone out of her way to steer clear of the Ho Ho or the Jingle Bell Bistro when she hears through the grapevine that Jake and Bridget are there together.

"She and Old Slugger made a pretty cute couple, too," Bonnie says, referring to River O'Leary, the former pro baseball player who'd visited Christmas Key the previous summer and swept Holly off her feet. "But our girl here obviously hasn't found what she's looking for yet." Bonnie pauses. "Hey, sugar, what do you think about a fling with a pirate? They aren't all crusty old men of the sea, you know—I saw a couple of young ones without wedding rings." Bonnie examines her manicure.

"No, thank you. I'll leave the buccaneers in breeches to you, Bon. I'd rather stay single for the time being and focus on work."

"That a girl," says Millie, squeezing Holly's shoulder as she guides her into the stylist's chair. "You work on you for a while, and the man situation will sort itself out."

"I think you've gotta have a man to have a 'man situation,'" Bonnie cautions. "I just don't want to see this beautiful young thing miss the boat, so to speak."

"She won't miss the boat, Bonnie," Millie says. "This girl has a face that could launch a thousand ships." Mill spins the chair around so that Holly is facing the mirror.

"Thanks, Millie." Holly pats the hand that Millie still has resting on her shoulder. "I appreciate that."

Millie pulls a comb and a pair of scissors out of her drawer. "Now how about some bangs to frame that pretty face?"

By one o'clock, Holly has eight different messages on her phone.

"Holly? Are you there, or is this a machine? Why don't people pick up their telephones anymore? This is Maria Agnelli. I damn near broke my ankle this morning on White Christmas Way. I stepped in a giant hole on my way to Pinecone Path, and I'd probably still be lying there if Iris hadn't come along and picked me up. Now I've got to see Dr. Potts about this ankle and probably be on crutches for—" Holly listens to the rest of the message and then presses the button for the next one.

"Mayor. It's Cap. Couldn't find you in your office this morning and no one seems to know what the hell is going on with these blasted holes. Come by the cigar shop, will you?"

"Hi, honey, it's Glen," says a sweet voice on the next message. All three of the triplets—Glen, Gwen, and Gen—look and sound the same, so it honestly could have been any one of the three of them speaking and Holly wouldn't have known the difference. "I'm very concerned about the holes all over this island. I've had four different people stop by the gift shop this morning to complain. Do you think we should call an emergency village council meeting?"

Holly saves the messages she's heard and puts her phone back in her purse. She's pulled into the parking lot behind the B&B, and her plan all along has been to spend the afternoon spray painting a bunch of wooden prop boxes with stencils so that they say "rum" and "whiskey" on their sides. She's also been wrapping blue glass jars with netting and filling each one with sand and a votive candle. With luck, her decorations will look pirate-y enough for the dinner she's planning for their guests that night on the beach. But now she's got mysterious holes to deal with, and a potential village council meeting to call.

With a glance in both directions, Holly holds her purse between her elbow and her body and jogs across Main Street. Cap's cigar shop is kitty corner to her B&B, and she can see him through the front window as he bends over his front counter to read the newspaper. Marco, Cap's parrot, is propped on his shoulder, chattering into his ear.

"Well, isn't this a surprise," Cap says expansively, standing up as Holly enters the shop and sets the bells on his door chiming.

"It shouldn't be too much of a surprise," she says. "You did call and tell me to come by."

"But my days of getting beautiful women to come when I call have long passed, Mayor. So I'm always pleasantly surprised when it works."

Holly would love to banter with Cap more—particularly after the recent battle they'd waged over her mayoral seat and the hiccup it had created in their relationship—but she's out of breath and running out of time. She glances at the tank watch on her wrist.

"Tell me about the holes. I went to get a haircut this morning and then to run a few errands, and suddenly I have eight messages on my phone about Mrs. Agnelli falling into a ditch and nearly dying, and about the whole town converging on Tinsel & Tidings Gifts to lodge formal complaints. I'm trying to figure out what's going on."

"If I knew, I'd tell you." Cap spreads his arms wide and shakes his head. In response, Marco shakes his own small head back and forth, imitating his master.

Holly sighs and runs a hand through her freshly cut hair. "Can you just tell me where these holes are, and then I can go investigate?"

"There's one on the way to Pinecone Path; one on Ivy Lane; and another up near your place."

"By my house?" Holly frowns.

"Apparently. Jake was driving out that way and says he drove his cart right into it. He was looking for you, too. But you probably knew that, since one of those messages had to be from him."

"Right. Yeah." Holly thinks for a moment. "Thanks, Cap. Will I see you on the beach tonight?"

"Wouldn't miss it. The gents have been by to put in their orders, and I always aim to please my customers. I'll be handing out cigars after dinner is done."

"Great," Holly says, patting the door frame as she steps back out onto Main Street. She pulls her phone out of her purse and goes back to her voicemail. Sure enough, after Glen's message is one from Jake: "Hey, stranger." She has an immediate physical response to the voice of her ex-boyfriend and her cheeks get hot. "There's something going on around here that we need to talk about. Unless we have a sudden infestation of prairie dogs, then I think we have a mystery on our hands. Call me."

Holly is about to dial Jake's number when he pulls up next to her in his golf cart. "What, you don't call people back anymore?" he teases, slowing to a crawl so that he's keeping pace with her.

"I was listening to your message right now. But Cap already filled me in."

"Let's take a run around the island and have a look at these weird crop circles," Jake suggests, patting the seat next to him. "Hop in."

"Crop circles?" Holly uses the running board on the passenger side of his cart to step up. She sits next to him and puts her purse on the floor of the cart between her feet. "I thought we were talking about a few small holes."

"Yeah, that's all it is. I'm just trying to imagine that it's something more interesting, like aliens."

"Prairie dogs on an island with no prairies wouldn't be interesting enough?"

"Hell, it'd be interesting enough for me if Ray Bradford was trying to move around the bottle of whiskey he likes to hide outside his house," Jake says.

"Ray hides his hooch outside?"

"Yeah. He doesn't want Millie to find it." Jake turns the wheel and takes Holly up Ivy Lane to check out the first hole.

"But Millie doesn't care if he drinks," Holly argues, confused. "They're always at the Ho Ho or at Jack Frosty's for cocktail hour."

"Right, but it's more *fun* for him if he's doing something she doesn't know about. You see?" Jake parks the cart.

"I guess," Holly says. "Is that all marriage is? Doing dumb stuff when the other person isn't looking so you can feel like a rebel?"

"Apparently."

"Then maybe we dodged a bullet, huh?" Holly leaves her purse in the golf cart and follows Jake. She regrets the crack about dodging a bullet as soon as it leaves her lips.

"Maybe," Jake agrees, hands on both hips as he stands in front of the first hole. It's about three feet deep and three feet wide, and they look down into the empty pit in the sand with no clue as to why or how it got there.

"Pucci is the biggest dog on this island," Holly says, referring to her beloved golden retriever. "But he doesn't roam the island without me, and he's never been much of a digger."

"Do donkeys dig holes?" Jake asks with a smirk. Just a few months earlier, Carrie-Anne and Ellen—the proprietors of Mistletoe Morning Brew on Main Street—had adopted a female donkey and brought her to Christmas Key.

"It seems kind of unlikely that she could escape her pen and wreak this kind of havoc all over the island." Holly pushes her sunglasses up on top of her head and looks up and down Ivy Lane. All quiet. "I doubt anyone saw anything unusual."

"If they had, we'd have heard about it by now," Jake points out.

"Can you take me to the other holes?"

Jake drives Holly around so she can inspect the damage, and then he drops her off in front of the B&B.

"So what's the verdict, boss?" he asks, resting his left wrist on top of the steering wheel while he waits.

"It's strange," Holly decides. "I don't know what to think, but I have a few things I've got to get done for the dinner party we're throwing on the beach tonight. Will you be there?"

"Ay, ay, matey. I'll be there." Jake leans back in his seat, ready to pull away.

"And you'll call me if you hear about any more holes?"

"I will," he promises.

Holly watches Main Street for clues as Jake drives off, but nothing seems out of the ordinary. Ray Bradford isn't wobbling down the sidewalk, secret bottle of whiskey in hand as he tries to find a new hiding spot for his booze. Nobody drives by with a shovel sticking out the back of their cart, and no family of prairie dogs ambles past.

It truly is a mystery, but one that'll have to wait for later, because right now she's got jars to fill with sand, and wooden boxes to stencil. Holly grabs a handful of gold-sprayed Oreos on her way past the front desk, cramming one into her mouth as she heads back to her office.

CHAPTER 3

I ris Cafferkey calls while Holly is finishing the decorations for the beach party. She's on her knees in the B&B's sandy parking lot, spraying the last stencil onto a box when her phone buzzes from the seat of her golf cart. In one swift move, she stands and grabs the phone, using her paint-covered fingers to tap the screen.

"Iris?"

"Hi, love. Sorry to bother you—I know you're always busy," Iris apologizes in her Irish-tinged lilt.

"No, it's fine." Holly looks back at the stack of boxes she's painted and then down at her filthy hands and knees. "What's up?"

"I was wondering what you thought of naked men, lass," Iris says without preamble.

Holly doesn't miss a beat. "I'm pretty fond of them under the right circumstances. And you?"

"Oh, much the same. Much the same." Iris laughs at the other end of the line. "Glad we can agree on that one. But I certainly don't think a midday walk with my sweet, innocent Emily is the time or the place for naked men," Iris says, referring to her daughter, who is Holly's oldest friend, and—as Iris has said—the sweetest, most innocent person on the island. "We went for a stroll on the beach and happened upon a group of naked, grubby pirates frolicking down at Snowflake Banks."

Holly wrinkles her nose. "Naked?"

"As they day they were born," Iris confirms.

"That's not sexy." Holly shakes her head, thinking of the middle-aged men with ungroomed beards, their bellies distended by grog. "I'm afraid to ask, but what were they doing?"

"Sunning themselves like lizards on a log."

Holly gags at the image.

"Wee lizards, some of them," Iris adds. "Just helpless little lizards flopping about in the sun—"

"Okay, okay," Holly cuts her off. "Got it. I'll go over there, and...I don't know what. Ask them to put their breeches back on?"

"Maybe make sure their lizards aren't shriveling up in the hot sun?" Iris offers with a cackle.

"I'll see you tonight, Iris. Thanks for letting me know." Holly pauses. "I think."

She hangs up and tosses her phone back onto the bench seat of her golf cart. Naked pirates. This was *not* part of her plan for the day.

"GENTLEMEN!" HOLLY CALLS OUT, STOPPING HER CART. SHE SETS the brake and steps onto the sand. "There's a lady present!"

"Can't say I see one," Sinker McBludgeon yells back, making no move to cover up. "Just a brassy girl who likes to play mayor."

Holly resists the urge steal Sinker's clothes and drive away with them. "We aren't zoned for a nude beach anywhere on Christmas Key," she says with force, grateful for the impenetrable lenses of her polar blue sunglasses. "You'll have to put your pirate's jewels back in their pouches if you want to stay at Snowflake Banks."

"But this is a private island," Sinker argues. He stands up and faces Holly. She tries not to flinch as she gets the full view of his unadorned frame.

"It isn't, though. We're a municipality—a part of Monroe County—

and we're governed by laws and rules just like every other part of Florida."

"So get that cop out here to write us some tickets," another pirate pipes up, cracking open a can of beer and letting the froth overflow onto the sand, "or take off your dress and join us." The other pirates whoop and cheer appreciatively. Holly's face goes up in flames.

"I'll do no such thing," she says, lifting her chin. "And I'm going to ask you one more time to cover yourselves."

The men don't move. Some are sprawled in the sand, others stand around with cold beers in hand. Most have their backs turned to Holly, and she tries to avoid looking at the variety of middle-aged male bottoms that stare back at her. She swallows hard, thinking of the way they'd behaved at the Ho Ho Hideaway the night before.

"Aw, we're just having some fun with you, Mayor," one of the guys says. "We've probably gotten enough sun today anyway." As if this decides it, the men begin assembling their clothes, most stepping into pants without putting anything on underneath them. "Don't want to go home to our wives and have to explain why we're red below the waist."

The other men laugh. "That'd end our days on the sea for sure," chortles a short, balding pirate.

Holly nods, taking a few steps backward. She's done her job here, and been completely traumatized in the process.

"Thank you." She gives a curt nod. "See you all at the barbecue on the beach in a few hours."

"You'll see a little less of us than you have just now, but we'll be there. Oh, and make sure you tell my favorite redheaded wench that I'm expecting to see her tonight!" shouts Sinker McBludgeon.

Holly grits her teeth and holds up a hand as she puts her cart in gear, pretending not to hear him.

DINNER IS A HUGE HIT. THE KITCHEN CREW HAS WORKED tirelessly at the B&B all afternoon to put together a pirate-worthy meal of giant turkey legs, greasy onion rings, and corn on the cob, and

Leo Buckhunter has dragged huge barrels full of ice out to the beach and filled them with bottled beer. As promised, Cap is there with his cigars, handing them out around the campfire as the sun dips below the horizon on the water.

"You look devilishly good tonight," Sinker McBludgeon growls, closing in on Bonnie. She's standing next to Holly behind the wooden picnic table that serves as their buffet. The women have just gathered the paper plates and plastic utensils from the drunken pirates, and Holly is sweating after filling the giant garbage bags—one with glass bottles, the other with trash. She wipes her forehead and readjusts the red bandana that's tied around her head.

"I don't know that I take too kindly to unwashed men getting in my personal space," Bonnie shoots back, tilting her chin up at Sinker defiantly. "But thank you anyway."

"But we did wash, milady," Sinker says with a twinkle in his eye. "Or didn't the mayor tell you how she caught us in our natural state this afternoon, sunning our loins and bathing in God's bathtub?"

Bonnie turns to look at Holly, eyebrows arched. "No, she neglected to mention that."

"Tryin' to keep that little gem all to herself, I see," Sinker says, moving in closer to Bonnie.

Bonnie does look good, Holly thinks, admiring her friend's makeshift costume. She's wearing a square-necked white blouse with cap sleeves, and an ankle-length black skirt with a scarf tied around her waist. Under the skirt she's sporting black lace-up boots, and Holly has loaned her a pair of hoop earrings that make her look kind of like a saucy gypsy.

In between getting the props and decorations set up on the beach, Holly had raced home to change into something that she hoped fit the mood, tying the red bandana around her hair and slipping on a pair of tight black pants and black knee-high boots. For a top, she's settled on a loose-sleeved cream blouse with puffy shoulders that's belted with a piece of rope. As usual, the other islanders have gone all out, and there are men with eye patches and women in flowing skirts and bangle bracelets. Everyone looks amazing.

Holly takes a few steps away from Bonnie and Sinker as they

banter. She might find the pirate's demeanor abrasive, but Bonnie is a big girl. Besides, Holly knows that nothing can stop the freight train that is Bonnie Lane when she has her sights set on a man.

"Holly!" Holly turns to see Bridget coming her direction. She's wearing a white lace wrap dress with jagged edges on the hem and the cuffs, and she has on white ankle boots to match. The look is more 80s-era Madonna than pirate, but Holly mentally grants her an A for effort.

"Hi, Bridget." Holly's stomach sinks. The unresolved feelings she has about her ex swirl in the pit of her stomach like battery acid and motor oil, feeling just as heavy and corrosive as she plasters a smile on her face and greets Jake's new girlfriend.

"Great party. It feels like Halloween!" Bridget is holding a bottle of beer in one hand.

"Shh, don't let the pirates hear you calling their outfits 'costumes'— they get very touchy about that. I found out the hard way."

Bridget's face goes serious, her mouth forming a delicate O. "Really?"

"Yeah. That one over there offered to 'love me so hard I'd wake up with scurvy.'" Holly nods at one of the pirates.

"Gross," Bridget whispers softly, eyeing the group of men that have to look—to her—like a bunch of grandfatherly docents at a pirate museum. "Thank God I have Jake. I'm sure he won't let any of them give me a disease." Her expertly made-up eyes widen comically. "Omigod, wait, I hugged one of the pirates on Main Street yesterday— do you think he already gave me scurvy?"

The huge bonfire crackles loudly behind Bridget, sending up sparks into the night sky. Holly looks over to see Jake tossing logs onto the flames. "If your teeth start falling out or you wake up with a rash, go see Dr. Potts," Holly says sagely, patting Bridget on the lacy shoulder of her dress.

"Okay, I will." Bridget nods, holding her beer in front of her chest.

There's a simplicity to Bridget that throws Holly off: on the one hand, she has a look of naïveté in her eyes that is completely disarming, and on the other, there's a calculating flash that appears every so often when it seems like no one but Holly is watching. It's been hard for Holly to separate her feelings about Jake from her feelings about Bridget as a person.

"You might want to check on your girlfriend," Holly says to Jake as she steps through the loose sand, grains of the powder sticking to her black suede boots. "She's worried she might be catching an eighteenth century seafarer's disease from all these salesmen with plastic swords."

Jake frowns at her. "Huh?"

"Never mind. Any new holes pop up that I should know about?" Holly stops next to the bonfire to watch as Jake rearranges the burning logs with a long stick. "I'm kind of worried that one of the islanders is going crazy and trying to dig their way to China. If anyone is frothing at the mouth, then I think we might have a culprit," she jokes, pretending to eye everyone warily. Jake pokes the fire, not taking the bait.

"No new holes," he says.

"What's eating you?" Holly takes a step closer, hoping he'll confide in her.

"Nothing. I'm good." Jake jams the long stick he's using on the fire into the sand. "Everything is *bueno*," he says unconvincingly.

"Okay, if you're sure..."

"I am." He gives her a tight smile. "I'll let you know if I hear anything else about the holes." Holly stands there, completely puzzled, as Jake leaves her to go and stand with Bridget. The fire crackles loudly again, and she jumps a little.

Off shore—way past the banks of Candy Cane Beach, where the dinner party is taking place—Holly can see the masts and sails of the pirate ship that their guests have anchored out in deeper water. She wanders to the edge of the shore to look at the ship. It's massive against the blue of the night sky, and the off-white canvas of the mainsail stands proud under the moon. The Coast Guard has granted special permission for the boat to stay anchored there for four days, and Cap had run back and forth in his much smaller boat to retrieve the pirates and bring them to shore when they'd arrived.

The moon is nearly full, and it hangs over the calm waters, sending glitter skittering across the waves. The whole scene looks like the cover of a pirate's adventure novel. Holly watches the wooden hull of the ship with its darkened portholes. Way up high, she spies the crow's nest of the ship, tethered in place with lines for support. A long rope ladder runs from the nest to the deck of the boat, and Holly can see clearly from shore that a man has climbed the ladder and is observing everything from a perch in the nest.

She squints into the distance, trying to make out which of the pirates is on the boat, but all she can see is the flicker of moonlight against the gold telescope he's got trained on the island. It's unsettling, the feeling of being watched from afar, and a shiver runs up Holly's spine. She folds her arms over her chest and takes two steps back.

There are moments like this one that somehow deflate her overall dream just a little; things that remind her that they are, in fact, inviting complete strangers to their island by hosting fishing excursions and pirate weekends, but it's a necessary risk if Holly has any hope of making her island a real tourist destination and of creating a self-sustaining economy.

Holly keeps her eyes on the ship as she walks away from the shoreline, heading back to the knot of people laughing near the fire.

CHAPTER 4

The island is quiet the next morning. Holly brews a fragrant pot of coffee in her kitchen, watching the breeze play with the trees outside her window. It was unsettling seeing a person watching them from way off shore the night before, but she'd felt the dark moment leave her as soon as she'd gone back to the bonfire and been pulled into Bonnie and Sinker's banter. By the time Joe Sacamano pulled out his acoustic guitar and started strumming every jaunty song and pirate ditty he could think of, Holly had loosened up considerably and was making the rounds and chatting with everyone.

The electric kettle whistles on the cool, marble counter top, and Holly walks across the room in her slippers to pour the boiling water into the French press. With the coffee steeping, she moves out to the front porch. Pucci follows at her heels.

It's a crisp winter morning and she hugs her sweatshirt around her body, peering at her uncle's house across the grass. Leo Buckhunter has turned out to be an amazing uncle and friend in the six months that they've known about their blood relation. Holly smiles at the closed curtains of his bungalow; if he isn't up yet, it probably means that

Holly's best friend, Dr. Fiona Potts, has spent the night at Buckhunter's.

She was amused when Fiona had nurtured a crush on the rangy, somewhat mysterious man who'd turned out to be her mother's halfbrother, but it makes Holly happy to know that a) her best friend has found someone to make her happy, and b) the man living next door on what she'd always thought of as "family property" actually has the right to do so.

Holly blows out a puff of breath and watches to see if it will form a cloud in front of her. It doesn't. This is the only time of year where things occasionally get chilly on the island, but it's entirely relative: when the normal temperature hovers in the upper seventies and skyrockets into the nineties, a 50-degree morning feels stark and wintry in comparison.

"Should we go for a walk after I pour my coffee?" Holly asks Pucci, looking down into his brown eyes. She knows the answer to that question is always *yes,* so she puts her Yankees cap on top of her unbrushed hair, trades her slippers for the beat-up Converse on the front porch, and pours her coffee and some half-and-half into a travel mug. "Let's go, Pooch," she says to him, leading the way down the front steps in a pair of gray sweats that she's chopped off above the ankle.

The forested side of the island always feels like the safest place on earth to Holly. When Frank and Jeanie Baxter bought Christmas Key in the 80s and decided to move there permanently, they'd spent a small fortune running utilities to the island and making it livable. Holly's entire childhood was centered around the development of the island, and the years of her life are marked in her mind not by ink marks on a doorjamb, but by which islanders moved to Christmas Key or which business opened the year she turned seven, or ten, or thirteen. By the time Frank and Jeanie both passed away, Holly was back from college and ready to take on the running of the island. In fact, she was more than ready: Frank had been grooming her for the task for years, and the knowledge he'd imparted, combined with her deep love of the island, are what makes her a passionate and devoted mayor.

Holly sips her coffee now, ambling down Cinnamon Lane with Pucci by her side. The rising sun is behind them to the east, and its rays poke fingers through the thick trees, splintering the shadows with light. Holly can already hear the rush of the waves racing to shore, only to break and retreat again. Pucci takes off at a slow jog as they near the sand, but Holly keeps walking, holding her mug in front of her chest. She smiles at her dog's enthusiasm.

Pucci stops just beyond the tree line, his hind end in the air as he sniffs inside the branches of a low bush. The smile fades from Holly's face as she gets closer; a pair of battered leather boots are sticking out into the sandy path.

"Hello?" she calls out. No response. "Good morning!" Nothing.

Pucci backs up from the unmoving body, planting himself in front of his mistress. He assumes a protective stance, though an aging golden retriever isn't the most intimidating creature.

Finally, a loud groan and an unintelligible string of words come from somewhere inside the bushes. "Who's out there?" the man grumbles.

"It's Holly Baxter. I run the B&B and I'm the mayor of the island." She sets her coffee mug on the sand, twisting it to wedge the bottom of the cup in place. "Here, let me help you." Holly puts her hands on the ankles of the man's thick boots, pulling firmly as he pushes his body out with both hands. When he finally emerges, red-faced and bleary-eyed, he scowls up at her.

"And you are?" Holly asks, ignoring the look on his face.

"Brian Bedowski." He pushes himself to his knees and waves away the hand of assistance that Holly offers. With some effort, he gets to his feet. "I own a State Farm agency in Pensacola."

"Ah, Brian Bedowski," Holly says. "Not Mad Jack Barnacle? Or Captain Patch O'Malley?"

"Nope," he says sheepishly. "Just Brian Bedowski. Of the Cleveland Bedowskis."

"Of course. The Cleveland Bedowskis. The most well-known branch of the tree, I assume?" Holly bends over and picks up her coffee mug, scratching Pucci between the ears to let him know everything is okay.

Brian considers this. "Well, we do own all the Burger Kings on the west side..."

"That'll do it." Holly scrutinizes Brian closely. He's wearing dusty black pants tucked into his equally dusty boots, and from beneath the placket of his partially unbuttoned shirt peeks the front of a faded black concert t-shirt. "Metallica?" Holly guesses, nodding at the letters that are visible across his chest.

Brian looks down. "Yeah," he says. "Big metal fan here." He nods rapidly, his thinning, sandy blonde hair barely covering a reddened scalp. "I make a better Metallica fan than a pirate," he laments, buttoning up his shirt to cover the band name.

"I think you're doing fine," Holly says, taking a sip of her coffee. "I mean, you passed out after a night of beer and cigars and then slept in a bush on an unfamiliar island. I bet Captain Kidd did that once or twice."

"And probably Sir Francis Drake," Brian adds, warming to the idea. He trips on a wayward branch as he follows Holly. "Hey, how far am I from civilization?"

"Not far: you fell asleep about a hundred yards from my house. And my uncle lives next door," she adds, not wanting Brian to get any ideas about showing up at her house for a visit. They walk back towards Holly's house together with Pucci still watching Brian warily. "Hey, what's your pirate name? You don't want me calling you Brian in front of your buddies, do you?"

"I guess not," he says. "They call me Bucko Chumbucket."

Holly wrinkles her nose. "Ew. That's not a good name."

"I know. But my wife made me be a pirate. The other guys think I'm kind of a joke, so Sinker named me Bucko Chumbucket."

"Huh. Okay. So why did your wife 'make' you become a pirate?"

Brian kicks a shriveled piece of husk that's fallen from a palm tree. "Because she thought it was weird for a dude in his forties to spend all his nights and weekends playing *Space Invaders* and eating Burger King," he admits. "But the Burger King is free—I have a special pass that lets me eat at any BK I want, no charge." Brian is clearly under the impression that this is a point in his favor.

"Bonus," Holly says. "So, this wife—what's her name?"

"Anita."

"Anita isn't feeling the flame anymore when she has to step over her middle-aged husband—no offense." Holly shoots Brian an apologetic look.

"No worries," Brian says.

"Anyway, she has to vacuum around a guy who comes home from the insurance agency, changes into sweats, and then sits around eating fast food and playing video games from the 80s."

"*Space Invaders* came out in 1978," Brian corrects her. "And I always play in my boxers and a t-shirt."

"My bad. Okay, so Anita isn't feeling the passion, Bri," Holly says. She stops walking and turns to him. "She married a handsome, swashbuckling stud of a man, and after a couple of kids—"

"Four," he adds.

"—after four kids, this hunky dude turns into Brian from State Farm."

"Well, I have to pay the bills," he says sadly. "And I like my job."

"That's awesome; you *should* like your job. And you should be proud of what you do. But you need to think about Anita. Does she read romance novels?" Holly is just guessing here, but she's feeling lucky.

"Yep. In bed at night. Always the ones with the man tearing off the lady's dress on the cover," he says, making a face that says he can't imagine why anyone would touch something so crass.

"Brian," she says, "it's simple: *ladies love romance.* They want to be swept off their feet. And understood. And desired. And made to feel beautiful. You can do all that without being a pirate."

"But she always jumps on me after a pirate weekend. As soon as we get the kids to bed, she makes me put on my boots again and—"

"Got it." Holly holds up a hand to stop him before he gets to the part where he pulls out his sword. "So then what's the big deal? You get to spend a weekend away with the guys every so often, drinking rum and smoking cigars on a *freaking pirate ship*, and then you go home to find Anita feeling frisky. It all sounds like a win-win to me," Holly says.

"I guess...when you put it that way." Brian gives a weak, hungover smile. "I just wish these other guys would let me stop someplace for a burger every so often," he says, patting his slightly rounded belly.

"You know what? I can set you up with a burger fit for a rockstar today, how does that sound?"

Brian's eyes light up like a little boy who's just been offered a cookie.

"Great. Let's get you back to the B&B so you can shower and meet up with the other guys. Hey," Holly stops walking. "How did you get all the way over here? We had dinner on the other side of the island last night, and when I left, you all were still sitting around the bonfire."

A grin spreads across Brian's unshaven face, and the combination of his impish look and the gold stubble on his cheeks gives him the look of a frat boy who's partied a little too long and hard. "I was looking for a cheeseburger."

CHAPTER 5

"Holly, you have got to make this stop," Carrie-Anne Martinez demands. She steps out from behind the counter at Mistletoe Morning Brew and walks across the coffee shop to meet Holly at the door.

"Make what stop?"

"The damn holes—they're everywhere!" Heads turn all around the shop, and the chatter dies down.

"More holes?" Holly closes the door gently with her right hand, trying to keep the bells on the handle from banging loudly against the wooden door frame. "Where?"

"This morning Ellen and I got up at four like we always do, and we went out to feed Madonkey and the turkeys before coming here to open the shop." Carrie-Anne is nearing breathlessness as she starts her play-by-play of a morning spent feeding the menagerie that she and her wife, Ellen, have adopted.

"Uh huh," Holly prompts, furtively scanning the coffee shop crowd. The Bradfords are present, as are Heddie Lang-Mueller, Cap Duncan, two of the triplets and their respective husbands, a smattering of other islanders, and Mrs. Agnelli. Holly is about to say more when she hears a light rap on the glass of the door behind her; she turns to see Jake and Bridget waiting patiently for her to move out of the way so they don't hit her with the door.

"Sorry," Bridget whispers, tiptoeing in theatrically after Holly steps aside. "We just need coffee."

"Come in, come in," Holly says. Her patience is wearing thin. "We almost have enough people for a mini village council meeting," she says, counting heads. "Bonnie isn't here, and we're missing—" She points at the triplets. "Which one of you are we missing?"

"Gwen," Gen says.

"Okay, we've got a good crowd here and no visitors amongst us." Holly slides onto a tall chair at the bistro table where Heddie is sitting. "So let's talk about these holes."

Loud discussion erupts all around the coffee shop. Holly lets it go on for a minute or so before she speaks. "Let's figure out what's going on and what we need to do."

The sea of gray and white heads turn to face her. Eyebrows raise and arms are folded as the islanders wait for Holly to go on.

"Who can tell the rest of us where the new holes are?" Holly asks.

Maria Agnelli steps down from her tall chair and stands, all four-foot-eleven inches of her poised for battle. "Someone is messing with us, Holly, and it all started when these blasted pirates got here."

Holly can't help but nod in agreement, and her mind instantly jumps to Bonnie and the cantankerous Sinker McBludgeon. Her entertaining discovery of Brian under the bushes that morning has been the most lighthearted part of the pirates' visit so far, but she isn't sure why one of them might be trying to turn their island into Swiss cheese.

"I can see the correlation," Holly allows, trying to be fair. "But why would a bunch of guys from Winter Park and Tallahassee come all the way down here to dig in the sand? It just doesn't make sense."

"I know why," Maria Agnelli says wisely. "Buried treasure, that's why."

The crowd leaps to action again, tossing around wild tales of Billy Bowlegs Rogers and his chests of gold and treasure. Cap adds what he knows about the legends of markings on trees and sunken pirate ships. Holly puts her fingers to her temples and presses lightly; she really needs another cup of coffee.

"I've never heard any rumors about buried treasure on Christmas Key," Holly says firmly. "I feel like that's the kind of thing my grandfather might have mentioned had there been any stories about pirates ever coming here."

"Look, no disrespect, Mayor," says Cap. "But maybe these guys know more than you do about this topic. They probably spend all their free time trying to figure out where the treasure is buried, and obviously there's some squirreled away here that we don't know about."

"That sounds like hogwash!" Heddie Lang-Mueller says, but her German accent makes the w in 'hogwash' sound like a v. Holly smiles at her across the table.

"You might call it hogwash, but think about it," Cap says. "What if they're really into this pirate business? What if they intend to pillage our island while they're at it?"

"They aren't very nice," Bridget adds, her face reddening as the crowd turns to look at her. She's still standing by the door with Jake, her legs sticking out from under a floral skirt that barely covers her assets. On top of that she's wearing a denim shirt with snaps and a white baseball hat. "I think that guy who's always hitting on Bonnie tried to give me scurvy at the bonfire last night."

Looks of confusion are exchanged all over the shop, but Bridget's comment doesn't really matter, because the seed of distrust has already been planted.

"Listen," Holly says, standing up. "This is getting ridiculous. We have a group of visitors here paying good money to hold an event on our island. Most of them are play-acting this pirate fantasy on the weekends after spending their weeks as high school teachers or accountants. They aren't here to hurt us or steal from us—this isn't the sixteenth century."

Holly's eyes rake through the crowd; some of the faces are starting to look more neutral and less accusatory.

"But we need to figure out where these holes are coming from. They're dangerous," Cap says, leaning back in his chair and shoving his hands under his armpits. His presence is imposing anyway, but when he speaks with purpose, the chatter stops and all eyes go to him. "The newest ones are along December Drive on the north side of the island,

Holly. If you take Ivy Lane up to December, you can run along the road and see that a bunch of holes have popped up overnight."

"I'll go check it out," Holly promises. "I've been trying to fill in the holes myself when I find them, but this is getting to be a bigger job than I'm equipped for."

"I'll come along and help," Jake offers, raising a hand. "I've got a shovel and an hour to kill."

"Thank you, Jake," Holly says formally, not looking at Bridget. "Now," she turns back to the crowd, "are we good for the time being? I'd like for us to finish out this long weekend with our guests and have everyone feeling both safe and hospitable. Can we do that?" In truth, what she wants to say is that everyone needs to be on their best behavior, but because being mayor is sometimes like being an elementary school teacher, she chooses her words carefully and aims for positivity over blatant redirection.

People are nodding. Some look unconvinced, but most have returned to their coffee and breakfast pastries.

"Good," Holly says to herself, heading for the counter. She really does need that coffee.

"I SEE THEM—JUST UP THERE," HOLLY POINTS, HOLDING HER PAPER to-go cup in one hand. She's left her cart behind in the B&B's sandy lot and ridden along with Jake in his police cruiser to find the new holes. They've got two shovels in the storage bin on the back of Jake's cart.

Sure enough, as Jake pulls off the unpaved road and parks next to a sand dune, they can see a string of holes. The craters zigzag across the street crazily like the footprints of a drunken giant.

"This mystifies me," Holly mutters to herself. "I really don't think this is the pirates."

"Then what do you think is going on?" Jake gets out and grabs the shovels. He meets Holly on the passenger side of the cart and hands one to her. As she takes the shovel from him, her hand brushes against his; he doesn't seem to notice.

Jake is already focused on filling the holes and Holly ends up talking to his back as he walks away. "I don't know what I think yet," she says, "but it seems pretty far-fetched that we wouldn't have heard about Christmas Key having a pirate history. I honestly feel like that would've come up at least once in all the years I've lived here." She sets her coffee in the cup holder of Jake's cart and follows him over to the first hole.

"It wouldn't be the first time your grandparents kept important information to themselves," Jake grunts, spearing the sand with his shovel and heaving the first pile into an empty hole. He's obviously alluding to the fact that Frank and Jeanie Baxter had chosen to keep the existence of Frank's illegitimate son a secret. Holly gets that it's salacious and interesting, but it's also her family that he's talking about, and she doesn't like it.

"You know what, Jake?" she says, setting the tip of her shovel in the sand and resting against the handle while Jake works. "I think the hat is dumb."

"What hat?" Jake stops digging and frowns at her. He's already broken a sweat filling the first hole.

Holly realizes that she's jumped from a perfectly reasonable topic of conversation to an emotionally loaded one, but it's too late to turn back now.

"Bridget's. The baseball hat." She points at the Yankees cap sitting on top of her own head. "The hat is *my* thing."

Jake rolls his eyes and moves on to the next hole. It's far enough away that Holly has to take her shovel and move closer to him in order to carry on the conversation.

"You don't have a trademark on girls wearing baseball caps, Holly." Jake dumps a shovel full of sand over the next hole and looks at her with annoyance. "Are you going to help me here, or what?"

"I'm *trying* to help you," she says. The words spill out of her mouth like vomit and taste just as bad. "I think you've punished me enough."

"Punished you? How? For what?" Jake walks over to her, the shovel held tightly in one hand. Holly can see the veins of his arm as he grips the wooden handle. "Why is this even about you?"

Holly dips her chin, letting her baseball hat hide her face as much as possible. She knows she's gone too far, and the anger in Jake's eyes confirms it.

"I'm not trying to punish you, Holly. We broke up. You said you didn't want to marry me, and then you drove the point home by sleeping with some guy who showed up on the island, like, a month later."

"It was more than a month," she says in a small voice, knowing that this won't help her case.

"Whatever. You moved on, and now I have. That's not punishment," he says, jamming the shovel into the sand. "That's life."

Holly's been waiting to get Jake alone like this so she can talk to him, but she never imagined it going like this. She nods slowly, her eyes fixed on the scuffed toes of her gray Converse. Jake is right—about all of it.

"Listen, you should be doing this. You're the mayor, and I'm just a police officer," Jake says, walking back to the cart and tossing his shovel into the storage bin with a clang.

"What?" Holly spins around, staring at him as he climbs into the cart. "But mayors don't do construction."

"Neither do cops," Jake says with a smirk. "And if we're going to split hairs, I think road improvements fall more within your purview than mine. Have fun."

Jake pulls away from the sand dune and swerves to miss the remaining holes. His cart disappears around the bend in the road, leaving a cloud of dust and sand swirling in the morning sunlight.

Holly walks over to the nearest hole and stares at it for a minute, silently cursing her own inability to simply keep her mouth shut. With a sigh, she starts to fill the hole with sand.

CHAPTER 6

Buckhunter is squatting on the roof of his bungalow when Holly pulls into her driveway that afternoon.

"How do, Mayor?" he shouts out to her, removing the cigar he's smoking from between his teeth.

"I do just fine, Buckhunter. What's going on up there?"

"Thought I'd get a better view of the hole-digging bandits from up here," he shouts. "I can't sleep at night thinking about pirates tearing up my island."

"Really?" Holly almost laughs out loud.

"Nope. Couple of shingles blew loose the other night and landed in my yard." He holds up a hammer with the hand that doesn't have a cigar in it. "I'm just fixin' stuff."

"Where's Fee?" Holly leans across the bench seat of her cart to grab her purse. She hasn't seen Fiona much lately, and they'd only waved at one another during the bonfire the night before.

"She's got some harebrained idea about swimming from Key West to Cuba," he says, jamming the cigar back into his mouth and positioning a nail over a shingle. "Says she needs to get out in the water every day to work on her endurance."

"I'm sorry, I thought you just said Fiona wanted to swim from

Key West to Cuba. There must be something wrong with my hearing." Holly stands in the grass of her uncle's house, looking up at him as he taps the nail in smoothly with his hammer. Fiona has a great figure, but she isn't big on working out. In fact, Holly and some of the older women on the island are known to walk the beach together once a week, and Fiona doesn't even like to get out of bed early for that.

"Yep, that's what I said." He grabs another nail and holds a different shingle in place.

"But, why?" A hesitant gust of wind blows through the trees and rustles the leaves and palm fronds. As it reaches Buckhunter, the breeze lifts three of his shingles and sends them flying across the gabled roof; they land on the grass near Holly's feet.

"Damn," Buckhunter says. "I needed those."

Holly sets her purse down and gathers the shingles. "Want me to come up there?" she offers.

"I'm not sure you're the kind of gal who belongs on a rooftop," Buckhunter says with a wink.

"I just spent the day filling fourteen holes on December Drive," Holly says, holding up her hands to show Buckhunter the blisters she got from the wood-handled shovel. "I can probably manage the roof."

Buckhunter whistles at her raw, red palms. "Did you do that alone? You should have asked for help," he says, moving over to the edge of the roof to hold the ladder steady for her.

"Yeah, I'll remember that for next time." She tucks the shingles into the back pocket of her shorts so that she can hold on to the sides of the ladder with both hands as she climbs the rungs. "So why is Fiona swimming to Cuba? Iris and Jimmy know how to make fried plantains and *arroz con pollo*. She doesn't need to breaststroke all the way to Havana for that."

Buckhunter leans forward and offers Holly a hand as she reaches the top of the ladder. "She's raising money for the hospital she worked at in Chicago. I think it's for the cancer center. Her cousin just passed away, and she wants to do her part. She's been pretty upset," he says with a grunt, pulling Holly up so that she can sit next to him on the slanted roof.

"Fiona just lost her cousin?" Holly says, sinking into a sitting position. "I didn't know. We haven't had much time to talk lately."

"So she says."

Holly turns her head to look at her uncle. They're sitting so close that their shoulders nearly touch. "Is she mad at me?"

Buckhunter chuckles. "No. I don't think so. Life is busy, kid—she gets that."

"Oh. Good." Holly turns to look back out over the family property. "You can see a lot from up here," she says, pointing to Cinnamon Lane and over at the beach to the left of the property.

"Yep," Buckhunter confirms. "Sure can."

"So how is Fiona raising money by swimming ninety miles through shark-infested waters?"

"Getting sponsors. Carrie-Anne and Ellen have signed on, and I think she's asked her family to do the same."

Carrie-Anne and Ellen choose a different cause each month to donate to with the funds they earn from their themed items at Mistletoe Morning Brew. Their support doesn't surprise Holly.

"Maybe she should call Coco and see if some of her bored housewife friends want to pitch in. They've all got money to burn," Holly says, bumping into her uncle lightly with her shoulder. They haven't heard from Holly's mother in a while, and neither is sure where she stands at the moment in terms of her plans to sell the island. Their three-way ownership of Christmas Key is basically all that's stopping Coco from turning it into a giant waterpark, and even the intervention of her lawyer hasn't helped to further her cause with Holly and Buckhunter.

"Let's not poke the sleeping beast," Buckhunter says with a gruff laugh. "She's hibernating in a cave somewhere up in New Jersey. Probably wise to leave her be."

Holly wraps her arms around her legs, pulling her knees to her chest. "So what do you make of all this pirate talk?" She shivers as the breeze picks up again.

Buckhunter puffs on his cigar, filling the air with sweet-smelling smoke. "Bupkis," he says definitively. "This island is full of imaginative old timers and a few mildly-cracked young people," he says, his gray-blonde goatee twitching as he holds back a grin. "These dudes in breeches and velvet coats are just here for a good time—nothing more."

"What if that good time really does include hunting for some treasure we've never heard of?"

Buckhunter shrugs. "What if it does?"

"Then it feels like we're being robbed."

"But we aren't. Treasure buried by pirates doesn't belong to any of us."

He's right—as usual. The thing about Buckhunter is that he can joke around and tease you until you want to punch him, but when he gives advice it's always solid.

"So we should just ignore their digging and keep filling the holes?"

Buckhunter squints out into the treetops. "I think *you* should keep filling those holes, Mayor," he says, sticking his cigar between his teeth and reaching for one of Holly's hands. He turns it over and examines her palms. "But maybe wear some gloves next time, huh?"

As soon as Buckhunter finishes his roof repair and heads off to open up Jack Frosty's for happy hour, Holly sends Fiona a text.

She's humming along to the Pet Shop Boys on her stereo and folding a pile of laundry in the kitchen when her phone buzzes on the wooden tabletop next to the stack of hand towels. *Yep. Swimming to Cuba. Must have lost my mind.*

Holly snaps a green t-shirt in the air and folds it in half, then in half again. She sets it on top of a pile of clothes and picks up her phone. *Want to be my date for the gathering at Jack Frosty's, or will that derail your training and conditioning?*

Pucci's bark pulls her attention out to the front porch. The door is open to the cool January evening, and the smell of a tropical winter filters through the house.

"Whatcha barking at, boy?" Holly coos, phone in her hand as she bends over to scratch Pucci on the head. He's standing at attention, ears perked up. His bark rings out again into the twilight of the evening, and suddenly Holly would rather close the house up than have it wide open. She takes a step back and pats her thigh, hoping Pucci will follow. "Come on, let's go in," she says. Pucci barks again, this time more insistently. "What, Pooch?" she asks, sliding her phone into the back pocket of her shorts. "What is it?"

There's a rustle in the trees near Buckhunter's house, and Holly's head whips in that direction. His windows are dark. Pucci is crouched at her heels, and he lets out a low growl. Holly wraps her arms around her body and clears her throat.

"Who's there?" she calls into the near-darkness. "Brian?" She hopes that the harmless, wayward pirate has just wandered back to her side of the island again. "Is that you?"

In response, a branch snaps loudly and Holly jumps back. Pucci has the opposite response and he springs forward, leaping from the top step of the porch and scaling all three stairs like he's clearing a hurdle. Before Holly has a chance to react, she hears a man's voice and a commotion from the trees on the side of Buckhunter's house.

"Ouch! Get off me!" The leaves rustle loudly as Pucci lunges at the unseen visitor. "Shoo! Get away!"

Holly doesn't recognize the voice, but the gravelly sound and the low pitch both conjure up the image of an older man. She rules Brian out.

"Pucci!" Holly shouts, taking one step down and forcing herself to be brave. "Pooch!" She hopes that Pucci has at least gotten a jaw full of pant leg and that he's holding their guest hostage. "Whoever you are, you'd better show yourself." Holly holds her cell phone in the air. "I'm calling Officer Zavaroni now, and he'll come over here immediately. It'll be better for you in the end if you just come out." She's shaking, but manages to hold her voice steady.

With as much courage as she can muster, Holly holds her head high and steps down from her porch. Her fingers punch the screen as she pulls up Jake's number. The phone rings. She walks through the grass, heart pounding. "I'm calling," she says loudly, approaching Pucci and the bushes.

She's only steps away from her dog when the leaves rustle again, shaking like a tree full of angry gorillas. Pucci growls, lowering the front of his body so that his hind end is up and his stance is aggressive. Between the barking and the shaking tree, Holly's anxiety level is about as high as it's ever been. She hears the click of Jake picking up her call just as a dark figure springs from the bushes.

In panic and fear, Holly drops the phone. "Jake!" she shouts. "Jake, help me!" The person who's been hiding bolts across the yard and through the trees. Pucci gives chase, bounding after a stout man with an odd, lumbering gait.

"Jake, there's a man here." Holly reaches into the grass for the glowing screen and puts it to her ear. Her hand is shaking. "I'm outside my house, and Pucci took off after some guy who was hiding in my bushes."

"I'll be right there."

CHAPTER 7

The lights of four golf carts illuminate Holly's property. Jake had come right away, followed by Cap, Fiona, and Jimmy Cafferkey. Everyone has their headlamps trained on the bushes in question, and Holly shows them where the man went, miming her surprise and how she'd dropped her phone in terror.

"I think you should stay with me tonight," Fiona decides. "Grab Pucci and some clothes, and we'll go to my place."

Holly nods, hands tucked under her armpits to stop the shaking. "Yeah, okay," she agrees. "But I need to pull it together. This isn't a big deal. It's just that it's dark and I was alone. I'm not used to being scared."

"That's the beauty of Christmas Key, lass—you have no reason to be fearful." Jimmy's face is full of concern. "But Fiona's right: let's get you out of here for a night, and then you can come back in the light of day and reclaim your property from the boogeyman."

"It's not a joke, Jimmy," Jake says protectively as he surveys the scene.

"I'm not laughing," Jimmy shoots back, his voice deep and serious.

"No, I get what Jimmy means." Holly drops her arms to her sides and forces herself to take a deep breath and relax. "There's a weird feeling that won't go away until I come back here and walk around during the day. I'll get my stuff and we can go," she says to Fiona.

Pucci sits next to Holly in her hot pink golf cart, and they trail after Fiona and the string of other carts in the dark. The flickering electric candles that Holly's attached to her cart are especially spooky on the thick, forested part of the island, and the black netting that hangs behind her blows forward and tickles the back of her neck like the fingers of a ghost. Holly shivers.

She's convinced everyone that she's fine, and as she grips the steering wheel, Holly tries to make herself believe that it's true. The only thing in recent memory that's rattled her is a visit from her mother, or something contentious that's happening on the island, like Cap Duncan's recent run against her for her seat as mayor. That had shaken her foundation, but not much else has—ever. Part of what she loves most about her island life is the solid feel of it. There's safety in knowing that she controls almost everything about her life (aside from the odd tropical storm), and that security is something that Holly depends on.

She carries her overnight bag into Fiona's house and fills a water bowl for Pucci.

"Are you sure you're up for this?" Fiona stands in the middle of the kitchen, looking at her best friend quizzically.

"Yeah. I need to show up and look some people in the eye. Not only that, but it would be unprofessional to drop the ball after I've put so much work into this pirate thing."

"Okay, boss. If you say so."

Fiona drives them over to Jack Frosty's, where everyone is meeting for an evening of bar food and drinks. Joe Sacamano and Buckhunter had torn through a round of Rock, Paper, Scissors to see who got to host the pirates at their bar first. Joe won the best two out of three, so Buckhunter has the honors on Sunday night.

Main Street is already lined with carts, and Fiona slows down, searching for a spot to park. Buckhunter had agreed to let Holly take over the decorations for the occasion, and she's done the same thing to Jack Frosty's that she's done everywhere else: turned the lights down low, covered the tables with black cloth, and set flameless candles all around the room for ambiance. In addition to her usual props, Holly has also hung black flags with white skulls around the bar, and she's created a playlist that resembles the soundtrack of a rollicking pirate movie full of adventure to play in the background all evening.

"Just park in the B&B's lot," she instructs Fiona. They pull in under a tall streetlight, and Holly frowns. "That's weird...Bonnie's here." But it isn't just that Bonnie is parked in the B&B's lot—which could simply mean that she couldn't find parking on Main Street either—it's that she can see the light on in the B&B's back office. "What is she doing here on a Sunday night?" Holly enters the B&B through the back door, her curiosity piqued.

Light from the office spills into the dark hallway, but when Holly pokes her head into their workspace, it's empty.

Fiona follows her to the front desk, where Maggie Sutter is once again working the night shift. Maggie closes a slip of paper in the spine of the book she's reading and sets it on the counter. "Evening, ladies," she says, pushing a glass bowl shaped like an oyster in their direction. "Malted white chocolate balls?"

The dish is full of little round candies that look like pearls. "Clever, Maggie, I love it. But no thank you," Holly says.

Fiona reaches over and takes a handful of chocolates. "I swam a mile today. I'm eating the chocolate," she says.

"What's the scuffle out at your place, Holly?" Maggie asks. She takes off her square reading glasses and sets them on top of her head like sunglasses.

"You mean tonight? How did you already hear about that?" Holly reaches over and wipes a layer of dust from the base of the lamp that rests on her front desk. She's had a hard time lately staying on top of both the cleaning and the office work at the B&B, and she makes a mental note to reestablish some order in the front of the house.

Maggie gives a scoffing chuckle. "Mayor, I can hear the gossip about stuff like that even *without* my hearing aids." Maggie taps her left ear with one finger. "Plus Jake already stopped in and had me print out a list of all the pirates and their home addresses."

"Did they check in under their real names, or their pirate names?" Fiona asks, swiping another handful of chocolate.

"Real," Maggie confirms. She takes the reading glasses from the top of her head and slides them back on as she consults the computer on the desk. "Want me to tell you the names their sweet, unsuspecting mothers bestowed upon them all those years ago, long before they grew hair in every crack and crevice and started belching smoke and whiskey?"

"Maybe later," Holly says distractedly. "Hey, have you seen Bonnie? Her cart is in the back and the lights are on in the office."

Maggie busies herself with the computer. She lowers her chin and peers at Holly over the rims of her glasses and then she clears her throat—twice. Holly taps on the counter with her fingernails while she waits for an answer. For as much gossip as the islanders engage in, there's a streak of loyalty that sometimes gets in the way of their willingness to share information about one another, and it often pops up at the most inopportune times.

Just when it seems that Maggie's not going to give Holly an answer, the sound of Bonnie's laughter trickles out to the front desk.

"Oh, honey, *stop*," Bonnie says, her tone begging whomever she's speaking to to do anything *but* stop. "I just got this corset tied again!" Bonnie comes around the corner and stops short when she sees Holly and Fiona's surprised faces. Fiona pops another malted chocolate in her mouth like she's eating popcorn and watching a movie.

Holly looks Bonnie up and down, noting that her hair is tousled and her lipstick gone. In her eyes is a wild, happy flame. Sinker McBludgeon nearly plows into her from behind as he comes around the corner on Bonnie's heels, buttoning the cuffs of his loose, white pirate's shirt.

"Ladies," Bonnie says breathlessly. "I was just headed over to Jack Frosty's and I thought I forgot something here." She runs a hand through her hair, patting it back into place.

"And? Did you find it?" Holly asks pointedly. Sinker grins from behind Bonnie's shoulder.

"She found exactly what she was looking for," Sinker says, putting a possessive hand around Bonnie's waist. He pulls her to his side and nuzzles her neck. This move sends an instant jolt of irritation through Holly.

"I'll see you at the bar," Holly says, grabbing Fiona's hand. "Come on, Fee." She yanks her best friend down the hallway, reaching into the office and turning off the lights as she passes.

They stalk down the street to the bar in silence, but Holly's feelings about Bonnie and Sinker ooze from every pore of her body.

"Well, I guess Sinker has a good alibi during the time that someone was prowling around outside my house. But it really disgusts me, Fee," she says. "The whole thing makes me sick."

Fiona slows down on the sidewalk as they approach Jack Frosty's. A song about sea shanties and buried treasure spills out of the bar as fully-dressed pirates march up the steps from Main Street, ready for some grog and a good time.

"Holly," she says softly. "Bonnie is a grown woman. You've got to let this one go."

"But he's a terrible person! I've seen the way he talks to her, and she *barely knows him*," Holly laments. "I've already told her: Wyatt is right here waiting if all she wants to do is flirt with someone who antagonizes the crap out of her."

Fiona tilts her head so that she's looking up into Holly's eyes. Even though Fiona is petite and about six inches shorter than Holly, her tone is firm and serious.

"Holly," she says, grabbing her friend's hands and holding them. "Sometimes a woman has a man right in front of her who everyone thinks is a perfect match, but for some reason, he just isn't." Fiona tugs both of Holly's hands for emphasis, making her shake like a rag doll. "And then some guy shows up in town and sweeps her off her feet. Some people might think she's moving too fast, but the only person who can truly judge that is her."

A man in breeches and a horizontally-striped shirt steps around them on the sidewalk.

Fiona's words have penetrated the surface, and Holly is getting her meaning, loud and clear. "You're right," she says. "I know you're right, but Bonnie is like...she's like..." Holly searches for the right words, not knowing how to formulate an appropriate description of how she feels about her assistant.

"She's like your mother. I mean, she's not like *your* mother—no one is quite like Coco," Fiona clarifies. "But she's like the mother you wish you had."

"Exactly," Holly whispers. "And I only want the best for her."

"Which this guy clearly isn't. At least not from where you stand," Fiona says, tugging Holly's hands again. "But as a girl who fancies the tough, mysterious type, I can kind of see the appeal," she says.

Holly laughs. Though she doesn't know much about Fiona's ex-boyfriend in Chicago, she does know that he was controlling and that it didn't end well between them. And now that her best friend is dating Buckhunter, she can see that Fiona is right: even though she doesn't personally take a shine to biker boys and tattooed tough guys, some chicks do seem to dig them. But *Sinker McBludgeon*? She swallows hard against the bile rising in her throat.

"It still seems really fast. He's only been here for forty-eight hours, and Bonnie is totally swept-up in this pirate game."

Fiona shrugs and lets go of Holly's hands. "How long did it take before you spirited River away to your bungalow during his first visit?" Fiona narrows her eyes, mentally calculating.

Holly takes a deep breath. She knows she's got this coming. "Okay, but—"

"But nothing," Fiona counters. "If you adjust the timeframe to account for their waning years, then Bonnie is actually right on schedule. What took you a week to accomplish only took her two days. That seems fair, given that she's, like, twenty-five or thirty years older than you."

Holly exhales loudly. "I have to get over this, don't I?"

"Well, you don't have to, but it's going to make this pirate party a lot less festive if you're sulking in the corner while the rest of us are trying on each other's eye patches and passing around a bottle of rum."

A loud cheer goes up in the bar as if on cue, and the sound of glasses clinking together in a rowdy toast echoes out into the night.

"Let's go in," Holly finally says, linking her arm through Fiona's. "And if I didn't say it earlier," she lowers her voice, leaning down to Fiona's ear. "I'm sorry about your cousin."

Fiona looks up with soft and teary eyes. "Thanks." She squeezes Holly's arm. "Let's have a drink in her honor."

"Deal."

"Two rum and Cokes!" Fiona shouts to Buckhunter as they enter the bar, still arm-in-arm. "You've got a couple of thirsty wenches here!"

THE BAR IS SPINNING AS HOLLY REELS AROUND THE ROOM, laughing and joking with the pirates as they tell stories of the sea and their travels. She drags Fiona along behind her, stopping to talk with men who introduce themselves as Fishkill Ahoy, Two Toes O'Morgan, and Mad Spot of Atlantis.

"There's Bucko Chumbucket!" Holly shouts over the music, pointing at Brian, the insurance agent with a wife and four kids.

"Bucko Chumbucket?" Fiona says with disbelief. "Are you kidding me?"

"No. He passed out by my house and I found him on the beach. I thought he was dead."

"How did I miss this?"

"You were busy swimming. Come on. I'll introduce you."

"Hey, Holly," Brian says, waving at her as she approaches. "Good to see you."

"Bucko, this is Fiona, my best friend, and the island's only doctor. Fee, this is Brian—he owns an insurance agency."

Fiona giggles. The rum has clearly gone to her head as much as it's gone to Holly's. "So on the weekend you look like this, and during the week you look like Jake from State Farm?"

"Do you wear khakis?" Holly snorts, falling against Fiona as they laugh.

"Right," Brian says, laughing good-naturedly. "Just like Jake from State Farm. And yes, I wear khakis."

"Hey," Holly says, sobering up. "Where's that one guy—the really tall one with the long beard and the old-fashioned glasses?"

"Bowman Sparrow," Brian says. "It's his turn to man the vessel."

Holly and Fiona sway slightly in unison, hanging onto one another as their drinks slosh like they're on a boat that's sailing through choppy waters.

"What does that mean?" Fiona frowns at him. "Is that some code that really means it's his turn to dig the holes?" Holly pinches Fiona's side.

"We never leave our ship completely unattended." Brian frowns at her. "A pirate has to protect his booty, you know?"

"So, wait," Holly says, thrusting the hand that's holding her rum and Coke in Brian's direction. "Someone stays on board all the time and does what? Surveys the horizon?"

"Exactly," Brian confirms. "Somebody stands guard in the crow's nest, watching the land and sea. It sounds like a crappy job, but it's actually pretty cool. It's peaceful."

"So the other night when we had the barbecue on the beach," Holly says, putting her thoughts together in a boozy, disjointed fashion, "someone was on board, maybe watching us with a telescope?"

"Right," Brian says simply. "It was Fishkill's night, I think." He points at Fishkill Ahoy, who is currently dancing a drunken, rhythmless jig in the middle of Jack Frosty's.

"Listen up—I have an announcement to make!" Sinker McBludgeon holds his beer glass high in the air. "Fellow pirates, friends, and wenches, I'd like you to be the first to hear what I have to say." The talk in the bar lowers to a smattering of whispers and Buckhunter cuts the music. Holly's eyes go directly to Bonnie, who is tucked under Sinker's left arm. She's got a shiny glow to her that's reflected in the adoring gaze she's got trained on Sinker as she waits for him to share his news.

"What's this all about?" Fiona hisses, leaning in to Holly.

"No idea."

"Friends," Sinker goes on. "This lovely woman here caught my eye the very second my boot touched land here on Christmas Key." Bonnie's cheeks flush with pleasure. "She's a feisty, demanding, sexy lady, and I'd like nothing more than to take her as my bride." Sinker leans down to plant a wet, rummy kiss on Bonnie's lips.

The pirates in the crowd whoop and catcall, but the islanders all turn to one another and launch into immediate discussion. Holly's jaw falls open and she turns to Fiona, stunned.

Fiona looks just as surprised. "That's fast, even accounting for the shorter timeline I gave her based on advanced age."

"But, no," Holly protests drunkenly, her head shaking back and forth like she can't make it stop. "No. Not this guy," she says, jabbing a finger in Sinker's direction. "We don't even know his real name, or what he does, we don't know anything about him—"

"Bonnie does," Fiona interjects.

"She doesn't know enough," Holly laments. "Not what really counts. All we know is that he's a bossypants jerkface, and that he thinks he's a freaking *pirate*."

"A 'bossypants jerkface'?" Fiona laughs. "Let's get you another rum and Coke, Hol." She takes the half-empty, watery drink from Holly's hand and sets it on the nearest table. "Actually, let's get you out of here before you make an ass of yourself and try to jump on Sinker's back and beat him to a pulp."

"Ooh, that's a good idea," Holly slurs, changing direction. "Let me go and give him a piece of my mind."

"Nope." Fiona throws Buckhunter a look and he's around the bar in seconds, intercepting his niece as she cuts a path towards the tall, burly pirate who's still holding Bonnie under the crook of his arm.

"Hey, kiddo," Buckhunter says, wrapping an arm around his niece's waist. "I'm going to ask someone to drive you and Fiona home." He steers Holly through the front door of the bar and onto the sidewalk where she immediately trips over a crack in the pavement like it's a giant speed bump.

"How did this happen, Buckhunter?" Holly moans, holding onto him for support.

"You were drinking with pirates, kid. You're a lightweight who got carried away."

"Not *this*," Holly says impatiently, motioning at her own body. "*That*." She points back at the bar. "Bonnie and that, that *pirate-wannabe*. She isn't supposed to marry him, Buckhunter. He's just a weekend fling. A gross one, but still." Holly feels the tears come on like someone's flipped a switch in her ducts. Suddenly she's choking on salty tears and snot is running down her face. She's a mess.

"Maybe people are supposed to find someone," Buckhunter says in a hushed voice, pulling his niece to his chest and holding her. He motions at Fiona behind Holly's back, waving her over. "Maybe it's the next step for Bonnie. You want her to be happy, don't you?"

"Yeah, but I don't want her to leave me." Holly's words are muffled against the fabric of her uncle's shirt, and her tears quickly wet his chest. "People are always leaving." The tears turn into wracking sobs as she contemplates island life without Bonnie. Holly can feel her right ankle give way as it twists beneath her weight; Buckhunter tightens his grip and holds her up so she won't fall.

"I'm going to get Jake to drive you ladies home," Buckhunter says, walking Holly over to the curb and sitting her down. "Hang on a sec."

"But I don't want Jake to take us home," Holly protests, holding up a hand weakly at Buckhunter's retreating back. "He left me, too."

Holly's arm drops to her side, her palm resting on the cool pavement. She leans her forehead on her bony knees and closes her eyes. *That's wrong*, she thinks, *Jake didn't leave me, I left him. And I sent River away. That's why I'm alone, not because Bonnie wants to...*but her thoughts trail off, and before her final epiphany can crystallize in her mind, the world around her starts to spin again and it's all a jumble of people she has to live without: Jake, River, her grandparents, Bonnie, her own mother.

Her own mother. Her mother hadn't even wanted to live with her and take care of her, so why should anyone else? Holly still has her forehead pressed to her knees, and the self-pitying tears fall from her eyes and onto her bare thighs. She waits for Jake to come and take her and Fiona home, and when he does, she refuses to speak to him.

In the morning, she remembers nothing.

CHAPTER 8

"Well, I can't just sail away into the sunset on a rickety old boat full of unshaven men, sugar," Bonnie says the next morning. "That's not how a real Southern lady does things."

Holly's managed to drag herself out of bed at Fiona's and get to the B&B by nine-thirty, and now she and Bonnie are sitting across from each other at their shared workspace. Everything seems annoyingly, painfully bright to Holly's eyes, and she's kept her Yankees hat on, brim pulled low to cut the bright sunlight that's streaming through their big office windows.

"Did you really think I was going to leave like that?" Bonnie laughs. "It does paint a picture, but I have things I need to do here before I move to Clearwater."

"*Clearwater?*" Holly repeats with obvious distaste, reaching for a pencil and examining the lead point to make sure it's sharp enough to write with.

"Yes, honey—Clearwater. It's where Doug lives."

"*Doug?*" Holly blanches. Sinker McBludgeon's name is *Doug?*

"Mmmhmm," Bonnie says dreamily, choosing to ignore Holly's disgusted face. "Douglas P. Beatty."

"What's the P stand for? Pri—"

Bonnie cuts her off with a sharp look. "Philip. The P is for Philip."

The women tap at their respective keyboards in silence for a few minutes. Bonnie answers emails about room availability over spring break, and Holly pretends to be busy as she scrolls through the island's Instagram feed, looking at the photos she's posted of her pirate decorations. The tapping of the keys is making her headache even worse. She reaches for her iced latte and takes a long sip through a yellow straw.

"What do your kids think?" Holly asks, trying to pull back on the throttle and keep her emotions in check.

"My boys don't know yet—it's all pretty sudden, doll." Bonnie stops typing. "But I think they'll be happy for me. I haven't been head-over-heels in years, and it makes my stomach feel like I'm on a rollercoaster. You know that feeling?" Bonnie's face lights up as she describes it.

"Yeah, I vaguely remember that feeling." Holly closes the Instagram page and pulls up her email. She stares at her inbox blankly. River O'Leary's been gone for over a month after their awkward Christmas Eve parting, and a general sense of melancholy has set up camp in Holly's heart whenever she thinks about the excitement of new romance. But she and River were different: he was no Sinker McBludgeon, and their relationship had been based on months of long-distance communication, not a steamy, rum-soaked, two-day fling in the B&B.

When Holly glances up from her computer screen Bonnie is looking at her sympathetically. "Are you okay today, sugar? You don't look so hot." Bonnie reaches over the seam that divides the two white wicker desks that Holly's pushed together to create one large table. "And I mean that in the nicest way." She pats Holly's forearm.

Holly gives a half-hearted smile. "Too much to drink last night," she says. "There's something about drinking with pirates that brings out the worst in me."

"You aren't the only one," Bonnie says, pointing out the window at Main Street. "Check out Dr. Potts." Their eyes follow Fiona as she drags herself toward Poinsettia Plaza. A pair of dark sunglasses covers her eyes, and her strawberry-blonde hair is pulled into a sloppy, damp bun. She's bypassed the usual summer dress and sandals that she wears under her white lab coat in favor of a pair of baggy olive green cargo pants and a t-shirt.

"Ouch," Holly says, tapping her pencil against the notepad on her desk. "No more rum and Cokes for me and Fee."

"Drink that coffee, honeypie, and then go get you another—we've got company today, and the pirates are shoving off before sunset."

Holly doodles a wavy spiral on her notepad. "What company?" She frowns.

"Girl, you need to snap out of it! I sent you the details on your Outlook calendar," Bonnie says, patting the top of Holly's laptop with her hand.

Holly drops the pencil and double-clicks her calendar to check the alerts. Sure enough, there's an update from Bonnie: *Millie's interview arriving at 1:00 on ferry. Staying in the Seashell Suite. Calista & Vance Guy + 2 kids.*

"I totally forgot about Millie's interview!" Holly says, pushing back her chair slowly like she's in pain. She stands. "And they have two kids?"

"That's what Millie says. I don't have any other details, but I think they're young."

"How long are they staying?"

Bonnie is looking at her email again. "Outlook, sugar," she says, pointing at the computer like it holds all the answers.

Holly looks at the alert. *Starts today at 1:00, ends Wednesday 3:00pm.* "They're staying for two days? But we don't have anything set up for the kids to do," she says, pacing the office in her flip-flops.

"We've got sand, golf carts to ride around in, the ocean, and about a hundred people who miss their own grandkids. We'll make do," Bonnie says.

"What about chicken nuggets? And crayons? And Disney DVDs?" Holly hates being unprepared, and the idea that children will be arriving on the island with nothing planned to entertain them sets her in motion.

"Why don't you run around and see if you can put together goodie bags for them?" Bonnie suggests with a mischievous smile.

"Oooh, that's a good idea," Holly says, chewing on her lower lip as she paces.

"I bet Cap would donate a couple of cigars, and you could get some gift cards for lattes from Ellen and Carrie-Anne. Maybe Jake can teach them how to shoot his gun, and Joe and Buckhunter could throw in some sippy cups full of tequila."

Holly stops walking. "Funny, Bon." She rolls her eyes and starts moving again. "On a more serious note, we could probably get Fiona to donate a couple of free 'island health exams' where she makes them stick out their tongues or something and declares them half-human and half-dolphin. And the triplets might have colored pencils or buckets and shovels at the gift shop," she says.

"I bet you could get Iris and Jimmy to make up some chicken strips and fries in little baskets or something."

"Definitely. And maybe Cap could introduce them to Marco." Holly kind of likes the idea of entertaining these kids for a day or two, and a part of her is secretly hoping it will keep her busy and distracted so that she doesn't have to think about the monumental mistake that Bonnie is about to make.

"There you go, sugar. You've got a plan." Bonnie snaps her fingers in the air. "Just like that. Now go and get another coffee and some fresh air," she advises. "And maybe throw on a little mascara and some concealer. Your little friends are arriving in a couple of hours and you look like something the cat dragged in. No offense," she adds.

"Believe me—none taken." Holly tosses her nearly-empty iced latte in the trash on her way out the door. "I think I'll run by home and do that, and maybe I'll grab Pucci while I'm there. Kids love dogs."

"Okay, hon," Bonnie says, already tapping away at her keyboard. "Sounds good."

HOLLY WAVES AT WYATT BENDER AS SHE DRIVES DOWN MAIN Street in the direction of her house. He holds a hand aloft, face tired and serious as he gives her a tip of his cowboy hat. A loud cannon booms in the distance and Holly jerks her steering wheel in automatic response, swerving slightly as she pulls onto Cinnamon Lane.

"Good lord," she says to herself, putting a hand over her heart. She hasn't been home yet since spending the night at Fiona's, and she knows that Bonnie is right: a shower and some make-up are in order. The loud reverberations of the cannon shot ring in her ears as she presses down on the gas pedal and takes the bumpy road at full speed. It doesn't do good things for her unsettled stomach to thump over the pits in the road and crunch over the little sticks and branches from the heavy tree cover, but she's eager to get to her house and see it in the light of day.

Buckhunter's cart is in his driveway when she pulls in. Holly pats her thigh for Pucci to follow her into the house, but the dog has already bounded down from the passenger seat and run over to Buck-hunter's yard where he immediately starts to sniff the bushes that the man had hidden in the night before.

"Come on, dude," Holly says to him, giving a short three-part whis-tle. "Let's go in." Pucci gives one last distrustful look at the bushes and follows his mistress.

Inside, the house is just as she left it. Her half-folded laundry sits in piles on the kitchen table, and a glass of water whose ice cubes have now completely melted rests on the counter. Holly sets down her bag and goes to dump the glass into the sink. Her house feels the same as it had before the scare she'd gotten the night before, and there's a sweeping sense of relief as Holly realizes that she doesn't feel the urge to check the locks on all of her windows or look under her bed for intruders. Whatever happened the night before had been a one-off and hadn't been meant to frighten her—she can sense that now. Even Pucci relaxes almost instantly, sinking onto his dog bed in the corner of the front room and falling into a comfortable dozing state.

After a hot shower, two Advil, and a tall iced tea, Holly sits on her lanai with a pad of paper and a pen. She jots down the ideas she has for the kids' visit, and then looks out into the trees around her property. It's almost eleven o'clock, and she wants to have at least a couple of meals arranged and something for the kids to do that afternoon while their parents meet with Millie and Ray at the salon. There's no guarantee that things will even work out with this family, but it's always Holly's goal to make every visitor to the island feel welcomed and like Christmas Key has been expecting them.

She puts her bare feet up on the glass table and leans back, looking at her half-finished shell wall. It's been a while since she's had time to gather any shells on the beach, and she's actually been sleeping well enough lately that she doesn't need to wake up and spend a couple of hours working on her lanai wall in order to fall back to sleep. In fact, the last time she can remember getting up at two a.m. to mix up a batch of mortar and glue her shells to the wall was shortly after River had left the island. It had been a cold night just before New Year's, and she'd gotten up to the sound of cicadas and a hooting owl to busy her hands and to free her mind from wondering whether she'd just made the biggest mistake of her life by letting him leave.

River was a whole other issue. There have been a lot of things on her mind lately, and he's one item that she's had to take off the menu for the time being. Between River and her mother, "out of sight, out of mind" has been mercifully true of late, and this ability to focus only on the tasks at hand has allowed Holly some time to gain perspective on her non-existent love life. With Coco keeping a distance and not bringing up any talk of investors coming to look at the island, and with no word from River whatsoever, Holly's turned her attention totally to Christmas Key business: her mayoral duties, planning the pirate weekend, and keeping up her campaign to advertise and promote the island as a travel destination. The only time she's let the blinders drop and her attention shift is when it comes to Jake and Bridget.

As if on cue, Holly's phone lights up on the table next to her feet, and a text from Jake appears on the home screen: *Couple more holes popped up near Hal Pillory's place, and we've got an injured pirate in Fiona's office. Just FYI.*

Holly reads the text and sets the phone down again. Excellent—more holes, a broken pirate, and visitors set to arrive in just over an hour. She sighs and swings her feet down from the table with resignation. Hangover be damned, she's got places to go, things to do, and people to greet.

CHAPTER 9

H al Pillory is circling his front lawn in a white men's tank-top and a pair of plaid shorts held up by a white leather belt. He's got black dress socks pulled halfway up his liver-spotted calves, and his feet are shoved into a pair of slip-on sandals.

"Nice wife-beater you got there, Hal," Maria Agnelli says, stopping to watch the scene. She's got her little dog, Noodle, tucked under one arm, and a gold sequined beret resting jauntily on her white head of hair.

"Heh?" Hal says, tottering over to where Mrs. Agnelli is standing. "Couldn't hear ya, Maria."

Mrs. Agnelli waves her hand with a flick of the wrist. "Nothing. Carry on with your investigation or whatever."

"It is an investigation," Hal confirms, nodding. He has more hair in his nostrils and ears than he has on his head, and his bushy, dark eyebrows are a stark contrast to the few wisps of white hair left on his balding pate. "Damn holes keep popping up around here. I showed Maggie this morning when she was walking home from her night shift at the B&B, and she agrees with me: it's the pirates, for sure. Who can help me fill these holes?"

"Okay, Hal," Holly says, stepping onto the lawn. "We don't know for sure that it's the pirates, and they're leaving this afternoon anyway. If they haven't found whatever they've been looking for this weekend, then they're just going to have to leave without it."

"But what about my lawn?" Hal moans, holding out a hand with bent fingers and knobby knuckles. "I work damn hard to keep my lawn nice, and these criminals show up and make it look like I got gophers living under my grass."

"You should be so lucky," Mrs. Agnelli says. "Been a helluva long time since anybody tried to burrow into *your* grass, Hal."

Hal turns to Holly with a confused look on his face. "What is she even *talking* about?" he asks.

Holly takes off her Yankees cap and touches the thin skin under her eyes with the pads of her fingertips. "I'm not sure, Mr. Pillory, but I'm guessing you wouldn't like it." She shoots Maria Agnelli a look to let her know that she isn't helping the situation.

"What are you going to do about my lawn, Holly? You invited these burglars here, and I heard they're Peeping Toms, too," he adds, pointing a finger at her.

"Hal, the girl has no control over whether the people who visit our island are burglars. She can't ask for a background check on every person who sets foot on Christmas Key, you know."

Hal jabs one finger into his ear and wiggles it around. "Well," he says in his deep, raspy voice. "Then maybe she needs to stop inviting them."

Jake pulls up in front of Mr. Pillory's house, screeching to a stop and jumping out of his cart. "What's up?" he asks brusquely, looking past Holly and speaking directly to Hal.

"Pirates came by and dug up my damn yard," Hal says, patting his protruding belly through the white tank top. "Dug it up like a bunch of grave-robbers looking for gold teeth."

"Okay, Hal," Jake says, clapping the older man on the shoulder gently. "Looks like you've got a couple holes here, but it's nothing we can't fix."

"How many hours until these people leave the island?" Mrs. Agnelli asks, setting Noodle on the ground next to her feet. "I'd like to swing by the B&B and get another look at that fella who wants to drag Bonnie off on some high seas adventure."

Holly sets her baseball cap back on her head. "They leave in a few hours," she says. "And in the meantime, we have guests arriving on the island for a couple of days, and I'd like to make sure we're all in the right mood to welcome them."

"Aww," Hal says, swatting at the air in annoyance. "More visitors. That's the last thing we need."

"It's a black family," Mrs. Agnelli says. "Heard all about it from Millie. Black ladies have such nice skin," Maria adds, her thoughts obviously rambling in several different directions at once. "Hey, I wonder how old the kids are? We haven't had little ones around for a long time."

"We're going to find out soon," Holly says, reaching for Maria Agnelli's elbow and steering her down the street. "I'm going over to the dock in about ten minutes." Holly flips her watch over on her wrist and checks the time. "Why don't you finish walking Noodle and then come over to Main Street so you can meet the family with me, okay?"

Maria Agnelli totters off down the street with a wave. Her little white dog follows obediently, tail twitching behind him.

"You go on and meet the boat, if that's what you're going to do," Jake says. "I've got Hal. I'll help him get these holes filled—"

"And set up a video camera system," Hal shouts. "I want a security camera on my property now."

Jake blinks slowly, and with great patience. It's not an eye-roll, but it's close. "We'll talk about how to make Mr. Pillory feel safe," Jake says, "and you go on and greet the new guests."

"Thanks, Jake." For the briefest second, she's tempted to hug him. But then she remembers his anger as he drove off and left her to fill the holes on December Drive, and she thinks about how he rushed over to her house when she called, scared and alone, and the way he drove her home when she got drunk. No wonder her feelings about him are so jumbled up, so complicated: they always have been. Instead of reaching for him, she takes a step back. "I appreciate your help," she says before walking away.

"Holly." Jake jogs behind her to catch up. He's left Hal standing in the middle of the yard, gaping at the holes in his lawn. "Listen, we need to put this behind us."

"Put what behind us?" Holly says, looking up at him as he blocks the driver's side of her cart.

"Whatever is eating you. I don't know why you hate Bridget, but I feel like it isn't her—it's something you've got to deal with."

Holly snorts. "I mean, it's kind of her," she says.

The muscles in Jake's jaw clench and unclench as he nods, processing this. "Okay," he says. "Okay. Well, I like her. She's fun, and she has a good sense of humor."

"Fine." Holly shrugs. "I want you to be happy. I'm trying not to be bitchy, Jake."

"Then you should try harder," he says honestly. "Because it's coming across...badly."

"Ouch."

"Yeah." Jake kicks the tire of her cart, his hands shoved into his pockets. "I always feel like you're looking for something that's wrong with Bridget so you can gloat about it. I didn't do that to you when you —" he pauses here, swallowing uncomfortably, "—dated someone else. I tried to take the high road."

Holly is instantly filled with shame; Jake is right—he was protective, he was appropriately suspicious, and he warned her that he wouldn't wait around for her in the event that things didn't work out with River—but other than an alpha-male arm-wrestling match between the two men, Jake had kept his distance. He hadn't sneered or pouted the way she's been doing, and while he'd obviously been hurt, he hadn't acted the way Holly's been acting.

She focuses on a spot on the ground next to Jake's feet. "You're right," she says. "I'm sorry. I'm just...confused."

Jake's stance changes and he sighs with loud disbelief. "About *what*, Holly? What are you confused about?"

"Jake?" Hal calls out, wandering around the yard again with both hands on his hips. "I think this tree right here would be a good spot for the video camera," he offers helpfully.

"Be right there, Mr. Pillory," Jake says without turning around.

"I'm confused about stuff," Holly says. This clarifies nothing, and she knows it.

"Okay, fine. You're confused about stuff." Jake folds his arms across his chest. "But you need to get a grip on that." He pulls one arm out and looks at his watch. "And you also need to get over to the dock."

Jake turns and stalks away. Holly looks at him for another second before getting into the cart. He's right: she does need to get a grip on whatever emotions are playing tug-of-war with her heart right now, and she definitely needs to get to the dock. With one backward glance at Mr. Pillory in his knee-high black socks, and Jake in his fitted police shirt and shorts, Holly pulls away from the house and heads back to Main Street.

BONNIE IS SITTING AT HER DESK IN THE OFFICE AT THE B&B WHEN Holly pulls up to the curb. She sits in the golf cart for a minute watching as Bonnie stands and walks over to the white board to write something on their to-do list, and there's a sharp pang in her heart as she realizes that at some point in the very near future she'll be the only person working in that office. The phone will ring and she won't hear Bonnie's cheerful Southern accent as she says, "Christmas Key B&B, this is Bonnie!" There'll be no one but herself to run and get coffee for, and when she sees something interesting out on Main Street, her commentary will be to an empty room.

Holly sets her brake and grabs her purse, giving Bonnie one last look before she heads over to Poinsettia Plaza to check on the pirate who reportedly ended up in Fiona's office.

"Knock, knock," Holly says, poking her head through the door of the waiting room. "Anyone home?"

"Be right out!" Fiona calls from behind the closed door of her exam room. Holly sits in a plastic chair and picks up a back issue of *People* magazine to flip through while she waits. About ten minutes later, the door opens.

"Keep it elevated as much as you can, and take the ibuprofen as needed, okay?" Fiona guides the injured pirate back into the waiting room. He's got one arm crooked at the elbow, hand held up and bandaged.

Holly drops the magazine onto the table in front of her and stands up. "Wow, what happened?"

The man—one of Sinker's main crew—looks at Holly with embarrassment. "Machete accident."

"A machete?" Holly puts her hands over her mouth. Even minor talk of blood and bodily injury make her feel faint. "What happened?" she asks, not sure if she really wants to know.

"I'll let you tell her," Fiona says, one hand in the deep pocket of her lab coat, the other on the shoulder of the pirate.

"Bunch of guys dared me to crack a coconut with a machete, and I accidentally cracked my hand instead."

Holly immediately sinks back into the chair, her knees giving out beneath her.

"Whoa." Fiona pulls her hand from her pocket and kneels in front of Holly. "I've got you, girl." She puts her cool hands on the sides of Holly's face. "Should I get the smelling salts?"

Holly shakes her head. "I'm okay," she whispers, trying not to look at the fat, bandaged hand of the pirate. "But more importantly, is he?"

"I'm fine," he assures her, lifting the arm as proof. "Ouch."

"Keep it steady there," Fiona warns him. "And get your buddies to do things for you as much as possible. We don't want you pulling any of the stitches."

"Stitches?" Holly groans, leaning her forehead towards her knees the same way she'd done the night before outside Jack Frosty's.

"Let's get you out into the fresh air," Fiona says, helping Holly to her feet.

The smell of antiseptic and bandages leaves Holly's nostrils the minute they step onto the sidewalk.

"Here we go." Fiona's voice is full of kindness and patience. "The hangover can't be helping with the nausea," she adds. "Breathe in and out a couple of times."

Holly does as she's told, nodding to let Fiona know that she's going to be fine.

"I'm good. You need to deal with your patient." Holly points at the door to the building. "I have to pop into Scissors & Ribbons anyway."

Just then, Ray Bradford steps out of the salon that's at the front of the plaza. "Mayor," he says, holding the door for her. "Good to see you. And you as well, Dr. Potts."

"Hi, Ray. Can you make sure she gets to Millie and doesn't pass out on the sidewalk here?" Fiona hands Holly off to Ray. "I need to get back to the office."

"Got it." Ray reaches for Holly's arm. "Feeling a little under the weather?"

"Blood," Holly says simply, making a face as she lets Ray lead her into the salon. "Stitches and blood."

"We've got the pirates leaving today, huh?" he asks conversationally as he guides her through the shop.

"Yeah, I think they're planning on getting out of here around six or seven."

"Ahh, sailing off into the sunset," Ray says. He runs a hand down the front of his button-up shirt. "That's a nice touch. And one of them taking a bride home with him is even better."

Holly's stomach plummets. "Right. It...it just..." And she's suddenly at a loss for words. Her eyes fill with the tears that have been threatening to fall all day.

"Oh," Ray says, looking at her with confusion. "Oh, no. Don't cry. Did I do this?" He looks around the salon helplessly, searching for his wife.

Holly swipes at her tears roughly. "No, it's fine. I just drank too much last night and I'm feeling kind of morose today."

Ray smiles. "Morose. Now, there's a good five-dollar word, kid. I'm sorry to hear it though."

"I'll be fine." Holly sniffs. "Sorry to cry on you, Ray."

"Don't give it another thought." Ray squeezes her shoulder encouragingly and points at the back of the salon. "Millie is down the hall."

Holly passes the row of empty black leather chairs and stainless steel shampoo bowls. The big hair dryer domes are pushed up over their respective chairs, waiting for wet heads to dry, and the front counter is tidy and unmanned. Jazz music is playing over the speakers, and the floor has been swept and mopped.

"Millie?" Holly calls out.

"Back room!"

Holly walks down the short hallway and past the restroom. There's another door that's propped open slightly, and she finds Millie inside, crouched on her hands and knees as she searches for something underneath a massage table.

"This looks great." Holly gestures at the small room. When the salon first opened, the space had been used to store boxes and supplies, but Millie has painted the room a soft amber color and set up a trickling fountain on a stand in the corner. There's a series of shelves on one wall with a variety of scented candles, and a massage table covered with a crisp white sheet and pillow.

Millie looks around. "Thank you. I've been putting in some evenings after the salon closes so I can have it ready. I wanted to show it to Calista today when she comes in."

"And Calista must be our potential new masseuse?"

"That's her. She and her husband have two little boys—twins—and they're coming down from Toronto. We've been corresponding so much lately that I'm getting excited to meet her in person."

"I'm sure." Holly watches as Millie feels around under the table. "Do you need some help down there?"

"No, it's fine," Millie runs her hands along the floor. "I lost one of my earrings while I was making the bed. It'll turn up." She stands and brushes her hands against her thighs. "Anyhow, they're going to be here soon, so I'm heading down to the dock to meet their boat."

"I was planning on doing the same," Holly says.

Millie's face breaks into a pleased smile. "Really? Oh, I'm so glad, Holly. You're such a good mayor—always making people feel welcome here. I love that about you."

"I wish everyone felt the same." Holly leans against the doorframe. The calm atmosphere of the dim room is soothing after racing around in the sun with a pounding headache all morning.

"Are we back to this nonsense again?"

"Seems like we are. People are up in arms over the pirates and the holes, and I'm worried they'll be closed off and not as friendly when your family from Canada arrives."

"Oh, they'll be fine," Millie assures her. "You get a bunch of old people in one place and they've got to have something to complain about. Right now it's some holes in the road, two months ago it was the camera crew on our island that wasn't making them famous movie stars."

Holly gives a hard laugh, remembering the fervor over the *Wild Tropics* camera crew. The issue had become a real source of contention.

Millie closes the door to the massage room and leads the way through the salon. The women walk out onto Main Street and back into the brilliant sunlight of a winter afternoon. There are a handful of people on the sidewalks, and several locals are driving their golf carts down the only paved road on the island. Millie stops to wave at Cap through the window of his cigar shop. Holly catches a glimpse of Brian the pirate in a pair of ratty khaki cargo shorts and his Metallica t-shirt. He's got his hands in his pockets and he's ducking into Jack Frosty's alone. Holly had taken him there for one of Buckhunter's famous burgers with grilled onions the day she'd found him sleeping in the bushes, and she figures that he's probably stealing away for another one now before the pirates shove off at dusk.

"Things have been good again with you and Cap, huh?" Millie asks, watching from under the hand that shields her eyes as the ferry crosses the water. Over the holidays Cap had taken Holly to task when he ran against her for her seat as mayor, and some old secrets had bubbled to the surface, resulting in a particularly emotional village council meeting at Christmas-time.

"He's back to his old self," Holly says. "Still on the wagon, still spending time with Heddie, I think."

"That was a doozy, wasn't it?" Millie wiggles an eyebrow. "Never thought I'd see those two looking cozy again after all the years they spent acting like they barely knew one another."

"I'm glad they made up," Holly says. She never knew about the rift between them, and to see them out having dinner together, or walking to the beach arm-in-arm is nice.

"Looks like we've got an on-time arrival." Millie looks at her watch.

"I'm so excited to meet these people, Holly. It's been a long time since we actively recruited people not just to visit, but to live here."

"I know." Holly immediately thinks of Bridget, but realizes that she doesn't count, since they didn't so much *recruit* her as *acquire* her. Before Bridget's arrival, the last person who'd moved to the island full-time had been Fiona, and that was nearly two years ago. "If they decide to stay, we need to take them around and show them the available houses."

"There aren't many," Millie says. "And it's not going to be a popular opinion, but my thinking is that we're going to want to start considering some spots to develop in case we get more people looking at Christmas Key as a potential home."

Holly knows she's right. As they stop and wait at the dock for the ferry to pull up and anchor, she considers possible locations on the island that would work for new housing. They already have Turtle Dove Estates, a small community of houses near Candy Cane Beach, and there are a few houses scattered up Ivy Lane. Her part of the island is family property that she isn't willing to divide up and sell, but there's a good plot of land on the north side of the island that's ripe for development.

"Look—I see them!" Millie says, waving as the boat pulls up. Two little boys in matching striped shirts are jumping up and down, hands flailing in the air.

The captain passes off a small delivery of groceries and newspapers to Holly, then helps the family disembark.

"Calista? It's so good to finally meet you," Millie says, approaching the woman with open arms. She appears to be around thirty, with smooth skin and eyes the color of jade. Her hair twists and curls into an afro with a wash of blonde on its tips, and she's petite, with a purple sarong tied around her narrow hips.

"It's good to meet you, too," Calista says, her eyes crinkling happily as she returns Millie's hug. "This is my husband, Vance." She steps back and puts a hand on the arm of possibly the largest man Holly's ever seen, "and these are our six-year-old twins, Mexi and Mori."

Vance is at least six-foot-six, with the build of an Olympian and a straight, white smile. In contrast to Calista's delicate figure and lighter coloring, Vance is as dark as mahogany and as solid-looking as a hundred-year-old oak tree. When he breaks into a smile, his eyes twinkle just like his wife's. Holly likes them immediately.

"Vance Guy," he says in a deep, rumbling voice. He offers Millie a giant hand. The twins make a wild tandem leap from the dock onto the sand, tumbling like puppies and rolling around with laughter. "It's hard to tell them apart at first, but they go pretty much everywhere together, so we just refer to them as M&M most of the time." He points at his sons, watching them with obvious pride.

"This is Holly Baxter, our island's mayor," Millie says, remembering that Holly is standing at her side. Holly steps forward and shakes hands with both Vance and Calista.

"It's wonderful to meet you both," she says. "We're excited to have new faces visiting the island, and your boys are adorable." She looks at the twins as they get up from the ground and give one another playful shoves. "What did you say their names were?"

Calista motions to her boys to stop the horseplay. "Mexi and Mori —short for Mexico and Moritz."

"Very cool," Holly says, grinning at the rambunctious kids. "I love unique names."

"Well, we got married in Mexico and loved it, and Moritz is after a famous Canadian poet, A.F. Moritz," Vance says, putting his large hands on the shoulders of one of his sons. The boys are a perfect blend of both parents, with the bright smiles and happy eyes to match, and identical heads of hair that look like mini versions of their mother's.

"Welcome to the island, guys," Holly says, bending her knees and sinking a little lower so she can look them in the eyes. They gaze back at her with unreadable faces, their hazel eyes wide. "Are you hungry?"

"I'm sure they are," Calista answers for them. "They refused to eat anything before we left Key West, and it's past lunchtime."

"If it's okay with you, I'd love to take them over to the restaurant on Main Street for lunch while you guys are across the street at the salon," Holly says to Vance and Calista.

"That sounds good to me." Calista looks up at her husband. "What do you think?"

"Sure. That would free us up to ask some questions and talk to

Millie more," Vance says, putting one hand on top of each boy's head. "What do you say, men? Can you go with Miss Baxter and be good for an hour or so?"

"It's okay, you can call me Holly," she says to Mexi and Mori. "And we'll be right across the street from your parents. My uncle owns the restaurant, and he said he'd make you guys anything you want."

The twins turn and look at one another. "Sushi?" says the one on the left. "Spaghetti bolognese?" asks the one on the right.

Holly blinks a few times. "Oh," she says. "I was thinking more like chicken strips or cheeseburgers."

"The boys are actually vegan," Calista says apologetically. "But they watch the food network a lot, so they're always coming up with stuff they think they want to eat."

"Vegan." Holly wracks her brain for the parameters of a vegan diet.

"No dairy or animal products of any kind," Vance says in a helpful tone. "So just fruits, veggies, nuts, grains—stuff like that."

"Maybe a quinoa bowl with avocado and a poached egg?" Calista offers. "That might keep things easy."

"Quinoa." Holly stands up straight and glances at Jack Frosty's. There's virtually no chance that Buckhunter has quinoa on hand. Or that he even knows how to cook it. "Would rice work instead?"

"Sure." Calista pulls each boy to her and kisses him on the forehead. "Be sweet for Holly," she warns them. "Thanks for giving us a little time for adult conversation," Calista says to Holly. "We're just with Millie if you need us."

"No problem," Holly assures them.

With a final wave and a reminder to listen to their new friend, Calista and Vance follow Millie up to Scissors & Ribbons.

"So, what do you guys think? Pretty cool boat ride, huh?"

One twin turns to the other and makes a face. "I don't think she has kids," he says, wrinkling his nose.

"I don't think she knows our names," says the other. And without another word, they take off running in opposite directions, one down the dock, the other into a patch of bushes behind the shops on the south side of Main Street. "Come and find me, lady!" says the one who pointed out Holly's inability to tell them apart. "I'm hiding from you!"

"I'm jumping in the water!" shouts the other. "I'm going to swim back to Canada!" Holly isn't sure whether he'll really jump in, but her gut response is to follow the child who's closest to danger.

It crosses her mind briefly that she could scream for Vance and Calista, but the independent, unwilling-to-fail part of her takes over and squelches that desire. She might not have kids, and she might not know which of these little monsters is which, but she'll be damned if she's ready to throw in the towel sixty seconds after their parents disappear.

Holly watches the land-loving twin dive into the bushes. *He'll be fine*, she thinks. Without wasting any more time, she turns and breaks into a sprint, following the other mop-topped munchkin to the edge of the dock with her arms outstretched to grab him.

CHAPTER 10

"And one time I had to put a giant turtle in the back of my cart and drive her over to the beach so she could swim away and find her home again," Jake says, lifting one of the twins and setting him behind the steering wheel of the police golf cart.

"But where are all the bad guys?" asks the other twin. By now, Holly has figured out that this one—Mori—has a bit of a lisp, and so his question comes out sounding like, "But where are all the bad guyth?" He also refers to his brother as "Mek-thee," the cuteness of which helps to mitigate the impishness of both boys.

"We don't have bad guys on Christmas Key. This is the safest place on the planet," Jake promises. He'd been driving down Main Street when Holly spotted him, and he'd pulled up to the curb curiously, eyeing the two smallest visitors he'd ever seen on the island.

"Then why do you have a gun?" asks Mexi.

"I think it's for the pi-wats," Mori says, pointing across the street at a group of four pirates heading into North Star Cigars.

"Oh, those aren't real pirates, guys," Holly says in a casual tone that she hopes will let the boys see that there's nothing to be afraid of. "They're just men who are visiting our island, and they like to dress up like pirates."

Mexi and Mori both look at her like she's crazy. "But they have *swords*," Mexi counters. "Big ones."

Jake lifts Mori so he can sit on the bench seat of the police golf cart next to his brother. "Eh, fake swords," he tells the boys. "I bet you have some fake guns or something at home that you like to pretend with, right?"

The boys exchange a confused look. "No," says Mexi. "Our mom thinks weapons enforce a patriarchal ideology."

Holly and Jake share the most incredulous look that any two humans have ever shared. "What?" she asks, assuming that she's completely fallen into a different plane and hallucinated the last ten seconds of her life. What six-year-old on the planet talks about patriarchal ideologies?

"Itthh true," Mori lisps. "Thee does thay that."

"Huh." Holly is still speechless. They let the boys pretend to drive the cart for another minute or two, and a companionable silence falls over Holly and Jake. It's almost like the confrontation they had at Hal Pillory's just hours before never happened.

"Hey, pumpkins!" Calista shouts, stepping out the door of Poinsettia Plaza. "Have you been good boys?" The twins slide out of the cart and run across the street to their mother. Holly looks both ways and follows them over. "Did they behave?"

"Yeah, they were fine," Holly lies easily. "We gave them rice with veggies, and they got to meet Christmas Key's only police officer," she says, pointing in Jake's direction.

"Excellent. Thank you so much." Calista smiles at Holly warmly. "And Millie tells us that not only are you the mayor, but you also run the B&B we're staying at."

"Millie speaks the truth. I've got you all lined up to stay in one of our suites, and I planned a few things that I thought the kids might like."

"You guys are fabulous." Calista looks back and forth between Millie and Holly. Vance is hanging back in the doorway, talking to Ray Bradford and keeping an eye on the boys as they chase each other up the sidewalk. "I'm blown away by this place."

"You're blown away and you're exhausted," Vance adds, coming up behind his wife and resting a hand on her shoulder. "And so are the boys. Why don't we take a short siesta and then explore the island after?"

"I'll go and make sure everything is ready for you," Holly says, stepping off the curb. She's happy to be done with her babysitting duties for the afternoon, and is seriously rethinking the other activities with the boys that she's planning on being involved with. "Come on over anytime you're ready."

"We'll be there in a few," Vance promises.

There's no one at the front desk of the B&B, so Holly sits down in the chair that looks out onto Main Street, resting her elbows on the desk. It feels like a million years since she woke up on Fiona's couch that morning, and it's only three o'clock.

"Sugar? Is that you?" Bonnie pokes her head out of the hallway that leads back to the office. "Oh, it is. I was wondering when I'd see you again."

Holly wants to tell her that if she'll just stay on Christmas Key she can see her anytime she feels like it, but she isn't in the mood to open that particular can of worms. The headache Holly's been holding at bay all day is threatening to strike again, and she pulls open the drawer at the front desk, hoping to find a bottle of Advil.

"I met the potential new masseuse and her family, and I watched her kids and fed them lunch."

"Ooooh, the new people. What are they all about?"

Holly searches for the right words as she rifles through the tin of rubber bands and paperclips in the drawer. Behind a small stack of envelopes and a metal letter-opener shaped like a mermaid, Holly finds a beat-up, rusted tin of Tylenol that looks like it washed onto shore in 1957. It'll have to do.

"They're all about vegan food and poetry, as far as I can tell." She pops a chalky Tylenol tablet into her mouth and tries to swallow it dry.

Bonnie's upper lip curls. "As in bean sprouts and Shakespeare?"

"More like quinoa and contemporary Canadian poets." Holly makes a *cacking* sound as the pill sticks in her throat. "Water," she croaks. She scours the front counter for some of Maggie's grog and realizes that all traces of pirate decor have been removed. No grog, no gold-painted

Oreos, no candy. All that's left is the black netting that Holly hung from the mirror behind the front desk.

Bonnie ducks down the hall and comes back with an unopened bottle of water from their mini-fridge in the office. "Here you go, doll."

Holly twists off the cap and takes a long swig. She hadn't even eaten lunch while she watched the twins, and she suddenly realizes she's dying of thirst, too.

"Thanks, Bon." She screws the cap back on the bottle and sets it on the desk. "So the pirates are all checked out, right?" Holly taps on the keyboard at the computer and starts pulling up room information. "Top priority is to get the Seashell Suite set up for the Guys."

"What guys?" Bonnie puts a hand on her hip.

"Simmer down, lady. There aren't any new men arriving on the island—that's the last name of the masseuse and her family."

"Guy?"

"Uh huh," Holly says, clicking the mouse to mark all the rooms as checked-out. "Calista and Vance, and their 6-year-old twins Mexi and Mori."

"Mexi and what-y?" Bonnie's brows knit together.

"Mexi is short for Mexico, and Mori is short for Moritz. Apparently he's named after some poet from the Great White North."

Bonnie huffs and looks out the front window at Main Street. "I'll be damned with all these weird kids' names," she says, shaking her red head in disbelief. "What ever happened to William and Jonathan? Or Mary and Theresa? I don't even mind Amy or Jason, but we're creating a generation of kids with names like Tennessee and Jingle—I don't know what to make of it." Bonnie walks over to the window and faces the street.

"Jingle?" Holly laughs. "I have never heard of a child named Jingle."

"You will," Bonnie says with force. "Or Gouda. Maybe Umbrella. I bet someone's named their kid Wind Storm already."

"That one is a definite possibility." Holly clicks out of the computer program and stands up, stretching her arms. "Is it just me, or does this feel like the longest day ever?"

Bonnie doesn't turn around. "It feels like a day where my closest friend on Christmas Key is avoiding me."

Holly's arms drop to her sides and she stares at the back of Bonnie's head for a minute. "You mean me?" she finally asks.

"Yeah, you." Bonnie turns to face her. "You got so tipsy last night that you had to be escorted out of the bar by your uncle and driven home by a police officer. And today you've been MIA. What gives?"

Holly shrugs.

"That's all you've got?" Bonnie's anger flares visibly. "I have a handsome man offering to sweep me off my feet and all you can do is shrug? No 'Congratulations, Bonnie!'—or 'I'm so happy for you!'...all I get is *this*?" She motions at Holly's dragged-down, hungover face and sagging shoulders. "I was happy as a clam when a man came to Christmas Key and lit your fire, but you can't feel the same way when it happens to me?"

Holly wants to speak, but she also wants to climb under her duvet and sleep for the next eighteen hours, so she weighs her words carefully. "I want to be happy for you, Bon," she says, her words plotted out like tentative footsteps across a rushing stream full of slippery rocks. "But I don't know what you see in him. Or how you think you know this guy well enough to leave the island and run away with him."

Bonnie puts both hands in the air like she's praying to the heavens; her eyes turn skyward as well. "For the love, sugar. *I am not running away with him*," she says in a slow, clear voice. "I'm taking a leap of faith and trying to follow my heart here. I find Doug exciting and dangerous, and when I'm with him I feel sexy and alive," she explains. Her hands drop to her sides.

"But you're sexy and alive *without* him," Holly says with a hint of challenge in her voice.

"Why don't you want me to be happy?" Bonnie's eyes are sad. "Is it because you're not?"

Holly rears back. "I'm not unhappy," she says, putting her hands on the edge of the desk. "I'm not...I'm *not*," she trails off, her eyes stinging like someone's just thrown sand in them.

Bonnie comes around the desk to where Holly is standing. "I'm sorry, sugar. I'm sorry," she coos, holding out her arms to her friend. "Come here. We'll work it all out."

Holly falls into Bonnie's arms and holds her tightly. She refuses to cry again. The past twenty-four hours have been an emotional roller-coaster, and she won't give in to the urge to collapse.

As the women embrace in a tentative cease-fire, the front door to the B&B bangs open and Mexi and Mori trip into the lobby. Holly lets go of Bonnie and puts on her best 'Totally In Control' mayor face.

"Hey," she says with a smile. "Welcome to the Christmas Key B&B. Let's get you all checked in!"

CHAPTER 11

T he day drones on as Holly races around the island. She checks in at home to make sure Pucci has food and water, moves the massive loads of linens from industrial-sized washer to industrial-sized dryer at the B&B, and follows up on the details for the pirates' send-off at sunset. She's invited the Guys to join everyone as the pirates push off in full regalia, thinking that Mexi and Mori might enjoy the festivities, but she's trying to scare up a couple of extra eye patches for the boys and hoping that the islanders will be receptive to seeing new faces in the crowd just as they're saying farewell to a group of visitors who've caused some upheaval.

"Brian!" Holly shouts from behind the wheel of her golf cart. She slows to a stop near the only pirate she's taken a real liking to. "I have a favor to ask, Mr. Chumbucket."

"Anything for you, milady," he says, making a swirling motion with his right hand as he bends at the waist theatrically. "For the woman who finds me a cheeseburger, I'd be willing to fall upon my own sword."

"I don't think gutting yourself will be necessary." She climbs out of the cart and meets him on the sidewalk in front of Poinsettia Plaza.

"I'm just looking for two eye patches and a promise that you guys are really sailing off into the sunset as planned."

"Done with us pirates, are ye?" Brian puffs out his chest and puts on a pirate accent.

"No, it's not that," Holly backpedals. "But I stripped all your beds and gave away a couple of your rooms, so I'm just making sure."

"Yeah," he assures her. "We're outta here at dusk. Our wives and bosses expect us home at some point, so—as with all good things—our weekend on the high seas must come to an end."

"You ready to get back to Anita and the kids?" Holly asks, remembering their conversation the morning she'd found him on the beach.

"I am. And I've taken your advice to heart: I'm going to embrace my weekends away from work and kids' soccer games, then I'll go back feeling refreshed and ready to be the man my wife wants me to be."

"Good," Holly says with a smile. "I'm happy for you, Brian."

"Eh," he says, raising both shoulders. "It's a good life. And *Space Invaders* will still be there when I get home."

"That a boy." Holly winks at him and climbs behind the wheel of her cart again. "Oh, and what about the eye patches? Any chance you've got some spares?"

"I think I can scare up a couple. I'll bring them to the beach with me tonight."

Holly gives him a thumbs-up as she pulls away.

Just a few more hours. If she can make it through the send-off on the beach, she can go home and finally climb into her bed for a good night's sleep. She looks at the sun making its descent in the winter sky. The end of this hungover, yucky-feeling day is near.

"Yo, ho, ho," bellows Sinker McBludgeon. He's standing on the beach near the skiff that Cap is using to ferry the pirates back and forth to their anchored ship. "'Twas a wonderful weekend of grog, wenches, and buccaneering, but it's time for us to set sail again, mates." He peers at his fellow pirates, holding a golden chalice in the air. The other men do the same. "Nothing compares to a weekend of merrymaking and exploring the sea, and certainly nothing can compare with the love of a woman." He gazes at Bonnie meaningfully.

Holly is standing near Fiona and Buckhunter, arms folded across her chest. She's working hard to keep her face neutral and her mind open.

"We've got some new recruits here," Sinker says, nodding at Mexi and Mori. They're wearing the black eye patches Brian found for them. "And I hope their parents don't mind them giving up their land-lubbing ways to become men of the sea."

Across from Holly, Vance and Calista smile at each other. The gold and pink sunset warms their faces and touches Calista's halo of hair, and Holly realizes that they'd make a great ad for the island. As surreptitiously as possible, she slides her phone out of her back pocket and opens the camera app.

"Christmas Key natives—you've welcomed us and let us plunder your island for treasure. For that, we thank you."

Holly looks at the faces of the other islanders and realizes that most of them are taking him literally. Maria Agnelli shakes her head, lips pursed angrily.

"Any more holes?" Fiona whispers, leaning closer to Holly.

"Nothing since Hal's front yard," she whispers back.

"And no leads on who was outside your house last night?"

A shudder runs the length of Holly's body. She's been able to put last night out of her mind while working her way through a busy day, but with night falling, the memory of Pucci growling in the darkness and of a shadowy figure running away from her house comes back full-force.

"Nope, no leads," she says. The last sliver of sun is fast disappearing, and Jake goes around, lighting the long-handled torches that Holly purchased for the occasion. They look like a bunch of island natives in the dusky night. Mexi and Mori are weaving through the crowd, playing tag in the sand.

"Now we'll shove off with the promise to return again, mates— maybe when you least expect it," Sinker says with a wicked laugh. He tips the chalice back and drinks. After his first sip, the rest of the pirates do the same.

"It's a pirate's life for me!" the men shout in unison, throwing their arms around one another's shoulders as they make their way to the water's edge.

In short order, Cap runs the skiff out to the big ship and back again a few times, collecting and depositing pirates with each trip. Sinker waits until the end, holding Bonnie in his meaty arms as he kisses her. The wind picks up the tail ends of the black scarf tied around his head, and there's a three-day beard covering his lined cheeks. Calista and Vance gather Mexi and Mori and lead them away from the passionate embrace.

Cap has room for Bonnie to join him on the last run out to the pirate ship. They skim the water on the small boat while Bonnie holds tightly to her man under the emerging stars. It's quite a scene, and even Holly has to admit—if only to herself—that there's a certain romance to a pirate ship in the night, lit up from within and glowing against the mysterious depths of sky and sea. Sinker pulls Bonnie close one last time before climbing onto the rope ladder that hangs from the side of the ship. It's worrisome to watch a man his age dangle against the side of a huge boat, and to know that the only thing standing between him and a perilous fall is his own unreliable agility. Holly squints as she watches, hoping for the best.

Finally, Sinker's up and over the side of the boat safely, and Cap pulls away. Bonnie's silhouette against the night is that of a heart-broken woman: she faces the big boat as Cap brings them back to shore, one hand held limply in the air in farewell.

It would be a more touching scene for Holly if she weren't so deeply exhausted. Before the boat even pulls up its anchor, she's said goodbye to Buckhunter and Fiona and is back in her cart with the headlamps on, driving herself home.

In her driveway, she finds another hole.

CHAPTER 12

"The details haven't completely worked themselves out yet," Calista says to Millie on Wednesday morning as they sit across from one another at the bistro tables outside of Mistletoe Morning Brew. "We need to find out more about online education and how we can homeschool the boys, but I think we want to do it."

Holly waves at them both and walks directly into the coffee shop. She'd spent the day before taking Mexi and Mori on a dolphin-hunting excursion, and had let them eat their rice and beans with their hands as they sat on a log on the beach. They'd gotten into three fights that ended in tears; Mexi had tripped and scraped his knee on the sidewalk, which necessitated a quick visit to Fiona's office for bandaging; and they'd helped Jake wash his golf cart while their parents scoured the island for possible houses to live in.

The hole in the driveway that Holly had driven into Monday night had required another patch job, but Buckhunter had done it in ten minutes that morning, swearing that he hadn't even heard Pucci bark at whomever was on the property.

"Think they're gonna stay?" Carrie-Anne asks Holly as she approaches the counter.

Holly glances back over her shoulder, watching through the front window as Millie and Calista talk like old friends. "I think there's a good chance," she says.

"Might be fun to have some young ones around." Carrie-Anne rinses out a coffee pot in the small stainless steel sink behind the counter. "Most of us don't get to see our grandkids enough, and there's a real energy that comes with the little guys, you know?"

"Yes, there is an energy," Holly agrees. "Can I get a peppermint mocha, please?"

"Iced or hot?"

"Hot," Holly decides. "And an iced latte for Bonnie."

"Oh, she's already been in, hon." Carrie-Anne starts to make Holly's drink with her back to the counter. "She got a box of pastries to take over to the office, so I think she's already a few steps ahead of you."

Holly smiles to herself. "She always is."

"Gonna miss that gal when she takes off for—where is she headed with that big oaf of a man?"

"Clearwater," Holly says. The word tastes bad on her tongue, and she wonders when she'll ever be able to say the name of Bonnie's new town without looking like she's sucking on a lemon.

"Huh. Not sure how I feel about that," Carrie-Anne says, pouring the hot coffee into a to-go cup for Holly. "How about you?"

"I'm not a huge fan of the idea." It's a grand understatement, but Holly is committed to keeping her real thoughts to herself when it comes to Bonnie leaving. She's already painted herself into numerous corners with both Bonnie and Jake by not keeping her true feelings about their love lives inside her own head.

"Well, a girl's got to follow her heart, I suppose," Carrie-Anne says, snapping a lid on Holly's coffee and then ringing it up. "Otherwise I wouldn't be living on a tropical island with a woman I fell in love with while I was still married to a man."

Holly laughs quietly. "True."

"And if my beloved didn't follow *her* heart, we wouldn't be living in a bungalow with a donkey and ten turkeys in our front yard, and we wouldn't be running a coffee shop that's decorated like—"

"Don't tell me," Holly says, holding up a hand. She looks around at the decor, taking it all in.

"Well, it's February first, so you can guess the basic premise of this month's theme."

"Love, obviously," Holly says. There's a shelf near the door that's stacked with books; Holly walks over to it and shuffles through the pile. "*Time Traveler's Wife*," she reads. "*Outlander. Almost Yesterday. Remembrance.*" She reorganizes the books and looks at the posters around the shop. They're all for movies like *Peggy Sue Got Married, Midnight in Paris, Groundhog Day,* and *Somewhere in Time,* which shows Christopher Reeve's handsome profile as he gazes longingly at an old-fashioned portrait of Jane Seymour on a red wall.

"I've got a playlist, too," Carrie-Anne says, holding up a finger to indicate that Holly should wait before she guesses. "Here we go." She pushes the button on the cd player behind the counter, and music blasts through the speakers in the ceiling. The opening notes of Cher's "If I Could Turn Back Time" fill the coffee shop.

"Time travel romance?" Holly guesses.

"Ding, ding, ding!" Carrie-Anne claps her hands. "You got it, girl."

"That's cool," Holly says, and she means it. She'd assumed there would be generic love songs and hearts pasted up everywhere, so this unexpected twist pleases her.

"Miss Baxter." Cap Duncan steps through the door of the shop. "Just the person I wanted to see." He closes the door behind him. "We got a village council meeting coming up?"

"February fifteenth," Holly says, sipping her hot coffee.

"I just wanted to give you a heads-up that people are talking again."

"About what?"

"Holes in the road, pirates, and," Cap lowers his voice here and tips his head at the window behind him, "having little ones on the island on a permanent basis."

"Is that a problem?" Holly's tone is slightly defensive.

Cap sighs. "Dunno. Haven't had kids here full-time since you and Emily were young. Guess we'll have to see."

"Guess so," Holly says. She nods at Carrie-Anne and heads for the door. "As always, if anyone has something to say, they just need to let Heddie know so she can put it on the agenda."

It's already about sixty-five degrees outside, and Holly breathes in the mild air as she walks up Main Street to the B&B. She hasn't had the nerve to ask Bonnie about when she plans to leave the island, and everything between them still feels fragile. They'd talked in broad strokes the day before about the things on the calendar for February and March, and Bonnie proof-read an email for Holly to send to Coco's lawyer about her intention to track revenue directly related to the reality show.

"Your mother's lawyer got back to us," Bonnie says the minute Holly's through the door of the office. She sets her coffee down on the desk and hangs her straw purse on the hook by the door.

"And?"

"Says you need to set up a system to find out whether people inquiring and booking stays on the island are are based on publicity from the show."

"But why?" Holly pulls out her desk chair and flops down. "Who cares?"

"Apparently Coco cares, sugar." Bonnie looks up from the laptop screen, gazing at Holly over the rims of her pink and yellow striped reading glasses. "And if she gets her lawyer involved, I think it's probably best to just comply. I'll figure out a system for tracking people who only heard about us from the show—don't worry about that."

But Holly does worry about it, because when Bonnie is gone, she's going to be left fielding all the calls, sifting through the information, booking the rooms at the B&B, planning events on the island, and organizing their advertising efforts. All of a sudden it feels like a weight is crushing her chest and blocking her windpipe. Holly stands up and walks to the whiteboard on the wall. She swallows around the painful lump in her throat.

"Last I heard, the show was set to air at the end of April, so I have some time to figure out a strategy for that." Holly uncaps the blue marker and looks at the space on the whiteboard in front of her. She's purposely tried out the singular there, talking about when *she'll* have to figure out a strategy, as she can't count on Bonnie being there to help her. Now that she's standing in front of the whiteboard, she doesn't even know what to write.

"Honey?" Bonnie says with concern. "You okay?"

Holly sets the pen back in the tray. With a forced smile, she turns around and faces Bonnie. "Yeah, everything is good. I've just got a lot on my mind."

"At least we're not listening to cannons firing off at all hours," Bonnie says. "That has to make you happy."

"*Me?*" Holly says, pointing at her own chest. "You were the one who freaked out about the cannons!"

"Oh yeah, that *was* me." Bonnie gives Holly her most winning smile.

"How are you going to get used to being with a pirate?" Holly asks, her hands resting on the chair back as she stands behind her desk.

"I'm not sure," Bonnie says. "Honestly, I'm going to take this crazy thing day-by-day. It's kind of out of left field, isn't it?"

Holly nods, looking at her hands. "I've never seen anything happen that fast," she says. "Maybe that's why it worries me so much. And it also bugs me that I never knew you were unhappy here."

"Unhappy?" Bonnie's jaw drops. "Honey, no! I'm not unhappy here —never have been. I just got bitten on the tail by a love bug."

"A love bug?" Holly makes a face.

"Oh, you know what I mean. And sugar, Doug *challenges* me. That man keeps me on the edge of my seat, and nothing fans my flames more than that."

Holly chews on the inside of her cheek, inspecting her long fingers with their short, filed nails as she leans on the back of her chair. "I guess," she says. "I mean, if he makes you happy, then that's what counts." It doesn't sound totally convincing, but it's the best Holly can do, given her general distrust of Sinker McBludgeon.

"Any man who can sweep you off your feet in forty-eight hours or less is worth at least a little more investigating, don't you think?"

"Sure, Bon. At least a little."

The warm Florida sun streams through the big windows that look out onto Main Street, and it touches Bonnie's red hair like the flames of an autumn fire on crackling leaves. There's a tenderness to the quiet moment in the office, and it fills Holly with longing for something that isn't even gone yet.

CHAPTER 13

H olly slides out the back door of the B&B on the morning of February's village council meeting. It's quiet on the pool deck, and she paces around the kidney-shaped pool, running through the possible objections the islanders might have to the items on the agenda.

In the weeks since the pirates' departure, Holly and Bonnie have worked to smooth the way for the Guy family, who have officially decided to make Christmas Key their home. They'd gone back to Toronto after their visit to make arrangements, and Holly's been working on the house they chose on White Christmas Way. She's spending all her free time painting, clearing the yard, and accepting the furniture deliveries as they arrive by boat. As owner of the property, it's Holly's job to get the house in shape for her new tenants.

"Holly?" A voice interrupts her thoughts. She looks over the fence and sees the top half of Bridget's face as she stands on the sidewalk on Main Street. "Can I come in?"

Stifling her knee-jerk response to say no, that she's too busy right now to talk, Holly nods. "Sure."

Bridget waits for Holly to lift the latch on the inside of the squeaky gate for her so she can come in. "Hi," she says as the gate slams shut behind her.

"What's up, Bridget?" Holly cuts right to the chase. She's got agendas to print and collate in her office, and she's promised Bonnie that when she comes back she'll have coffee and a muffin in her hands for her hardworking assistant.

"I just wanted to talk to you."

Holly pulls in air through her nostrils, hoping that they don't flare with obvious impatience. As mayor, she reminds herself, it's her job to listen to *all* of the islanders and to hear their concerns, and this extends to Bridget as well, no matter what her misgivings are about the girl.

"It's two things, really," Bridget says, smoothing her wavy, blonde hair with one hand. She sits on the edge of a pool chair without being invited to do so and stretches out her long, toned legs. There's a tiny, blood-red tattoo of a rose on one ankle.

"I'm all ears."

"Okay, the first one is...I need some advice," she says, pressing her palms together like she's holding a delicate piece of tissue paper between them. "As you know, there aren't many young women on the island—it's pretty much just you and me."

"And Emily and Fiona," Holly adds.

"Right," Bridget says, giving Holly an indulgent look. "But you and I have some things in common that are different than the other girls."

Holly starts running through her opening remarks for the village council meeting in her head while nodding and trying to look focused. "Uh huh. Go on."

"We find ourselves in certain *situations* that, you know, maybe the others don't. I mean, given age and circumstance," she says delicately.

"Okay."

"And there are some things that require confidentiality, which—I'm sure you know by now—isn't really a thing on this island."

Thoughts of the village council meeting fade from Holly's mind for the moment. "What exactly do you need confidentiality for?" She narrows her eyes at Bridget.

"I guess what I'm asking," Bridget says, lowering her eyes to look down at the frayed edges of the olive green skirt that barely covers her tanned thighs, "is whether I can trust everyone on this island."

Holly is completely at a loss. She has no idea where Bridget is going with this, and there's a loud warning signal in her head that's telling her to be on guard. "I think you can," she says defensively. "I trust the people on this island. I've known most of them my whole life."

"What about Fiona?"

"She's my best friend," Holly says, her haunches up at the mention of Fiona's name. "I trust her completely."

"As a doctor?"

"Of course."

"Okay," Bridget nods, standing. "Then I guess I'll trust her, too." She walks to the gate, the muscles of her young, shapely legs flexing as she pauses and turns back to Holly. "Thanks."

"Wait," Holly says, remembering that Bridget had come to her with two items to discuss. "What was the other thing?"

Bridget sighs. "I really hate to bring it up," she says, not quite meeting Holly's eye. "But I have some concerns."

"About?"

"About the people who are moving here."

"Huh," Holly says. She folds her arms and waits.

"You know I spent a couple of years in Hollywood," Bridget says. "And I got used to all kinds of things. I had to deal with people whose religions I didn't agree with, and I'm even fine with people like Ellen and Carrie-Anne."

"People like Ellen and Carrie-Anne?" Realization dawns on about a three-second delay. "You mean..."

"Right. Two women who are married," Bridget says flatly. "I almost don't even care about that anymore." She's on a roll now, picking up steam. "But I grew up in a small town, and I'm feeling kind of freaked out right now."

"By what?" Holly is beyond stunned, and there's no way to hide it.

"These people who are moving here." Bridget takes a couple of dramatic steps across the pool deck like she's trying to hit her mark on a film set. "Come on, Holly. They're *black*," she says in a stage whisper.

Holly stumbles—she actually takes two steps back and trips over her own heels like she's been socked in the jaw—and catches herself by grabbing onto a pool chair. "What?" she says hoarsely. "Are you kidding me?"

"I'm not kidding, I'm being honest with you. I know you've lived in this bubble of paradise your whole life," Bridget says, gesturing at the palm trees and sky around them, "but some of us come from a world of *reality*, Holly." Her voice has gone from the sweet, practiced lilt she normally uses to a flat, harsh tone that doesn't match her pretty face.

The taste of acid burns Holly's throat as she feels the thickening sensation that comes before vomit. She grips the metal of the pool chair tightly with one hand, keeping her distance from Bridget.

"Come on. Don't act like the thought hasn't crossed your mind," Bridget says with disdain.

But it hasn't. The thought that they'll have children on the island has crossed her mind. The notion that newcomers will always change the make-up and the interpersonal relationships of the population has crossed her mind. But the race of their new neighbors hasn't warranted more than a passing awareness. A sharp pain creases Holly's stomach and she holds onto the chair for support.

"I've got bigger things to think about now," Bridget says with a toss of her head. She places one open palm on her stomach. "If Fiona can confirm for me what I think is true, then I need to worry about the future for me and Jake and for—" she pats her belly, "well, for everyone else." A beatific smile melts the ugly look on Bridget's face.

The world shrinks in Holly's line of vision, and the ground feels unfixed beneath her feet. She watches as Bridget turns again and leaves. The gate clangs with her exit, and Holly sinks to the chair. She focuses on the ripples in the turquoise water in front of her, fighting back the waves of nausea.

Like a tsunami rushing the shore, Bridget had just confirmed for her in one fell swoop what she's been feeling all along: beneath the sweet, curious demeanor of Jake's new girlfriend is a person who Holly can't—and won't ever—like. This flip from the dingy girl who doesn't know what scurvy is to a blonde bigot in a miniskirt has left Holly reeling. Racism and ugliness have no place on her island, and neither does Bridget. But if what she's hinting at is true and a visit to Fiona confirms that she's carrying Baby Zavaroni, is there any way Holly can get rid of her?

She lays back on the pool chair and stares at the blue sky overhead with blank eyes, wishing she could get far, far away from this mess. What would her grandparents have done in this situation? Surely not have stood by and waited for hate to infect their island—and neither will she. Holly watches as a plane the size of a fruit fly crosses through their airspace.

CHAPTER 14

The village council meeting is short and to the point. Half a dozen villagers lodge formal complaints about unscreened visitors coming to Christmas Key, with accusations of prowlers and Peeping Toms leading the charge against large groups of tourists.

Holly debates the concerns with vigor, even putting herself up as an example of someone who *should* be afraid of prowlers (given the fact that she'd found a man rustling around in her bushes after dark) but isn't fearful of progress and the challenges it might bring. It feels like old news to her as she stands at the podium looking out at the faces of her neighbors, and a sense of weariness overcomes her. The only thing keeping her from dropping the pink marble gavel and walking out is the knowledge that a solid majority have moved beyond their initial concerns and are actively supportive of having people visit Christmas Key.

"Listen," Cap says, standing up. "May I speak, Mayor?"

Holly nods and leans on the podium with both elbows, fingers laced together as she waits for whatever Cap has to say. It hasn't been long since he'd actively spoken out against the reality show crew being on the island, so she's curious about what he might add to the conversation now, just a few months later.

"The pirates were a rowdy bunch, but no real harm's come of their visit," Cap says in placating tones.

"Is it you plugging the damn holes they drilled all over this island?" Maria Agnelli pipes up. "And did you hear they paraded around Snowflake Banks with their willies out and scared poor Holly half to death?"

Holly blushes; she didn't know that word of that incident had spread beyond her and Bonnie, but she isn't shocked—news travels like a virus around the small island.

"Well, it isn't like she hasn't seen a willy or two in her day," says Hal Pillory, standing slowly on creaky knees to address the crowd without invitation. "But those pirates certainly did a number on my yard."

"Oh, your yard again," Mrs. Agnelli rolls her eyes with disgust. "I'm less concerned about your damn lawn than I am about you making accusations about how many naked men Holly's seen."

The lightheaded feeling that rushes through Holly feels like the response she'd had to being in Fiona's office with a bandaged pirate. It also feels a little like the revulsion she'd felt that very morning when Bridget had talked to her on the pool deck. She clears her throat.

"We seem to have lost the plot here," she says into her microphone, hoping to calm everyone down and turn the subject away from her experiences with the male anatomy. "Thank you for your input, but I've recovered from both the surprise visitor on my property, and the accidental peep show I got at Snowflake Banks."

Hal and Cap sit down again, and Mrs. Agnelli clenches her jaw tightly, frowning at both men.

"I think if we look at this as another experiment, we can all agree that having people visit us adds a certain flavor to our lives that's lacking when we don't invite tourists to Christmas Key."

Without meaning to, Holly's eyes go to Bridget; she's sitting next to Jake, her hand resting on his thigh. There's an impassive look on Bridget's face that reveals nothing.

"And along these lines, I'd like to announce that we have a new full-time family joining us on the island. Calista and Vance Guy will be here next week with their twin boys, living in the pink house on White Christmas Way," she says, keeping Bridget's face in her peripheral vision.

"How old are the kids?" Hal Pillory asks, putting a finger in the air like he's trying to get a waiter's attention.

"Six," Holly says. She looks back at Jake and Bridget. He's leaning into his girlfriend, listening to her as she whispers in his ear. "The boys are six, and they're full of mischief and energy."

"That's little boys for you," one of the triplets adds. "Between my sisters and I, we have seven boys. I can tell you it's going to take a village to raise those kids." She looks at the identical faces next to her, and all three women nod wisely.

"What about school?" asks Iris Cafferkey. "We don't have Eleanor and Sadie with us anymore, and we couldn't have gotten you and Emily educated without them."

A warm feeling passes over Holly at the mention of the two retired teachers who'd given her and Emily the most fun, hands-on school experience she could have ever dreamed. They'd spent hours reading books in the shade with Sadie and Eleanor, and had learned to bake in their kitchens for home economics credit. They'd gone swimming in the ocean and done stretches on the sand to learn physical education, and had been taught to identify leaves, insects, birds, and plants in the thick trees as a way to learn science. After both she and Emily had gotten their high school diplomas and Holly had moved to Miami for college, Eleanor Smith moved back to Ohio to live with her kids. Sadie Pillory had passed away peacefully in her sleep, leaving her husband, Hal, to become the lonely, cantankerous widower he is today.

"School is something to consider," Holly says. "But lots of kids do distance learning these days, and homeschooling by the parents is a pretty popular thing right now. Calista mentioned that they're looking into that."

The older islanders exchange curious looks; in their day, parents educating their children at home was virtually unheard of, and they knew nothing about kids taking courses online from teachers they'd never even seen face-to-face.

"Let's assume that Calista and Vance will take on the concern for their kids' education at this point. We just need to worry about welcoming the family to Christmas Key and getting their house in order. Calista wants to get right to work at the salon when they arrive."

"What will the husband do?" Mrs. Agnelli asks. "Is he one of those new-style stay-at-home-dads?"

Holly shakes her head. "I'm not sure. He might be." There's still a lot she doesn't know about their new neighbors, and with each question, she's realizing that having children on the island is going to change things more than she'd imagined.

In the crowd, Jake snakes an arm around Bridget's chair and rests his hand on her shoulder, pulling her closer so that he can kiss her cheek.

"I think we've covered everything on this month's agenda," Holly says, looking away from them quickly and consulting the typed paper in front of her. "If no one has anything else to add, I'd like to adjourn and remind the ladies that we've got a function to attend at Jack Frosty's in honor of Bonnie."

"No men allowed?" Wyatt Bender hollers, cupping his hands around his mouth.

"Nope, no men," Holly confirms. "Just a going-away party that the ladies are throwing for our favorite redhead." She keeps the smile plastered on her face as she sets the gavel on its block. Having a send-off for Bonnie is a painful reminder that this move is actually happening. Even though Holly's been over at Bonnie's most nights helping her decide what to pack and what to leave behind for what Bonnie promises will be "frequent visits" to the island, it still hasn't felt as real as a going-away party.

The islanders get to their feet at varying paces, some leaning on canes as they make their way out of the B&B's dining room. Holly hangs back, chatting with the stragglers as the rest of the women head over to Jack Frosty's. She's let the triplets take the helm as far as planning the bash, and she's just as happy to show up after everyone is situated so that Bonnie can bask in the glow of her friends' well wishes, rather than stew under the storm cloud of Holly's disapproval. It's been hard to keep her feelings and tone about the whole thing neutral, but Holly's bitten back her words in Bonnie's presence on more occasions than she can count, saving the vitriol she feels for Sinker McBludgeon for the times she and Fiona share a drink on her lanai.

After everyone has gone, Holly sits in one of the empty chairs and looks around the room. There are discarded agendas on the chairs around her, and the double doors leading out of the dining room are open at different angles. The sound of the front desk phone ringing in the distance filters down the hallway and into the large room.

Some days feel uneventful and routine, and others have so much packed into twenty-four hours that Holly can barely believe all that's happened at the end of the day. It's only lunch time, but she's already had a horrifying discussion with Bridget, run the monthly village council meeting, and is about to go and pretend to be happy for the woman who's been her mother and confidant for most of her twenties.

Holly rests an arm on the back of the chair next to hers. There are tables pushed against the wall, covered with half-empty boxes of pastries and a coffee tureen. Everyone should be seated at Jack Frosty's by now, and Buckhunter has undoubtedly mixed up the first batch of margaritas for the ladies. Holly pushes herself out of the chair and walks around to pick up the agendas people have left behind.

She gives the dining room one last look as she stands in the doorway with a stack of papers in one hand, then flips out the lights and closes the door. She'll deal with putting the tables and chairs back later.

"Margarita with salt, or no?" Buckhunter asks as Holly steps up into Jack Frosty's. He's moved all the tables around and set up one giant seating area in the middle, where twenty-two women are currently drinking and toasting a smiling Bonnie. There are gift bags scattered around the long table, and someone has set a crown on Bonnie's head and wrapped a pink feather boa around her neck.

"Salt, please," Holly says, tucking her loose hair behind one ear.

Buckhunter salts the rim of her glass and pours the lime green concoction straight from the blender. "Key lime—Bonnie's request," he says, handing it across the bar. "You doing okay?"

Holly nods and grabs the drink with both hands. "I'm fine, thanks."

"They went pretty easy on you at the meeting," Buckhunter says. "But I think some of the questions were good ones."

"About the Guys and having children on the island?"

"Yeah." Buckhunter checks the burgers he has on the grill. He flips the front row of patties and sets his spatula down, wiping his hands on a towel before he looks back at Holly. "They were valid concerns. For the next twelve years or so, we'll have kids on the island. That changes things."

Holly puts the cold glass to her lips and tastes the salt. "I don't think it has to be a bad change," she says after swallowing her first sip. She reaches for a square cocktail napkin on the counter.

"No, but we need to be prepared," he says. "Their parents are coming here to live a dream, and as far as we know, they've never lived anywhere but in a big city. This is a huge change. They're going to need help."

"I see your point." Holly wipes the condensation off her glass with the napkin.

"It's just something we all need to think about." Buckhunter flips the second row of burger patties. "But it's going to be fun. I'm up for the challenge," he says over his shoulder.

"Thanks for hosting Bonnie's lunch," Holly says, watching her uncle's back in his faded Hawaiian shirt.

"No problem, kid. You should go and join the other hens. We can talk later."

There's an empty seat at the center of the table between Iris Cafferkey and Fiona, so Holly pulls it out with one hand and sets her margarita down.

"Hi, sugar!" Bonnie waves from the head of the table. Her cheeks are already pink from laughter and tequila. "Sit down—burgers are on the grill!"

Holly scoots up to the table and hangs her purse over the back of the wood chair.

"What do you think of all of this excitement, love?" Iris elbows Holly and leans into her. "Bonnie finding her soul mate and leaving us, new folks headed our way...big changes, wouldn't you say?"

"Yep. Big changes." Holly lifts her glass and takes another long drink, wishing immediately that she hadn't. "Ow, ow, ow," she says, pounding her forehead with the heel of her hand. "Brain freeze."

"Slow down, sugar," Bonnie says, laughing. "Last time you were here you overdid it by a long shot. Wouldn't want to have to call Jake to give you a lift home at two o'clock on a Wednesday!"

The other ladies giggle, but Fiona puts one hand on her best friend's arm protectively. "Sip it, girl, don't chug it," she says in a low voice that only Holly can hear. "You don't want to be wrecked before the food comes."

As if on cue, Buckhunter arrives at the table with two trays of burgers and fries. "I've got one with no ketchup and one with extra pickles and mustard," he says, passing out the burgers.

"No ketchup over here." Glen raises a hand.

"And I've got the pickles and mustard," Gwen says from across the table. It takes Buckhunter three more trips, but he gets everyone situated with burgers and fries, then disappears to mix up the next batch of margaritas.

"Tell us everything, Bonnie Lane. You're such a minx, moving off the island and taking up with a man you just met," Fiona says. The women all look to Bonnie as they take the first bites of their burgers. Heddie Lang-Mueller picks up a knife and fork and cuts a small piece off of hers like it's a steak.

"There isn't much to tell yet." Bonnie holds her burger in both hands. "Doug is waiting for me to get there, and we're going to set up the house with the stuff I bring."

"Are you taking everything?" Gwen asks, dipping a french fry in ketchup.

"No, I'm leaving most of it here. I want to come back to my house and visit as often as I can. And besides, I want to feather my new nest with things that Doug likes, too."

"Doug," Iris says, sighing dreamily. "I wonder what he looks like when he's not wearing pirate clothes."

"Well..." Bonnie's eyes dance with mischief.

"Iris," Holly warns, "you might want to re-think that statement."

Iris blushes. "I meant in his regular work clothes, lass, not in his birthday suit."

The table roars with laughter. Bonnie adjusts her rhinestone crown and holds the boa out of her way so that she can take a bite of her sandwich. Holly watches her assistant bask in the attention of their favorite neighbors. It's good, this send-off party. Bonnie deserves to know how much she'll be missed by everyone, but there's no way she can know how much she'll be missed by Holly.

The women's laughter tinkles through the open-air bar as they tease Bonnie, and Buckhunter brings more baskets of fries to the table to fuel a gabfest that lasts all afternoon.

CHAPTER 15

The pink house on White Christmas Way is nearly ready for the Guy family to arrive and move in. Holly has spent the week following Bonnie's farewell luncheon juggling B&B stuff and working on the house, and now, as she stands in front of it and looks at the turquoise paint she's just touched-up on the shutters, she feels accomplished.

"Looks nice," Jake says, pulling up to the curb in his golf cart. "But I think you missed a spot."

"Where?" Holly squints at the shutters flanking the front window.

"I'm kidding."

Holly lunges at him jokingly with the paint-tipped brush in her hand, pretending to smear him with turquoise.

"Ah, ah, ah—keep the paint on the house, Mayor." Jake holds out a hand. "I think that qualifies as assaulting an officer with a deadly weapon."

"A paintbrush?"

"Specifically one that could turn me into a Smurf."

Holly considers the paint on her brush. "Smurfs don't have this much green—they're more blue."

"You say potato, I say po-tah-toe."

Holly freezes; River had said the same thing to her once, standing in her kitchen as she'd rinsed the seashells they'd collected on a hot summer night. She thinks of him standing there, pouring their root beers into glasses while she'd run her hands under the cold water in her sink. She's been so preoccupied lately that she hasn't even thought about River, and all the sensations of that moment come rushing back on the heels of Jake's words.

"Yoo-hoo," Jake says, waving a hand in front of her from behind the wheel of his golf cart. "You in there?"

"Yeah," Holly laughs. "Sorry, I'm here."

"So the new family arrives today, and Bonnie leaves on Saturday," he says, trying to prompt her.

"Right. And Bonnie wants us to stop by her place every week or so and air it out."

"That seems weird, being in her house when she's not even on the island," Jake admits.

"I know."

"How're you handling her leaving?" Jake rests his wrist on top of the steering wheel.

"Not well," she says, looking at the paintbrush again. "But *que sera, sera*, right?"

"Sure." He looks at the pink house behind Holly, making no move to leave.

Holly isn't sure she's ready to ask, but the conversation she had with Bridget the day of the village council meeting has been gnawing at her incessantly.

"How's Bridget?" she asks.

Jake frowns. "She's been acting different. Last night I found her crying in the kitchen, and when I asked her why, she said it was because we didn't have any sourdough bread."

Holly's stomach turns. "Huh."

"And remember how you always used to hate that I kept my gun in the house?" he asks. "She was giving me grief about that, too. Said I needed to build a shed for it with a padlock or something because it freaked her out."

"Huh," Holly says again. "PMS, maybe?" she offers hopefully.

"I guess. And she's a little put out about having new people move to the island, I think."

"Which is weird," Holly says more emphatically than she means to. "Because she herself just moved here and changed the dynamics of the island."

Jake blinks a few times before speaking and then puts his cart in gear. "But you and I have had this conversation already—more than once," he says, rolling slowly along next to the house. "So I don't want to go there again. Plus you've got things to do." He points at the house and slides his sunglasses back on before hitting the gas and driving away.

But she doesn't, not really. The house has been deep-cleaned, the light bulbs checked and changed, the lawn mowed, and the paint fixed. All it needs now is a family to move in and give it life again. Holly stands on the lawn, the paintbrush dangling at her side.

She wants to run into the street and shout after Jake, "Ask Bridget how she really feels about the new family moving to Christmas Key! Ask her what she said to me—just *ask her!*"

But she doesn't. She doesn't do it because grown women don't act that way, and because she knows that with enough rope, Bridget will eventually hang herself.

"We're exhausted!" Calista says, dragging both boys and multiple suitcases through the door of their new house. "And this place looks amazing, Holly."

"Good, I'm glad you like it." Holly stands in the front room, watching as the boys break free of their parents and race through the house like cats with their tails on fire.

Vance Guy comes through the door last, arms laden with back-packs, duffel bags, and suitcases. "I think we've got enough clothes to stitch together and cover the state of Texas," he says, dropping every-thing on the tile floors with a thud. "Which seems unnecessary, because we're living in the tropics and we don't need much besides flip-flops and shorts."

Calista runs a smooth hand over her forehead and pats the blonde-tinged hair that haloes around her head. She's got silver rings and several silver bangles on both hands, and she's wearing a pair of wide-legged jeans and a tank top.

"I can't believe we're here," she sighs. "Like, I *really* can't believe we did this." For a moment, her face registers the shock of someone who's just made a major life decision and is realizing the enormity of it. "We're raising our boys on a tropical island."

"That's a fact, my love," Vance says in his deep, soothing voice. "And it's going to be great."

They exchange a glance that makes Holly think of the look new parents must give one another in the hospital as they gaze at their newborn baby for the first time. She suddenly feels like she's intruding on a private moment.

"Well, you should have everything you need to get through the first couple days. We put together some casseroles and dishes and left them in your fridge," Holly says, pointing to the kitchen the way a flight attendant points at exit rows. "And we stocked your bathrooms with toilet paper and bar soap."

Calista's hands fly to her face. There are tears in her eyes. "You did?" she says, moving toward Holly. She opens her arms and wraps them around Holly's neck, hugging her tightly and swaying back and forth. "Thank you. Thank you so much," she says into Holly's hair.

"You're welcome."

"That's very kind," Vance says, reaching out one arm and wrapping Holly in a side-hug after his wife has finished thanking her. "We appreciate the hospitality, and we're really looking forward to getting to know everyone."

Not everyone, Holly thinks. But hopefully she can shield this nice family from the ugliness that she saw on Bridget's face that day at the pool. And hopefully Jake will see Bridget for who she really is before it's too late—unless it already is too late.

"Listen, you guys get settled," Holly says, taking a step back as the twins race through the room and around her legs. "I'm only a phone call away if you need anything. My number is on that piece of paper on the kitchen counter, along with Jake's number."

The Guys walk out onto their new front porch to see Holly off. Vance and Calista stand there with their arms wrapped around each other, watching as she goes. Vance is so much taller than Calista that her head barely comes to his armpit. Mexi and Mori bound out the front door after their parents, somersaulting across the lawn and shouting as they dance around. Holly climbs behind the wheel of her pink golf cart and flips on the power. She notices a streak of paint on her left thigh and another on her forearm as she waves at the Guys and pulls onto the sandy road.

The sun is about to settle in for the night behind the trees, and the sky is streaked with fading trails of purple and mauve. Sunsets on Christmas Key slip by unnoticed sometimes, but tonight Holly takes it all in, letting nostalgia fill her as she remembers the way she used to watch the sunset on the beach with her grandpa. She hopes he'd be proud of the choices she's making, and that he'd approve of the things she's done. When Frank and Jeanie Baxter had moved to this undeveloped island nearly thirty years ago, they couldn't have dreamed of having a doctor and a cop—or of having a beauty salon and a cigar shop—on Main Street. They certainly couldn't have imagined a reality show filming there, or a bunch of pirates anchoring offshore for a weekend of drinking and partying with the locals. She's pretty sure they'd be impressed.

Okay, Holly thinks, pulling her mind back to the present. *The new family has arrived and gotten settled, and tomorrow is Friday. Bonnie leaves on Saturday, and...*but her mental check-list stops there, because as she turns right from White Christmas Way onto December Drive in the early evening twilight, she drives directly into another giant hole.

CHAPTER 16

F iona cuts through the water early the next morning like the hull of a ship splitting the waves. Her strokes are long and graceful, and her red one-piece catches Holly's eye every time she does a flip-turn in the B&B's pool and starts another lap.

Holly is on the second floor of the inn, delivering a stack of clean towels to the empty rooms, and the sight of her best friend in the pool lures her away from her work. She sets the linens on a cart and takes the stairs, cutting through the lobby and out the back door.

"Hey!" Holly says, hoping Fiona will hear her as she comes up for air. "Fee!" With a final stroke, Fiona reaches the wall and pulls her upper body out of the water, leaning on her forearms and looking up at Holly.

"Hey yourself," Fiona says, trying to catch her breath. She slides her goggles off and tosses them onto the pool deck before hoisting herself up and out of the water. "What are you doing here this early?"

"I woke up and wanted to start tackling my to-do list." The pool area is still dim and slightly cool before the sun rises enough to warm it. "When are you swimming to Cuba?"

"Not for two more months—the fundraiser is in April." Fiona picks up her towel from the pool chair and wipes off her face. She tips an ear toward the ground and shakes her head.

"Well, you look good."

"I'm a long way from ready, but fortunately it's a relay, so I can take breaks and one of my teammates will take over for a while." The ripples and waves from Fiona's previous strokes spread out like rings in a pond, eventually settling into near-stillness.

"I've been dying to talk to you," Holly says, sitting on a pool chair. "But yesterday at Bonnie's lunch didn't seem like a good time."

Fiona wraps the large towel around her body and tucks one corner of it in under her armpit; she sits on the chair across from Holly's.

"I was out here the day of the village council meeting, and Bridget showed up."

"Here? She came to the B&B?"

"Yeah. She walked right up to the gate." Holly points at the street entrance to the pool deck. "She asked if we could talk."

"Okay."

Holly scratches at a bug bite on the front of her calf. "I've kept it to myself for the past week or so because I wanted to process the conversation and make sure I wasn't twisting things around in my head."

"What'd she say, Hol? You're obviously freaked out by this." Fiona squints at her, tilting her head as she listens with concern.

Holly takes a deep breath. "Has she come to see you? As a doctor, I mean."

Fiona pulls her lips in and holds them there for a beat. "Well." Her pause speaks volumes. "You know I can't talk about my patients with you—or anyone. I mean, we can joke in broad terms about silly stuff like hemorrhoid cream and Viagra, but I can't name names. Or give details."

"Of course. It's just..." Holly trails off. She's back at square one, trying to swoop in behind the scenes and save Jake from potential disaster. It's the same thing she'd done with the reality show crew in town as they'd tried to manufacture an on-screen romance between him and Bridget (clearly she'd been unsuccessful with *that* venture), and now here she is, trying to mentally will a potential human out of existence so that he isn't saddled with a small-minded woman for the next eighteen years—or longer.

"What's going on? Just because I can't give you details doesn't mean that you can't tell me everything. You're my best friend, Hol," Fiona says. "If something's bugging you, I want to know."

The knot in Holly's stomach unwinds a little. Fiona's nearly ten years older than she is, and the fine lines around her eyes are off-set by the smattering of freckles on her lightly-tanned skin. Her long, strawberry-blonde hair is pulled into a wet braid, and without make-up, her blue eyes stand out like two chips of blue quartz.

"She hinted that she might be pregnant," Holly blurts out. "And she flat-out told me that she's a racist."

"Whoa." The softness in Fiona's eyes disappears. "Are you serious?"

"Yep. She said she was concerned about having people on the island who weren't white."

"Whoa," Fiona says again. "Damn."

"I know."

The women sit in silence for a minute, listening to the hum of the pool filter and the sound of carts driving down Main Street towards Mistletoe Morning Brew.

"I understand that you can't tell me whether she came to you for a pregnancy test—I get that. But I can't sit by and let Jake tether himself permanently to a woman like this."

"And you're sure he doesn't know?"

"No, I have no idea what he knows. Lately we either get along— almost to the point that it feels flirtatious—or we argue. We had it out over Bridget in front of Hal Pillory's a couple weeks ago, and I always feel like he's just waiting for me to say something bad about her."

"Then this news won't be well-received," Fiona says, shaking her head sympathetically. "He'll probably accuse you of having it in for her."

"Exactly." Holly stands up. "And I have another hole to fill over on December Drive—"

"Wait, aren't the pirates gone?"

"They're gone, but the holes keep showing up. Not as frequently, but I drove right into this one last night and I know it wasn't there before."

"Let me get dressed and I'll come with you," Fiona offers.

"No, it's Friday. I'm sure you have work to do, and you need to shower after being in the pool. I've got this."

"You sure?"

Holly nods at her friend, giving her a grateful smile. "I'm sure. I'll catch up with you later."

The hole takes twenty minutes to fill with sand and dirt. On the drive back to the B&B, Holly turns onto Cinnamon Lane and sees a small sign with a skull and crossbones that she's forgotten to take down. She'd hung the hand-painted signs on each street marker, and as she stops to remove it, she admires her own handiwork and the creativity that went into decorating the island. It isn't just the money that tourists bring—it's the planning and preparing for events and guests that really charges her.

Planning stuff. Organizing. Solving problems. Keeping her hands busy. Holly thinks about all these things as she slows to a stop at the end of her own driveway. Pucci is out on the porch, head resting on his front paws next to his silver water bowl.

"Here, boy!" she calls, giving a whistle. Pucci's head lifts and his ears perk. "C'mon!" Without hesitation, he's up and bounding across the yard to greet her.

It's Holly's last day at the office with Bonnie, and she knows that having Pucci there for moral support will be comforting, and that having him there to take on short walks will give her an excuse to leave if she starts to get choked up.

Holly pats the seat next to her and Pucci jumps onto it, settling quickly into his position as co-pilot. "All right, buddy. Let's go to work."

MIDDAY, BONNIE STEPS OUT TO ORDER A LAST WORKING LUNCH from the Jingle Bell Bistro. Holly sits behind her computer, a pencil jabbed through the twist of hair she's piled on top of her head. She's managed to keep things professional and to hold the tears at bay all morning while she and Bonnie work peacefully. Jimmy Buffet is playing through the bluetooth speaker that Holly's placed on the windowsill. She reaches down to pet Pucci, who's curled up next to her feet.

Her phone vibrates on the table next to her elbow. *I've been wanting to say hi and to check in on you. Hope you're doing well.*

Holly's heart stops. River. She reads the message three more times. When she doesn't touch her phone, the screen fades to black again. She and River haven't spoken in more than a month, and hearing from him now stirs up all kinds of feelings. Rather than grabbing the phone and responding, Holly gets up and slips her feet into her discarded flip-flops.

"Let's walk down to the dock and back," she says to Pucci. He hears the word "walk" and is up and on all fours before Holly has her sunglasses on.

Outside on Main Street, Vance Guy is strolling down the sidewalk a few steps behind Mexi and Mori.

"Hey, men!" Holly says to the twins, ambling over to them with her hands in the pockets of her cargo pants. "What's up?"

"Mek-thee lotht a tooth," Mori says in his adorable lisp, pointing at the gaping hole in his twin brother's mouth.

"The tooth fairy came," Mexi adds, falling to his knees and petting Pucci's face.

"That's pretty cool." Holly leans forward to admire the missing tooth. "What are you guys doing today?"

"We're out for a walk while Mom works," Vance says, "and I'm looking at this space right here." He points at the narrow storefront next to Mistletoe Morning Brew. There hasn't been anything in the space for years, though at one time an ambitious islander had hoped to turn it into a souvenir shop. Tourism hadn't been plentiful enough at the time and the shop had come and gone quickly.

"I've got an idea if this place isn't being used, and I'd like to run it by you, Mayor."

"Shoot," Holly says, watching from the corner of her eye as Mexi and Mori lead Pucci down the sidewalk to the dock. Vance seems unconcerned that the boys are heading for the water, so she turns her attention back to him.

"I'd like to open a book shop." Vance puts one of his large hands on the dirty window, cupping it so that he can see into the empty building. "It's long and narrow, but I think I can fill it with shelves and put some tables and chairs out front here like they've got next door at the coffee shop. I might even be able to clear another area out behind the store and do a reading garden or a back deck on the other side of the building."

Holly smiles at the picture he's painting. "You've been here a day and you're already thinking of ways to jump in with both feet. I like it."

"I'm not used to the laid-back island life, I guess," Vance admits. "I need to have my hands busy and my mind working on a project."

Holly peers into the dark shop next to Vance. "I'm impressed. Seriously." She checks her watch and glances over her shoulder to see Bonnie pulling into the B&B's little parking lot with bags of food on the seat next to her. "How about if I grab the keys from my office and we can check it out?"

"Really?" Vance grins. "So the mayor really *does* have the keys to the city?"

"This mayor has the keys to this city," she says, laughing, "because her grandparents bought the island in the eighties and groomed her from birth to run the place." Holly points at the B&B. "Give me a sec—I'll be right back."

"Hey, sugar," Bonnie says, pulling sandwiches from the white paper bags and setting up lunch on their desks. "I got you a diet Coke and a club sandwich with a pickle. Come and get it."

"Thanks, Bon. You start eating—I'll be back in a few minutes." Holly opens a desk drawer and fishes around for the ring of keys that she knows will open every door on Main Street.

"What's shakin'?" Bonnie sets a bag of potato chips on Holly's desk and one on her own. She's been in high spirits all morning, surely anticipating her departure the next day, but has wisely kept her excitement under wraps.

"Vance wants to check out the empty shop next to Mistletoe," Holly says. "He thinks he's got a good idea for the space."

Bonnie sits down and unwraps her own turkey sandwich. "I forget that little place is even there—I walk by it every day and think nothing of it."

"Let me show him really fast, and I'll come back so we can eat together."

Holly walks out the front door of the B&B and down the steps to the sidewalk, her flip-flops smacking the pavement behind her. She's left Pucci with the boys, who are back with their dad, holding sticks and rocks in their small hands that they must have found near the dock.

"Let me unlock it and we'll open the back door so we can get some light in here," Holly says, bending over and sliding the key into the rusty lock. The salty air is quick to corrode metal this close to the ocean, and the lack of use that some of the locks see only serves to speed up the process. She wiggles the key around and turns the knob. "Here we go."

The air inside the small shop is still and dusty. The boys cough dramatically as they step up and into the narrow space. Holly walks to the back and opens the door, throwing more light into the building.

"The power is off, obviously, but it's wired for electricity and phone, though that may not be necessary anymore, given the fact that we have cell service and WiFi," she says, holding the keys in her hand as she gestures at the walls. "You could probably run shelves along as much of the walls as you want. And out here," Holly says, stepping out the back door, "it's pretty overgrown, but there's a lot of potential." The trees and tall grass behind the shop give way to a thicket of palm and lemon trees, and Holly knows that if they clear it out, there's a good opportunity to use the space for a reading area.

"I can see it," Vance agrees, and it's clear that he's calculating cost, effort, and viability as he takes it all in. "Woodworking is a hobby of mine," he says in his smooth baritone, "and I could probably put together a pretty natty deck out here. Maybe string some lights up around it."

"Natty—nice word," Holly says, picturing the things he's describing. "If you tear out some of these bushes, there's a pretty view of the trees, and over there," she points beyond the building, which ends with

Mistletoe Morning Brew, "if we clear that out as well, there'd be a view of the water."

"The water?" Vance says with boyish excitement. "Oooh, this is getting good." He claps his hands together, rubbing his palms like he's rolling a marble between them. "I can see it all now, Holly. This is great."

"I can, too." There's a loud banging sound from inside the shop, and Pucci comes out the back door to join Holly and Vance on the uncleared patch of land. He looks up at his mistress warily.

"Boys?" Vance calls. "What are you doing?"

"Nothing!" they shout in unison.

"They're never doing *nothing*," Vance says conspiratorially.

"Maybe we should close up and come back when Calista is free?" Holly offers, leading Pucci back into the shop. Mexi and Mori are in there, pounding their rocks on the floor like cavemen trying to crack them and shape them into weapons.

"Mex, Mor," Vance warns. "Let's not bust up the shop before Dad even signs a lease." Holly can't imagine moving fifteen hundred miles with a couple of rambunctious six-year-olds, and the fact that Calista is spending their first full day on the island getting acquainted with her new job has to be stressful for Vance and the boys.

"I need to get back to work," Holly says, walking to the front door. "But why don't you holler at me when you guys want to look at it again, and we can crunch numbers and talk more about the logistics. I think a bookstore is a rock-solid choice for this spot, and I know everyone will be on board if we put together the details and bring it up at the next village council meeting."

"When is that?" Vance says, shepherding his boys through the shop by their shoulders.

"Third Wednesday of every month, so our next meeting would be..." Holly re-locks the store with her key, jiggling the rusty lock again as she bites her lower lip. "The next meeting would be March fifteenth."

Vance nods, thinking. "That gives us a few weeks to kick some ideas around. Thanks, Holly," he says. "I'm going to take these monsters out for lunch, and I'll talk to you in the next couple days."

"Perfect." Holly jingles the key ring on her hand. "You guys have a good day, okay?" she says to the boys. "Make sure Mexi orders something he can eat now that he's down a tooth." She winks at Mori.

"He can eat apple-thoth," Mori says, punching his brother lightly on the arm.

"I hate applesauce!" Mexi shouts back, running down the sidewalk in the direction of Jack Frosty's.

"Food time," Vance says apologetically. "Thanks again."

Holly waves as the boys race up the steps to Buckhunter's grill. They disappear into the open air bar with loud shouts and laughter.

Holly walks back to the B&B lost in thought. The idea of another new business on Christmas Key has her wheels turning. It isn't until she's seated across from Bonnie and unwrapping her club sandwich that she remembers there's a message from River on her phone.

CHAPTER 17

"I'm emotionally vulnerable right now." Holly watches the boat that's taking her beloved Bonnie to the mainland as it shrinks in the distance. "He caught me at a weak moment."

"You do have a lot going on," Fiona says.

Bonnie had gotten onto the boat with little fanfare, but with more than a few tears. Holly has been dreading this moment, but she stands there now with dry eyes, her heart heavy and sad.

"If I'd waited any longer to text him back it would have been rude."

"That's probably true," Fiona says, wrapping an arm around Holly's waist and pulling her close. The sun is sinking, and it's an uncharacteristically windy afternoon on the island. They stand there together, their summer dresses billowing wildly around them, looking like two women huddled together to stay safe in the middle of a storm. "What did he say?"

"He said he misses me." Holly squints into the wind, her hair flying around her; a piece sticks to her lips and she pulls it away. "He wanted to know if I missed him."

"Wow." Fiona doesn't say anything else. They watch the boat as it turns into a tiny speck on the horizon.

Saying good-bye to her friend has turned Holly inside out. She'd spent the previous night at Bonnie's house, and even though she's promised to call Holly as soon as she makes it to her new home in Clearwater, Holly is still feeling unsettled about the whole thing.

"Hey, it's after four," Fiona says, checking the waterproof watch she wears when she swims. "Wanna go to the Ho Ho? Everyone should be there tonight..."

Holly nods, arms wrapped around her body as she holds herself tightly against the wind. "Yeah, that would be fun." She glances at Fiona, whose hip is touching hers. "But don't let me drink, promise? Alcohol and this mood do not mix. I'll end up crying in a corner by myself or something."

"I promise," Fiona swears. "I'll make sure Joe only mixes you virgin drinks all night."

Holly takes Fiona's hand and they walk up the sidewalk together, past Mistletoe Morning Brew, which is closed for the day, and past the empty storefront that she'd shown to Vance the day before.

"Hey, did I tell you that Vance wants to turn this into a bookstore?" Holly points at the dirty window of the shop as they pass.

"Seriously? That would be awesome."

"He's got big dreams. We even looked out back and talked about building a deck where people can hang out and read."

"They could get their coffee next door and come over," Fiona says. "Hang out, read books, drink java...it all sounds very Portland, doesn't it?"

"As in Maine?"

"No, as in Oregon—where all the hipsters are."

"Oregon is also where you-know-who lives."

"Ohhhh, right," Fiona says. "I forgot River and his fishing buddies were all from the Northwest." She tugs Holly's hand to keep her moving. "Okay, so what else do we need to hash out with regards to Old Slugger?"

"*Bonnie* always called him Old Slugger," Holly moans, her face falling again. It feels like she's wandering around in the dark, trying not to run into sharp things, but at every turn she nearly impales herself. River. Bonnie. What next—Jake and Bridget? Her mother?

"Sorry, scratch that. What did you say when he asked if you missed him?" Fiona nudges Holly as they approach the B&B's parking lot. They're both parked there, and the rest of Main Street feels almost deserted because Bonnie had demanded that everyone say their good-byes before she went down to the dock, so only Holly and Fiona are still there. Most of the other islanders have already gone home for an early dinner or converged on the Ho Ho for the Saturday evening gathering.

Holly stops next to her cart. The wind blows the sand of the parking lot and it swirls around the two women, coating their sandal-clad feet in a fine dusty powder.

"I told him things had been hard since he left. I told him I hated the way it felt when he went home on Christmas Eve, and I hated that things ended so badly between us. I told him I felt like it was all my fault."

"But did you tell him that you miss him?"

Holly chews on her lower lip and pushes the hair out of her eyes as the wind works overtime to blow it back into her face. "No. Not yet."

"Woman, you're killing me!" Fiona throws both hands in the air.

"Why?"

"Because, you're, you're..." Fiona pulls her hair into a low twist and holds it over one shoulder to keep the wind from tangling it. "Because, you have these beautiful, amazing men who would do anything for you, and you can't commit. Like, you *cannot commit*. I feel like you came pre-programmed to be a lone wolf, and a part of you *wants* to have a man and be in love, and the other part of you is all 'Love. I cannot compute,'" Fiona says this last part in a robotic voice. "You have to make a decision."

"Says who?" Holly asks simply. And the weird part is, she means it. Who says she has to choose one guy and settle down forever? She isn't opposed to it, but who says it's that easy? Who says she *has* to do it that way?

"Says the universe!" Fiona argues. She looks around the lot and at the back door of the B&B. "I don't know," she finally acquiesces. "Maybe I'm the one who's wrong here. Maybe this island follows different rules than the rest of the world."

"Like the Bermuda Triangle?"

Fiona laughs. "Yeah. But my honest advice—as a woman nearly ten years older than you—is not to let great men and potentially great relationships pass you by. Not for progress, not for your duties as mayor, not for work at the B&B. I've known a lot of not-so-great men, and you've got two rockstar examples of the species in your orbit, but you're so blasé about it that it makes me want to throttle you."

Holly is holding back a smile. "But how do you *really* feel, Fee?"

Fiona reaches over and pinches Holly's upper arm. "Oh, come on." She takes the few steps to her own cart and slides behind the wheel. "I guess if you want my advice," she shouts over the rush of wind, "then you'll ask for it. Now let's go and do some non-drinking at the Ho Ho and pray that Joe takes the stage so we can dance a little."

"I can dance anyway," Holly says with a shrug, getting into her hot pink cart.

"Yes, you do dance to your own beat, my friend," Fiona says, backing up and looking over her shoulder. She puts the cart in gear. "I'll see you over there."

Holly waits for Fiona to pull out of the lot and turn right onto Main Street. When she's alone, she sits for a minute, watching the empty, dark windows of the B&B. They look back at her like unblinking eyes. She knows Fiona would never say the things she just said if she didn't really mean them and want her to be happy. Holly taps the steering wheel with her fingers, thinking about the way things ended with Jake and with River. She even goes back over the short relationships she had in college. Fiona's right—what is it about her that makes her push men away just when things are getting serious?

The wind whips the palm fronds around in the trees overhead. Bonnie's absence and the fact that she'll walk into an empty B&B office on Monday morning hits her hard, twisting her stomach and clenching her insides. She doesn't want to be alone forever, pushing people away as soon as they get close. She doesn't want to hang onto the childish feeling that just because her own mother left her, everyone else will eventually leave too. Fiona's words are worth considering, and River deserves an answer.

Holly reaches inside the purse on the seat next to her and pulls out her phone.

❋

THE BAR IS ALREADY FULL WHEN HOLLY GETS THERE. FIONA'S CART is parked next to the palm tree that's always wrapped in holiday lights, and Holly wheels into the unmarked spot next to it, putting her cart in park and shutting it off. The sun is hanging out over the water on the west side of the island, and she watches it for a minute, letting the roar of the ocean and the wind soothe her.

The islanders are always pleasantly rowdy on a Saturday evening at the Ho Ho, and Holly knows tonight will be no different. The only thing that's changed is that Bonnie's gales of laughter won't rise above the crowd as she and Wyatt Bender flirt with one another mercilessly. And when someone does something worth noting (as they almost always do), Bonnie won't be there to cock an eyebrow at Holly to remind her that they need to discuss the event over coffee at their desks on Monday morning.

It all feels so colorless and changed to Holly, but she's determined to put on a brave face and push forward. After all, life is about change and progress—two things she's been pushing for on the island in recent months, and two things she knows are painful, but necessary.

"I thought you got lost!" Fiona shouts, carrying two frosty glasses in her hands. "I got you a virgin daiquiri, though Joe says that's almost sacrilegious on such a gorgeous evening. Something about rum and wind going hand-in-hand." Fiona passes Holly a frozen drink. "Should we sit on the beach?"

Fiona leads them out the back of the open bar and onto the sand, where they sit facing the waves.

"Looks like this is the place to be!" Gwen, Gen, and Glen are trailing down the stairs with their own drinks in hands. "Mind if we join you?" asks Glen.

"Not at all," Holly says, kicking off her sandals and tossing her purse on top of them. She finds a spot in the sand and sits down. The fading sun warms her face, and a sweep of goodwill and peace floods her unexpectedly.

As the other women settle on the sand around her, Buckhunter shouts at them from the top of the stairs. "Is the party outside this week?" He's already barefoot and wearing an unbuttoned shirt, his tanned, wiry upper body exposed to the wind and the late winter sun.

"Come on out!" Fiona says over her shoulder. She scoots over on the sand, making room for her boyfriend. It's still strange to Holly sometimes when she takes a step back and remembers that her best friend and her uncle are dating. Pretty, petite, fiery Fiona, and rough, tattooed, mysterious Buckhunter. A doctor and a bar owner. A ball of energy and an enigma. But somehow it works.

Buckhunter sinks to the sand next to Fiona and leans over to kiss her through his neatly-trimmed silver-gray goatee. He puts an arm around Fiona's shoulders. "Since there are no guests on the island right now and I knew everyone would be coming over here, I thought I might as well close up shop and join you all."

"Glad you did," Holly says, smiling at her uncle as he gazes happily at Fiona's freckled face.

Before long, the triplets' husbands make their way onto the sand, and then Cap and Heddie sit on the bar's steps, watching the group from a distance as they talk quietly. Holly waves at them both and turns around again, closing her eyes and feeling the sun on her eyelids. It's only been a few months since Heddie and Cap started hanging out with one another again, and a whole history between them has been exposed and healed. The fact that they're both German and love the same books and movies doesn't hurt, nor does Heddie's gorgeous, regal presence. The echo of her youthful film star beauty is still evident in everything about her, and from the look on Cap's face, he's only too happy to be basking in her presence again after several years of estrangement.

Oddly, everyone goes quiet on the beach. The golden scenery and the dying wind are the backdrops to the gathering, with the islanders all facing the sinking sun. Holly takes a moment to appreciate the tranquility of the moment. It's a sliver of time she gets to share with the people who mean the most to her in the world. A second in their lives where there are no outsiders amongst them, only the few who know exactly what it means when one of the fence posts of their community takes leave of them.

Under the palm tree sits the Cafferkey family, with Emily between

Iris and Jimmy. She smiles happily at the ocean before her. To Holly's left is another knot of her friends and neighbors, with Hal Pillory sitting on his own lawn chair near a patch of seagrass. He's got flip-up shades clipped to the bridge of his glasses, and they're propped straight up like an open garage door as he watches the waves roll in and out.

Jake ambles down the steps, one hand in the pocket of his shorts, a beer in the other hand. Bridget is nowhere to be seen, and this makes Holly happy. This is a moment for the people of Christmas Key—the real islanders—and it's perfect in its unplanned simplicity.

As the sun slips towards the horizon, Holly swirls the melting drink around in her glass. Somewhere across that vast sea, Bonnie's sailing to a new life. One that Holly might not agree with, but one that she'll support if it makes her friend feel complete. And far away—across water and land—River's reading her text in Oregon, probably thinking of how he'll respond to her.

From inside the bar, Joe Sacamano hits the switch and the hanging lights around the bar go on, casting a glow onto the sand. The sound of his amplifier kicking on is an indicator that live music is coming, and a smattering of applause breaks the silence on the beach. People start to get up and brush sand off their backsides, carrying drinks up the stairs as they prepare for another night of music and dancing with their neighbors. Buckhunter offers Fiona a hand and they follow the crowd up the steps. Holly waves them off, taking a drink through her straw as she lingers on the beach.

She waits a while longer, listening to the chatter of happy people in the bar and the sound of Joe strumming his guitar in the twilight.

CHAPTER 18

H olly's almost survived her first week alone in the B&B office by blasting music whenever she isn't on the phone, taking Pucci out for several short walks a day, and forwarding her phones while she leaves for lunch. On more than one occasion she'd turned to tell Bonnie something or had started to forward an email on to her, but then she remembered that B&B business was no longer relevant to Bonnie.

On Thursday afternoon, the office phone rings just as Holly and Pucci are returning from a Mistletoe Morning Brew run.

"Christmas Key B&B, this is Holly," she says breathlessly, kicking off her Converse and folding her feet under her thighs on her office chair.

"Sugar?"

"Bon!" Holly shouts, jumping back up from the chair like she hadn't meant to sit down in the first place. She's gotten one text from Bonnie, just confirming that she'd arrived in one piece and would call as soon as she got more settled in. "How are you?"

"Oh, I'm fine, doll. How are you?"

"I miss you so much," Holly says. "It's been so weird being in the office without you this week. Even Pucci knows something is different."

"Awww, I miss the two of you," Bonnie wails. "How is everything else?"

"Other than us being heartbroken without you, everything is good. The new family is all settled in. Vance and I have been talking details all week about him opening the bookstore, and he's getting a pitch ready for the next village council meeting in a couple weeks."

"That's wonderful, sugar," Bonnie says with enthusiasm.

"I'm excited about it. But I'm less excited about the fact that Bridget is a hideous racist who might be carrying Jake's baby."

"Say what?"

"I didn't want to load you down with gossip and stuff while you were trying to leave, but on the day of the last village council meeting, Bridget showed up while I was sitting by the pool." Holly walks over to the bank of windows that looks out onto Main Street and settles in on the wide ledge to tell Bonnie all the stuff she's been holding back. She'd wanted to tell her everything before, but out of kindness to her friend, she'd tried to keep the focus on getting Bonnie ready to go, rather than on dragging her into more island drama.

She recounts the whole thing to Bonnie as people walk by her window and wave. By the time they're done talking, Holly's told her all about Bridget, the three new holes they've found on the island in the past week, and about the handful of bookings she has coming up at the B&B.

"I feel like there's a lot going on," Bonnie says. She hesitates for a second. "Hey, are you sure you don't need me there, sugar? I could maybe pop back over and give you a hand…"

"No, Bon. Of course not," Holly says hastily, her eyes focused on Mexi and Mori as they race down the sidewalk on the other side of the street. One of them has a soccer ball tucked under his arm. "We're totally fine."

"Okay, if you're sure," Bonnie says. There's a strong hint of disappointment in her voice.

"I'm sure. Everything is covered, I just wanted to catch you up on the gossip so that you didn't come back to visit in a few months and stumble onto a new bookstore and a pregnant Bridget without any warning."

"Well, thank you for that," Bonnie says. "I'm dying to hear how it all turns out. You'll keep me posted?"

"You know I will," Holly promises. As she watches, Mexi and Mori drop the ball and start kicking it around, shoving one another as they chase it down the sidewalk and nearly run into Mrs. Agnelli. Holly scans the area, but she doesn't see either of the boys' parents nearby. "Listen, Bon, I've got to go. I'll talk to you soon, okay?"

"Okay, sugar. Love you heaps."

"Likewise," Holly says. She sets the cordless office phone on the desk and shoves her feet into her tennis shoes. "Be right back, Pooch," she says to her dog when he lifts his head from the dog bed in the corner.

Outside, Mexi and Mori have nearly reached North Star Cigars with their soccer ball. Holly looks up and down the sidewalk, searching for Vance or Calista. In the split second that her eyes are off the boys, one of them boots the ball with a power she wouldn't have guessed he had in him, sending it sailing through the air and across the street. Holly's mouth drops open as she watches the ball heading directly for the golf cart that's driving down the road. She's poised to shout a warning when Hal Pillory notices the ball coming at him in his peripheral vision. He swerves wildly to avoid it, and plows into a parked cart. The force of the impact stops him like a brick wall. Hal plunges forward in his cart and hits the steering wheel with his chest.

Holly barely has time to realize that Bridget is sitting behind the wheel of the parked cart, because her eye is still on the ball as it spins through the air, the black and white hexagons a blur as it makes contact with the huge front window of Mistletoe Morning Brew. The shattering of glass fills the air like church bells, and everything on Main Street goes still.

Mexi and Mori are frozen in place on the sidewalk, eyes wide. Hal is bent over the steering wheel of his cart, moaning and bleeding from the forehead. Ellen and Carrie-Anne's faces are perfectly framed in the giant hole that looks in on their coffee shop, the jagged edges of glass surrounding them as they clutch one another in shock. Mrs. Agnelli is still standing on the sidewalk with one hand over her heart. The scene is interrupted by a shout from the door of Poinsettia Plaza.

"What the…Mexi! Mori!" Vance Guy booms loudly as he steps out onto the sidewalk. The door to the plaza swings shut. He breaks into a jog, reaching his boys in mere steps. "What's going on here?"

No one speaks as he leans down, holding each boy by the shoulders in turn and looking into his sons' shocked faces. Holly swallows hard and rushes down her side of the street to help Hal and Bridget.

"Everyone is okay," Holly yells across the street at Vance. "Can you get Fiona?"

Vance's face creases with concern as he takes in the various pieces of the puzzle and the whole picture starts to come together in his mind. "Stay here," he instructs his boys curtly, pointing at a spot on the sidewalk. "Do not move." He runs back to Poinsettia Plaza and disappears inside.

"Hal, are you okay?" Holly asks gently. She's afraid to move him. Hal moans back at her when she places a hand on his shoulder. "I'm here, and Dr. Potts is on her way." Without leaving Hal's side, Holly turns her attention to Bridget. She's sitting in the driver's seat of her own cart, phone in hand. "Bridget, are you okay?"

Bridget is shaking as she punches the screen of her phone. "Not really," she says. She's shaking and trying not to cry. "Did you see that?"

"I did," Holly confirms, trying to keep her voice calm. "You don't need to call anyone, Bridget. Dr. Potts is coming—everything is going to be fine."

"I need to call Jake," she says, finally looking up from her phone to glare at Holly. Holly looks around at the street. Mexi and Mori are obeying their father, standing exactly where he left them. Cap has emerged from his shop and is holding Mrs. Agnelli under the elbow, waiting to be called on if help is needed. The silent anticipation on the street reminds Holly of a showdown at high noon.

"I'm sure someone has already called him," Holly assures her.

"He needs to hear about this from me," Bridget says, holding up her phone as proof that she's calling him. "Jake?" she says, sounding mildly panicked. "Can you come to Main Street? I'm hurt. There's been an accident."

Holly turns her attention back to Hal and the blood that's running down his temple. His eyes are still closed tightly.

"Oh my God," Fiona says, rushing across the street with her open lab coat flying behind her. She's got a first aid kit in one hand, and her eyes are trained on Hal. "Anyone else hurt?" she quickly scans the area.

"Bridget got banged up a little, but mostly Hal," Holly says, stepping out of the way so Fiona can attend to him. Main Street springs to life again as carts pull onto the road and slow to a stop. The triplets emerge from Tinsel & Tidings and rush down the sidewalk, holding one another by the hand or arm as they survey the scene. Buckhunter steps down from Jack Frosty's, wiping his hands on a rag and looking on with curiosity.

"Everything okay?" Buckhunter shouts, tossing the towel into his restaurant and rushing towards the accident.

"Fiona's got it," Holly calls back, walking up the sidewalk to meet her uncle. "The boys kicked a soccer ball across the street and Hal swerved so it wouldn't hit his cart," she says breathlessly. "He ran into Bridget's cart, and the ball broke the front window of Mistletoe Morning Brew."

"Don't forget to mention that Bridget was *in the cart*," Bridget yells. "And Bridget got run into by someone who's probably too freaking old to even be driving." She scoots across the bench seat of her cart and climbs out the passenger side because Hal's cart is t-boned against her driver's side. "But I'm fine, don't worry about me," she says sarcastically, brushing off the front of her skirt.

Fiona continues to help Hal, asking him questions in her quiet, patient doctor's tone. She's already snapped on a pair of latex gloves and is dabbing at the gash on Hal's temple as she feels around for obviously broken bones.

"Why don't you have a seat, Bridget," Fiona says calmly, not looking away from Hal. "You're next on my list of people to check out."

"I kind of feel like I should be first," Bridget argues, "given that I count as two people, and we're both way younger than the old guy who can't watch where he's going."

"Let's get you inside so you can sit down and wait for Jake," Holly says through gritted teeth. Vance and Calista have both converged on the twins across the street, and Calista is on her knees in front of the boys, questioning them quietly with thunder in her eyes.

Bridget yanks her elbow out of Holly's grip. "I can walk," she says. "I'm just worried about my baby."

Holly chooses to ignore the talk of a baby, and instead pulls out a chair inside the coffee shop for Bridget. "Here. Sit." She points at the chair. "Ellen? Can we possibly trouble you for a glass of water?" Holly moves over to where the stunned women still stand, broken glass crunching beneath her shoes with every step. "I'm sorry," she whispers, picking up her feet and walking gingerly across the tiled floor.

Ellen is rooted to the spot, a rolled-up poster in one hand. "I was re-decorating for March," she says dumbly. "It's a new month and I need new decorations."

"I know." Holly steps up to Ellen and gives her a cautious side-hug. "I'm so sorry about this." She's purposefully calm, as she doesn't want to rattle Ellen in her current state.

"I'll get the water," Carrie-Anne says. She pours a glass from the tap and rushes it over to Bridget. Holly stands with Ellen, her arm still around the older woman as she holds her. Without discussing it, Carrie-Anne leaves her wife in Holly's hands and takes over Bridget duty. She sits with her at the tall bistro table, watching the action outside.

"What are we gonna do, Holly?" Ellen's words rise in pitch and volume as the full scope of the situation sets in. "We don't have a front window anymore! All the money I've been saving from our monthly fundraisers is going to have to pay for a new window."

"Shhh," Holly says, swaying slightly and rocking Ellen from side-to-side the way you might do with a distraught child. "Let's not get ahead of ourselves. The weather is good, we'll get the glass cleaned up from the floor and call a repair shop on the mainland right away. I'll find someone to help me cover your front window, and you know your shop will be safe until we get new glass—there's no question about that. We've got this," she promises.

Jake pulls up in his cart then, screeching to a stop in the middle of Main Street. He approaches Hal and Fiona with concern all over his face, bending over to talk to them while Fiona places a bandage on Hal's forehead.

As soon as Bridget sees her boyfriend outside, she slides off the chair and grabs her phone from the table.

"Did she say she was pregnant?" Ellen whispers to Holly, her shock over the front window subsiding. "I could have sworn she said something about a baby."

"I think so," Holly whispers back, pretending that it's news to her as well.

"Honey—" Carrie-Anne says. She sounds alarmed. "Wait!"

Holly and Ellen look at Bridget; she's reached the door just as Carrie-Anne's warning rings out in the shop. And then all four women look down at the same time to see the stream of blood that's running down the inside of Bridget's bare leg.

CHAPTER 19

The B&B kitchen becomes the gathering place that evening for anyone who wants to talk about the accident and pitch in to make casseroles to deliver. Holly stands at the center of it all, pointing out stations and giving hugs as her neighbors walk in.

Near the sink, the triplets are working on a three-layer casserole to take to Hal Pillory, who is back home and propped up on his couch with a sling on his arm and a bottle of ibuprofen. Iris and Emily are assembling a tray of dumplings and rice to drop off with Ellen and Carrie-Anne, and Wyatt Bender and Cap have shown up with offers to help put together sandwiches for Jake and Bridget, but Holly's noticed that they're mostly talking to the women and sneaking pieces of deli meat while everyone else does the work.

"Did you know?" Glen whispers to Holly as she passes by the triplets' work station. "Had Jake already told you?"

Holly stops. She has a block of cheddar cheese in one hand and a large tomato in the other. "No," she lies easily. "I had no idea. I feel terrible for them."

Bridget had been rushed to Fiona's office straight from the coffee shop. No one came out for several hours, though Jake had gone in as soon as he saw his girlfriend being led across the street by both elbows.

His face had gone white at the sight of blood, and he'd left the scene of the fender bender immediately, forgetting all about the debate over whether Hal should have let the soccer ball hit his cart, or whether swerving had been the right thing to do. Word of Bridget's condition had spread quickly, and everyone waited, talking in hushed tones. They took turns helping Hal get comfortable in a room at the B&B while he waited for Fiona to come back and check on him.

The second she'd seen Bridget bleeding, a huge wave of guilt had threatened to topple Holly. Isn't this what she'd been hoping for—no baby? Not like this, of course, but essentially for Bridget to somehow turn up *not* pregnant, and for Jake to see the light in time to disentangle himself from her grasp? Standing in the kitchen now, Holly's eyes feel tired as she stands and listens to the other women talk. A few traumatic stories of lost pregnancies and old sadnesses are passed around as those who've gone through a miscarriage try to make sense of how Bridget and Jake must be feeling.

"It's not that I don't feel bad for them," Mrs. Agnelli says, joining Holly and the triplets. "But a person has to wonder how a girl shows up here and is already pregnant a few months later."

"I think we know how it happened, Maria," Gwen says, shaking a bag of frozen peas over the casserole dish she's been preparing and sprinkling them across the concoction. "But it does seem..."

"Fast," Gen adds. The triplets always do this—finish one another's sentences, work fluidly together side-by-side, and share the same opinions on almost everything—and they all appear to be in agreement now. "It seems like a young lady ought to pace herself a little, and not have all the fun at once."

The other women nod knowingly.

"Well, it happened, and now we get to help them pick up the pieces," Holly says with a charity she almost feels. "Let's get dinner out to everyone and make sure no one needs anything else, then we can go down to the coffee shop and put some plastic over that window. I promised Ellen and Carrie-Anne I'd get that done tonight."

"How are the parents doing?" Iris asks as she passes on her way to the fridge. "They must be feeling pretty guilty about their wee lads causing such a ruckus today. Not to mention the outcome."

"I think they're okay." Holly had talked to Calista and Vance, who were beside themselves as the aftermath of the soccer ball incident had unfolded. They'd gone home with the boys, checking in once with Holly by text to see if there was anything—anything at all—that they could do to help. "They were pretty upset about it the last time I talked to them."

"As they should be," Mrs. Agnelli says, reaching for one of the crackers that Glen is about to crumble for the casserole's topping. "Those hellions need some discipline."

"Oh, they're just little boys, Maria. It was an accident. A tragic one, but an accident nonetheless," Gwen argues.

"But where were the parents?" Mrs. Agnelli demands. "Six-year-old boys shouldn't be left to their own devices. Not even on an island like this. It's not safe."

"For anyone," Iris adds as she passes by them again, heading the other direction with a bottle of rice vinegar in hand.

"I'm sure it won't happen again," Holly says, touching Mrs. Agnelli's shoulder and moving away from the group. She needs to excuse herself from the discussion and help to get everything prepped and out the door before it gets too late to deliver the meals.

But she isn't sure it won't happen again—she knows nothing about kids and parenting, and she has no idea how Calista and Vance are going to work and run a bookshop and watch over their boys. And even though they're kind and patient people, there's no guarantee that this incident hasn't soured the islanders toward having small children around. As Holly loads the rice and dumplings onto the seat of her cart to run over to Ellen and Carrie-Anne's, she wonders how she'll mend fences and make the Guys feel at home on Christmas Key after an incident like this.

It's dark outside when Holly finally leaves the B&B, and there's no one on Main Street. She pulls out of the lot and turns on her headlamps. Ellen and Carrie-Anne's bungalow is on the north side of the island, situated on a piece of property with enough room for two animal pens. Ellen is a die-hard animal lover who'd agreed to take on the ten live turkeys Holly accidentally ordered for Thanksgiving dinner, but then hadn't had the heart—or the stomach—to eat. On top of that, Ellen had convinced her wife to adopt a homeless donkey named Madonna, who'd promptly been christened 'Madonkey' by Holly.

She pulls up to their house and parks, lifting the tray of food by its handles and carrying it up the front walk. From the side of the house, Madonkey brays at Holly, sending the ten turkeys into a frenzy.

"Hey, hon," Carrie-Anne says, flipping on the porch light and opening the screen door as Holly approaches. "The animals are like our own private alarm system around here." She nods at the fenced-in pens that she and Ellen built for their pets. "Come on in."

Inside the house, Ellen is sitting at the small table in the kitchen, a cup of tea next to her as she scrolls through her laptop.

"Holly," Ellen says. She's looking less shell-shocked than she had that afternoon. "Can I get you some tea or coffee?"

"Nothing for me, thanks. I just wanted to bring a dinner by and see how you ladies were doing."

"Oh, that's so nice!" Carrie-Anne reaches for the dish and takes it from Holly's hands. She sets it on the butcher block counter of their galley-style kitchen. "You didn't have to do that."

"It's from all of us."

Ellen shuts the laptop. She picks up her mug of tea with both hands. "How are Jake and Bridget doing?"

"I'm not sure yet. Mrs. Agnelli and Iris are running dinner over to them, and the triplets are taking a casserole over to Hal's to check on him."

"Oh, Hal!" Ellen covers her mouth. "How is he?"

"He's pretty banged up, but we're taking turns checking on him since he didn't want to stay at the B&B. He was a little confused at first, and he kept asking for Sadie," Holly says, remembering how he'd pled with them to find his late wife and let her know he was okay. It had taken twenty minutes for him to remember that she was gone, and when he did, the sadness that settled in over his face had nearly broken Holly's heart.

"The poor button," Carrie-Anne says. "He's been keeping to himself so much lately that I don't think any of us really know how he's doing."

"I think we need to do better about checking on him. And on Maria, too," Ellen adds. "We've got some neighbors who are getting up there in years, and they need us—we all need each other." Her eyes get misty as she reaches out a hand from her spot at the table. Holly walks over and takes it.

"It's all going to be okay," Holly assures them both. "I'm meeting Cap and Wyatt back at Mistletoe here in a few minutes to cover your window, and we'll have everything back up and running like new as soon as possible."

Ellen lets go of Holly's hand and places a palm on the closed laptop in front of her. "I've been researching glass repair in Tampa and Key West, and I think I found a place that can come out to us early next week and fix the window."

"The good thing is that the weather isn't unbearable yet, so we can take down the plastic during the day and just run the ceiling fans to keep things moving in the shop," says Carrie-Anne. "I already turned off the air-conditioning and I think we can get through four or five days that way. We won't be able to keep the bugs out, but we'll have coffee."

"We'll be like the postal service," Ellen jokes, cracking a smile for the first time all day. "*Neither snow nor rain nor heat nor gloom of night...*"

"There shall be coffee!" Carrie-Anne holds up a triumphant fist.

"You two are the best." Holly gives each woman a quick hug. "Let me know if there's anything else we can do, okay?"

"You've done enough. Thanks for covering the shop window for us." Ellen blows on her mug of tea.

"And thank you for dinner," Carrie-Anne says, lifting the corner of the foil that covers the dish. "Mmm, we love dumplings and rice. And we forgot to eat tonight, so this is perfect."

"No problem. I'll see you both tomorrow."

Holly lets herself out the front door. She stops to put a hand through the fence so that Madonkey can sniff her. "Hi, girl," she whispers, petting the sweet animal on the top of her head. Madonkey looks back at Holly with big eyes. "What a day, huh?" she asks mildly, touching the donkey's silky fur. "Don't let these birds give you too much grief, you hear?" She nods at the pecking turkeys with the floppy wattles under their chins.

The porch light goes off, and Holly climbs back into her cart to make her next stop.

VANCE DUCKS UNDER THE ROUNDED ARCHWAY THAT SEPARATES THE kitchen from the front sitting room. He's carrying a pot of tea. The boys have already been put to bed at the back of the house.

"We feel horrible," Calista says. She's sitting on the edge of her new couch with her elbows on her knees, and she lowers her face into her hands so that her fingers rest on her temples.

Vance sets the pot on a trivet in the center of their low coffee table. "Honey or milk?" he asks Holly as he pours steaming tea into a mug for her.

"No, plain is fine—thanks." She picks up the cup by the handle and sets it on a coaster in front of her.

Vance sinks into the armchair next to the couch that the women are sharing. He dips a spoon into a jar of honey and sets it in his cup of hot tea to dissolve.

"I'm not even sure where to go from here," he says in his deep, rich voice. He leans back in the chair and steeples his hands beneath his chin. "We spent the evening having a long talk with the boys, and we haven't even told them that their actions caused a young lady to...to..." His eyes look glassy and faraway as he grapples for words.

Calista reaches out a hand and gently places it on her husband's knee. "They're six, Vance. I'm not even sure they'd understand at this point."

"It might be a lot for them," Holly agrees, lifting her mug of tea and holding it in both hands. "And I think the bigger issue at this point for everyone on the island is how to handle having two little guys underfoot." She takes a sip of the scalding liquid, preparing for what she has to say next. "And one of the main concerns going forward is how you two will supervise them."

Vance and Calista exchange a look. "Well," she says and stops there.

"Part of why we moved here was to escape the need for constant supervision for the boys," Vance says, lifting the spoon from his cup of tea and tapping it against the side of the mug before he sets it on a saucer. "Paradise for us is the idea that our boys will have the freedom to explore and to—essentially—raise themselves."

Holly swallows hard, trying not to blanch at the idea of two rambunctious six-year-olds"raising themselves."

"Studies have shown that children who are given freedom and decision-making opportunities often do better as young adults than those who are given too much structure," Calista says, going into parenting mode. "Mexi and Mori are busy little boys, yes, but they aren't bad kids. They just need to learn about action and consequence. For instance," she says, setting her own tea on the table, "they kicked the ball and nearly hit a man driving down the street, causing him to crash and hurt himself."

"And they do feel badly about that," Vance interjects, holding out a large hand, palm to the floor. "Make no mistake: they have a conscience."

"No one is questioning that," Holly assures them. "They're adorable, spirited boys, and having kids on the island has the potential to invigorate all of us. In fact, the future of our island *depends* on bringing young people to Christmas Key."

"Exactly," Vance says, putting the outstretched hand on his denim-clad thigh. He readjusts the tortoise-shell glasses on his face and crosses his legs at the knee.

"We need to come to an agreement about what that looks like so everyone is comfortable. Some of us haven't been around children in quite a long time." Holly knows that this discussion has to happen, but there's an awkwardness to a childless woman making demands and offering child-rearing guidance to a couple who've raised twins for the past six years.

"And what would make everyone comfortable?" Calista asks, an invisible defensive guard falling over her face. It's the automatic response of a mama bear whose children are being attacked, and Holly inhales through her nose, ready to lay it all out.

"I think everyone would like to know how they'll be accounted for on a daily basis. As you know, I grew up here—as did Emily Cafferkey —and we haven't had kids around since she and I put away the Barbies and stopped playing hide-and-seek in the trees."

The Guys nod patiently. Vance sniffs and reaches for his tea.

"We were fortunate enough to have two retired school teachers on the island to help guide us through our education. We don't have that anymore, so I think their schooling is a concern."

"But not yours," Calista says with a tight shake of her head. It's the first time Holly has sensed an edge to this gentle woman.

"Calista," Vance warns. "Let's hear her out."

"As mayor," Holly says, hoping to calm Calista's nerves, "it's my concern to address the services available on this island to all residents —and that includes Mexi and Mori. What I'm saying is that we don't have schooling to offer, and at their age, that's an issue."

"We're looking into online courses," Calista says. "There's no need to have certificated teachers on hand anymore with the different homeschooling resources out there."

"Okay," Holly says. "But who will make sure they're sitting down and doing their courses? If you're working at the salon and Vance is busy opening a bookstore, how is this going to work?"

Vance and Calista search each other's eyes for answers.

"We're working on that," Vance admits. "We are, I promise you. My mother is one option that we're exploring, and if the boys double up in one bedroom here then we'd have room for her to stay."

"She would move down here?" Holly asks, eyebrows raised over the edge of her tea mug as she prepares to take a drink.

"She could." He nods, working his lips as he thinks. "She's widowed and already missing us, and I think it would do her some good to be down here with her grandsons and other people her own age." Vance spreads his arms wide, indicating the neighbors all around them who are similarly-aged. "We just started kicking the idea around tonight, so we'll need to work on it a little more."

Holly considers this. Another older person on the island would certainly add something to the mix of the current population, and if they're going to push forward with progress and change, then it couldn't hurt to entertain the idea of Vance's mother moving to

Christmas Key. It would certainly ease some minds if she took over the daily care of her grandsons.

"That's an interesting proposition," Holly says. "Do you think she'd be open to it?"

"I think there's a reasonably good chance." Vance trains his eyes on his wife, and Holly can see the silent negotiations that pass between them. It's the dance of a well-seasoned couple: I'll trade you one mother-in-law for the freedom to work and not worry about the kids during the day.

"It's a possibility," Calista allows, turning to look at Holly next to her on the couch. "We're just starting that discussion, so we'll let you know if things go that direction."

"Fair enough." Holly sets her mug on the coffee table and stands up. "Anyhow, I should let you get on with your evening. I really just wanted to touch bases with you and make sure everything was okay."

"Thanks, Holly. We appreciate it." Vance stands up from the chair and puts his big hands into his pockets. "I'm hoping we can find a way to move forward from here, but we do understand the gravity of the situation."

"I'll talk to you tomorrow, probably," Holly says, picking up her purse from the couch and putting the strap over her shoulder. "Try not to worry too much. Accidents happen, and the people on this island are far more forgiving than you can imagine."

Vance and Calista wave at Holly somberly from the doorway to the pink house. They stand next to one another as Holly gets into her cart again to drive home. As mayor, she knows she should stop by Jake and Bridget's house to check on them, but as Jake's ex-girlfriend, she knows she shouldn't. With a glance at Jake's dimly-lit bungalow, Holly rolls past. She'll let them be for the night. After all, what could she possibly say or do that would make things better?

As she speeds up, the sound of her tires against the sandy road fills her ears.

CHAPTER 20

Holly opens her email at work the next morning to find a string of messages that Bonnie's sent in the middle of the night.

1:14 am: *Oh, sugar—I don't know what to think. Doug is so...different. I think I made a huge mistake.*

1:57 am: *Ignore me. I'm ranting and raving like a madwoman, and that's not fair to you. I knew where you stood on the whole thing, and I did it anyway. Now I should be forced to clean up my own mess here. Pretend you never heard from me, okay?*

3:03 am: *And you know what the worst part is? He isn't even a pirate—not at all! I knew he wasn't going to dress like one all the time, but he doesn't even act like the same man. Can I call you in the morning?*

5:13 am: *I'm so tired, Holly Jean. I haven't slept a wink tonight. Not a single bloomin' wink. I've been up and sitting on the lanai out behind Doug's condo (Yes, I live in a condo. In Clearwater.) and all I can think about is how dark and quiet it is on Christmas Key. It never gets that dark and quiet here. I think I'm losing my mind. I'm calling you in three hours. I know you'll be in the office by then.*

As Holly reads through the emails, she nibbles on pieces of her chocolate chip scone from Mistletoe Morning Brew. She brushes her hands together to get rid of the crumbs, and puts her fingers to the keyboard.

8:08 am: *Hi, Bon. I'm here. Call me. I hope you're sleeping now after that all-nighter you just pulled. Holler at me whenever you get this!*

Holly takes a sip of her hot coffee. The sidewalk outside the B&B is quiet. Fiona is unlocking the front door to Poinsettia Plaza across the street when the phone rings.

"Sugar?" Bonnie is already talking before Holly even says hello.

"Hi, Bon." Holly leans back in her chair and watches as Fiona disappears into the building across the street. "Tell me everything."

"Honey, I don't even know where to start." Bonnie sounds tired. "Doug snores like a freight train and I can't sleep at all. I haven't had a full night since I got here."

"That sucks." Holly picks up a pen and starts to doodle on the notepad next to her computer. Bonnie's spot across from her is empty, and the chair is pushed in. Everything is neat and organized. Her absence has felt like a gaping void in the B&B office, and hearing her voice now makes it almost feel like she's there. "Can you sleep on the couch or in a spare room?"

"He likes to wake up next to me," Bonnie says. "It must be nice to have some sleep to wake up *from*."

"Ouch."

"Yeah, it's painful. And he likes me to make him breakfast and coffee, which I haven't done for anyone but myself in years. It'll just take some getting used to. I didn't mean to flood your inbox with nonsense," Bonnie says, choking up. She stifles a quiet sob on the other end of the line.

"Bonnie," Holly says. "Don't cry. It's only been—what?—six days? Give yourself some time."

"I'm sorry, sugar. I don't mean to do this to you. I've just been so homesick."

"That's understandable. I felt the same way when I left the island for college. I cried so much that my roommates thought I was depressed. And I kind of was...but then things started to feel familiar, and I got used to Miami. It was never home, but it turned out fine."

"I don't think this is going to turn out fine, doll. Doug works at a desk all day and he hates his boss. He comes home mad as a hornet after being pushed around all day, and he takes it out on me."

"What?" Holly feels a bonfire of anger sweep through her body. "How does he take it out on you?"

"Not with his fists or anything—nothing like that. He just complains about whatever I make for dinner, and he hates the way I decorated his condo. I don't know. It doesn't feel the way I thought it would."

Holly flips the plastic tab on the lid of her to-go cup back-and-forth. "So do you think he acted all big and manly when he was dressed as a pirate as a way to make up for the fact that he's not like that at all in his real life?"

"I think that's it in a nutshell." Bonnie sighs. "And I let myself get swept off my damn feet like a fool."

"You aren't a fool, Bon. Wanting love and romance isn't wrong, and no one can fault you for wanting a little excitement."

"But you were right all along, and I didn't listen to you."

Holly resists the temptation to agree. What she says next almost causes her physical pain, but she knows what Bonnie has sacrificed in order to move to Clearwater and make a leap this big. "Do you think," Holly swallows a sip of coffee, "that maybe you should give it more time before you make any big decisions?"

Bonnie is quiet. "Maybe," she says in a small voice. "Maybe I'm not giving us a fair chance to try this thing. It is a lot of work to blend your life with someone else's, and it doesn't get any easier at our age. We've both got likes and dislikes; histories and memories; habits and prefer-ences—and trying to compromise with another person is hard work. You could be right," Bonnie says, though she sounds reluctant.

"Go and try to get a few hours of sleep while he works, then go for a walk or something and clear your head. Call me later?"

"You're right, sugar. I don't know what I'd do without you."

"And you'll never have to find out, because I'll always be right here, Bon."

"Okay, honey. I'll call you later."

Holly ends the call and sets her cell phone down on its face. This wasn't the time to fill Bonnie in on all that's happened in the past couple of days, but she knows that when her friend is well-rested and clear-headed, she'll be more than ready to hear about the twins and the accident, about Bridget and the baby, and about Hal and his cuts and bruises.

Outside the B&B, traffic is picking up on Main Street. Holly needs to go and help Ellen and Carrie-Anne pull the plastic from their front window and measure the glass for the company that's going to come and replace it. She's reminded once again—as she sits and looks out the window at the golf carts and at her liver-spotted neighbors wobbling over to the coffee shop and the salon—that living on this island is more interesting than any soap opera could ever be.

CHAPTER 21

Bridget keeps to herself for a full week after the accident, and Holly only sees Jake in passing. The window repair company from Tampa makes the trip over by boat with a huge pane of glass for the front of Mistletoe Morning Brew, and a crowd gathers to watch the four men use clamps and a dolly as they carefully wheel the huge window up from the dock and get it into place. Ellen and Carrie-Anne have emptied their fundraising coffers from the month of February (formerly earmarked for a donation to a wildlife preserve in upstate New York), and with the help of a box placed on the front counter of every business on the island, they raised another $479.18 towards the window repair.

With the window fixed and the carts barely dented, all evidence of the biggest accident that Christmas Key's ever seen are essentially erased. No new holes have popped up on the island recently, and a steady rotation of neighbors have lined up to drop in on Hal and make sure he's healing and eating regularly. As always, the islanders are working together to divide and conquer as a team, and they're moving forward without looking back.

The first time Bridget makes a trip to Main Street after the accident is for lunch at Jack Frosty's. She and Jake park his police cart at the curb and he helps her step out gingerly, one hand on her back, the other beneath her hand like he's escorting an elderly widow. Holly watches them as she sits on the bottom step of the B&B with her legs outstretched and crossed at the ankles. There's an electric air around Bridget that's nearly visible, and Holly snaps her gum, looking up and down the sidewalk to see if anyone else notices. Bridget has an angry, told-you-so edge about her, and as their eyes meet, the younger girl raises her brows questioningly.

Holly looks down at her phone. She's been waiting to hear from Bonnie, who's fallen off the radar after their last call. It's been on her mind to call or text and check in, but something's been holding her back. Holly knows that by constantly calling and keeping Bonnie in the Christmas Key loop, she isn't really letting her go. So instead, she deletes the first words of the text she's been typing and slips the phone into the pocket of her sweatshirt.

It's time to check on Jake and Bridget—both as the mayor and as an ex-girlfriend who cares—so she stands up slowly and straightens her skirt. This trip to Jack Frosty's is clearly Bridget's way of getting over the inevitable onslaught of sympathy greetings from everyone all at once, and it will be easy for Holly to blend in with the group of people who will be stopping by their table.

"Hey, chief," Buckhunter says from behind the bar. The grill sizzles as he tosses food onto the hot surface. Holly waves and stops at the jukebox, where she picks out a Springsteen song and punches the button. The opening notes of "I'm On Fire" fill the bar. When she can't reasonably spend any longer standing in front of the lit-up juke-box, she puts both hands into the pockets of her sweatshirt and walks directly to Jake and Bridget's table. Holly tightens her grip around the cell phone in her right pocket and pastes the type of subdued smile on her face that feels appropriate for the occasion.

"Jake. Bridget." She nods at both of them as she stands next to the table awkwardly. Bruce Springsteen croons in the background. "I'm so sorry for your loss."

Bridget stares at the plastic-covered menu and doesn't meet Holly's gaze. Jake looks up at her with tired eyes. "Thanks, Hol," he says. "It's been a shock."

She wants to ask if Jake had known about the baby and if he'd been happy about it, but as she looks at the bags under his eyes, she knows it doesn't really matter. Whether he'd known his girlfriend was pregnant and had rejoiced at the possibility of a family, or whether he'd found out about the pregnancy and its loss at the same time, he deserved her sympathies.

"Everyone has been worried about you guys, but I wanted to give you space, so I didn't drop by your house. If there's anything at all I can do..."

Bridget drops the menu and it hits the table with a loud smack. "There is," she says. "We can revisit the issue that you and I talked about that day at the pool."

Jake's head ping-pongs back and forth as he looks at the women.

"Okay," Holly says. She waits, giving Bridget the floor.

"I told you there were differences that would cause problems. These people obviously don't raise their kids the way they should, and look what's already happened. Next thing you know they'll be boycotting Christmas and they'll ask you to change the name of this place to Kwanzaa Key."

"What the...?" Jake looks like he's standing in the middle of the street with an 18-wheeler coming right at him.

"They'll be blasting rap music all up and down White Christmas Way—oh, excuse me," Bridget holds out one hand, propping her arm up on the table with her elbow. Her bony wrist droops as her fingers splay gracefully. "I'm sure they'll have some issue to bring up at the next village council meeting about the fact that they live on *White* Christmas Way. Maybe we can rename it for them."

Holly is speechless. The tables around them have gone quiet, and the only sounds in the restaurant are the loud hisses coming from the grill, and the song on the jukebox. Jake sits in silence.

"I don't know what to say," Holly stammers. "You voiced your concerns to me that day at the pool, and I'm hearing you loud and clear now, but I really don't have a response for you other than—" Holly is gearing up, ready to finally give Bridget a piece of her mind, when Jake stands abruptly.

"I don't think Bridget is feeling up to this. We'll just head out now and catch up with you another time. Thanks for stopping by, Holly." Jake has Bridget up and out of the chair so quickly that they nearly knock Holly over as they exit the restaurant. Holly looks around at the other diners, exchanging a look with Millie Bradford and Maggie Sutter, who are sharing a plate of nachos nearby.

Buckhunter has missed the entire conversation as he flips burgers and pours iced tea behind the counter. "You out of here already?" he asks his niece, setting a plate on the counter and adding a pickle to the hamburger he's been cooking. The Springsteen song ends and Roy Orbison's "Pretty Woman" drops into place and starts playing.

"I've got a family coming in this afternoon from Key West for a few days," Holly says. She consults her watch. "I need to get back to the B&B and make sure everything is ready, but I wanted to stop in and see how Jake and Bridget were doing."

Buckhunter glances at their empty table. "Did you scare them away?"

"No," Holly says, kicking at the leg of the tall bar chair with the toe of her shoe. "Bridget got mad because I don't have a plan in place to keep Christmas Key white."

"Come again?" Buckhunter picks up a bottle of ketchup and the plate he's just finished loading up. He runs the burger over to the table where Cap is reading a newspaper, passing Holly again as he rushes back behind the bar to flip another burger on the grill. A sheen of sweat covers his forehead.

"Apparently Bridget grew up in a small town with, like, zero diversity."

"Okay," Buckhunter prompts, spinning around his small prep area as he grabs onions to toss onto the grill.

"And she isn't a fan of having the Guy family here."

"Fiona mentioned something about that." He frowns at her as he works his spatula, flipping meat and grilling onions.

"And she just went on a mini-rampage over there and totally freaked out her boyfriend."

"So you don't think Jake knew how she felt?" He puts a glass under the tap and fills it with water before taking a long drink.

"Based on the way he just acted right there? No, I don't think so,"

Holly says. "And I'd kind of like to be a fly on the wall right now to hear what they're talking about."

Buckhunter shakes his head. "That's a doozy. It would be a deal-breaker for me if I found out my girl felt that way."

"I've known Jake a long time," Holly says. "And I don't think he's going to like it." They'd visited Miami together on a number of occasions while they'd dated, but one time Jake had taken Holly there for a weekend away on South Beach. As they'd sat at a table with an umbrella on the sidewalk one afternoon, a sleek-looking European man seated next to them had appraised their waitress to his table mate, assigning a derogatory term to her based on the color of her skin. Jake had nearly come to blows with the man, and Holly had never seen him as angry as he was at that guy for treating someone like that.

No, she thought, Jake won't be happy to find out that his girlfriend —and very nearly the mother of his baby—is a flaming racist.

"Guess we'll have to wait and see." Buckhunter pulls a stack of hot plates from the small dishwasher behind the bar. "Any new holes show up?"

"No," Holly says, thinking about it. "Not for a week or two. It's weird—they were popping up everywhere while the pirates were here, and then after they left it was kind of sporadic. And now there's nothing."

"Huh. Maybe old Bluebeard hid out in the trees and dug for his treasure when none of us were looking, then took to the seas again when he found it."

"Hey, as long as he isn't hanging out on my property at night like a creeper, then I'm fine with that."

"Let me know if there's anything I can do to help with the guests we have showing up today."

"Thanks. I think they'll be low-key. It's a family of four, and they're just here for three nights. They told me all they want to do is lay by the pool and walk on the beach."

"Sounds good." He turns back to the grill and scoots the spatula under a burger patty, lifting it off the hot surface and putting it on a plate. "I've got grub to serve, so I'll talk to you later."

Holly stops at the jukebox on her way out and chooses Springsteen's "Hungry Heart." Without turning around, Buckhunter holds a finger in the air and bobs his head to the beat.

"SO WHEN IS HE COMING BACK?" FIONA SHOUTS OVER THE ROAR OF the waves on Snowflake Banks. "I'm ready to see you with a smile on your face again."

Holly trudges through the sand barefoot. Pucci is right beside her. Her best friend is stretching on the sand, wearing a pair of sweats pulled on over a navy blue one-piece swimsuit. Fiona's hair is tied in a knot on top of her head.

"Who, River?" Holly sits next to her. She digs her feet into the cool sand as she watches the ocean.

"Yeah, River. I've been waiting to hear what happened after you two texted each other, and you never said anything. Are we hot and heavy again? Doing some long distance romance? A little telephone *lovvvve?*" Fiona says with a suggestive lilt.

Holly smirks at her. "Please don't start talking about naked Skyping —that was always Bonnie's favorite joke."

"Well, now that you mention it..." Fiona holds one arm straight over her head and grabs onto the elbow with her other hand to stretch her shoulders. "Thanks for coming to watch me swim. I hate going out into the ocean at dusk alone—it doesn't seem safe."

"That's because it isn't. I'm always happy to come and watch."

"So really, tell me what happened." Fiona stands and unties her sweat pants; they fall to her ankles. She kicks them off and goose-bumps immediately rise on her bare thighs and arms. It's the second week of March and not at all chilly, but with the sun disappearing fast, the water is colder than the heated swimming pool at the B&B.

"We've been talking a little. I told him some of the stuff that's been going on around here, and he even called one night." Holly drags her hands through the sand, lifting fistfuls and letting the fine, powdery grains sift through her fingers. "It feels different than before, and it's certainly not romantic, but it's nice to have someone to talk to who knows the island and who knows me."

"Interesting," Fiona says, squinting at the waves. "Is he seeing anyone?"

"No." Holly brushes the sand off her hands and reaches over to pet Pucci. "He's been fishing and coaching his spring baseball team," she says, referring to the foster kids that River volunteers to coach. "He wants to see me again."

Fiona bends her front leg and does a deep lunge. "And do you want to see him?"

Holly thinks about it: does she want to see him? Is she ready to face him after the way things ended on Christmas Eve? It was humiliating for her to be so transparent about the fact that she wasn't totally over Jake, and it was annoying that the man she'd broken up with still had that kind of hold on her. And the worst part was that she couldn't have realized it on her own, when there wasn't a gorgeous former baseball player who'd come to the island to spend the holidays with her. But with everything that's happened since then—the fact that Jake and Bridget have seemed so happy, and that they almost had a baby together—it's been easier to slowly let go of her feelings for Jake.

"Yeah, I think I want to see him. Sooner or later," Holly says.

"That really pins things down." Fiona lunges with the other leg. "Listen: he's obviously still into you or he wouldn't be calling and texting and talking about meeting up again. Jake is in deep with Bridget now, and it's obvious to anyone with eyes that you don't feel the same way about him that you used to. So don't screw this up." Without waiting to hear what Holly has to say, she dashes for the water, squealing loudly as the cold waves lap against her shins, then her thighs, and finally her torso. Fiona puts her hands together over her head and dives into the water.

The setting sun is warm on Holly's loose hair and bare arms, but she has no desire to be in the water. Instead, she watches as Fiona swims out and back, working to conquer the waves and tides. It's impressive the way she's taken on this challenge to swim to Cuba, and Holly admires the muscles forming in Fiona's upper back. The sun catches the water on Fiona's strong limbs as she cuts through the waves, and she glistens like a blade of grass covered in morning dew.

Holly pets Pucci as she thinks about how complicated human relationships are. There are so many intricate layers of drama and heartbreak that make people tick: Bonnie and Sinker—okay, *Doug*—and their desire to find romance and adventure; Jake and Bridget and the thrill of finding each other on a reality show, then the heartbreak of losing a baby together; Hal Pillory having an accident at his age and calling out for his late wife like she was just in the next room; and even Brian the pirate and his need to keep the fire alive with his wife in the midst of hard work and four kids.

And there's more, she thinks, catching sight of Fiona as she dives under a wave and surfaces like a dolphin, arms slicing through the water—what about her own mother and the way she always has to both keep a cool distance and still control everything like a puppet master from behind the scenes? And Buckhunter keeping the secret about Holly's grandfather being his biological father for so many years?

Secrets. Love. Loss. Fear. Loneliness. Regret. Euphoria. Joy. It's a rollercoaster that races through life, pulling its riders to gut-dropping lows, and then tearing them from the earth and hoisting them to unimaginable heights. Without the ride, it would be a long, eventless drudge from dark origins to dark endings. So will she take the ride and see River again? Probably. The promise of another unimaginable high on life's rollercoaster is too great to resist.

Fiona emerges from the water, red-skinned and dripping. With a thick towel in her hands, Holly jumps to her feet and races to meet her friend at the shore.

CHAPTER 22

Vance decides to put his plans for the bookstore on hold for the time being, and he and Holly agree to save their pitch for a different village council meeting. Their more immediate concern is how Vance and Calista will handle the care and education of their young boys on an island with no school and no daycare.

"We got so used to having options in a big city. It seems like there's a restaurant or a play center that caters to kids on every corner," Calista says to Millie as they work together in the salon. Holly is sitting in the corner of the room, hands splayed flat on Millie's manicure table. She's chosen a bright orangey-coral color for her short nails.

"Was the original plan for Vance to stay close to home and watch them while you worked?" Millie asks mildly, picking up Holly's right hand and setting it in a dish of warm water to soften the cuticles.

"I guess. We were just so excited to get down here and start living the island life that it seemed like it would all fall into place. I'd be here, Vance would be working on the novel he's been writing for the past few years, and the boys would be growing up wild and free under the sun." Calista dumps a small basket of freshly laundered towels on the front counter to fold as she talks. "It seemed ideal."

"It is ideal, sweetheart." Millie picks a fresh emery board from a cup on the table. "It's also unrealistic. They're six-year-olds and they need someone to be accountable for them and to teach them how to read and write and divide and sit still for five minutes." Millie has already experienced the whirling dervishes that are Mexi and Mori as they tore through Scissors & Ribbons on a visit to their mom's workplace. She told Holly in confidence that it secretly made her a tiny bit glad to know that her own young grandchildren were a safe distance away and wouldn't be dropping in for a visit unannounced.

"What happened with your mother-in-law, Calista?" Holly asks, changing hands and putting her left one in the bowl when Millie taps the table and motions for her to switch.

Calista snaps a towel with more gusto than is technically necessary, folding it into a crisp square. "Well," she says.

"Well?" Millie prompts, eyebrows raised.

"She's willing to come down."

"That's great!" Holly says with enthusiasm, aware that it's in stark contrast to the skepticism on Calista's face.

"Mmhmm." Calista purses her lips, her light eyes clouded over as she continues to fold. "But mothers-in-law are tricky beasts. And make no mistake: mine is the trickiest of them all."

"How so, hon?" Millie asks, wrapping Holly's hand in a small white towel.

"She feeds my boys meat and tells them that God didn't intend for little boys to grow up on nuts and forest berries," Calista says. "And she cranks up Motown to top volume on Saturday mornings while she mops the floors—have you ever been woken up at six o'clock on a weekend by Diana Ross and the smell of lemon floor wax? She won't listen to *anything* I say, and she always tells me that I'll never make Vance happy if I don't learn how to take an animal from alive and squawking, to cooked and glistening on a platter."

"We could have used your mother-in-law around here at Thanksgiving," Millie says, giving Holly a look over the edge of her wire-rimmed bifocals. "The mayor here accidentally ordered ten live turkeys who are now living pretty high on the hog out at Ellen and Carrie-Anne's place."

"Well, I guess you'll have my mother-in-law around now for any of your livestock or floor-waxing needs," Calista says, throwing up her hands in exasperation. "I'm ready for her to show up and start criticizing. She'll tell me that my floors aren't clean enough, that I should put on ten pounds, and that my boys need a haircut and a hot bath. But as long as it's what's best for everyone, then I'll just deal with it."

"You could always put in more hours here," Holly suggests. "I've heard from several people that you give amazing massages."

Calista's frown melts. "Yeah? That's good to hear, I guess." She folds another towel. "Do I have you on the books yet, Holly?"

"Oh, I don't know if I'm massage material." Holly shakes her head. "I can barely sit still for twenty minutes to get a manicure."

"She's not lying. I end up fixing her smudges every time she comes in," Millie says, pressing her palm against the top of Holly's hand to keep her fingers flat on the table.

"You should try it," Calista presses. "If you aren't good at relaxing and getting into a meditative state, then this would be the place to start. We could even do thirty minutes the first time, if you want."

Holly thinks about the bliss of being completely unavailable for thirty minutes. She'd have her cell phone switched off, and the door would be closed so that no one could barge in and rail at her about holes in the road, pirates with bad manners taking over the bars, or people who "don't belong" on their island. It does sound tempting.

"Okay, put me down for a half-hour. If it's going well, we can stretch it out to an hour," Holly decides.

Calista pushes the pile of towels aside. "What day and time are good for you? I have keys to the salon, so if you prefer an evening when Millie isn't open for business, we can always meet here and it would be totally quiet."

"That sounds nice," Holly says. "Okay, how about tomorrow? I'm always tense the night before the village council meeting, so maybe it would help. Can you do seven o'clock?"

"I can do seven," Calista says, tapping at the computer keyboard and bringing up her schedule. "Okay, the lady is set up for her very first massage," she confirms, saving the information and clicking out of the schedule. "Don't eat or drink a lot beforehand, and feel free to wear anything you want on the table—or nothing at all, if you prefer."

"I usually need a few margaritas before I'll climb onto a table in my birthday suit." Holly watches as Millie drags the small brush over her nail bed, leaving streaks of bright coral behind.

"Your choice," Calista laughs. "Most people feel comfortable with just a sheet draped over them, but I'm cool with whatever."

The door to the salon opens and Cap steps inside. His shoulder-length white hair and imposing presence make him seem too large for the shop—kind of like a cat who's squeezed himself through the door of a dollhouse. He stands there awkwardly, looking at the women.

"Hey, Cap," Millie says, still polishing Holly's nails as she talks. "You here for a spa day?"

"I don't think I need a haircut or a polish job," Cap says, holding up his hands and inspecting his nails.

"I beg to differ," Millie puts the brush back in the bottle, screws the cap on tightly, and rolls the bottle of polish between her palms to mix it up. "But you can't force a man to part with a mane of hair he's been cultivating since Reagan's first term in office, so I'll just keep waiting patiently for the day you ask me to chop off that ponytail."

"Won't happen, Mrs. Bradford," Cap says. He lumbers over to the counter. "I'm here to sign up for a massage with this lady here. I've got a knot in my shoulder that feels like a hot poker to the eye. When can you squeeze me in?"

"Let's see," Calista says, opening her schedule on the computer again. "I don't have anyone coming in until three today, so I could actually fit you in now, if you'd like. I just need ten minutes to prep my room."

"Ten minutes? I could do that." Cap looks at his watch. "I don't think anyone's going to have a cigar emergency in the next hour. Let me run down and close the shop. I'll be back in ten." He pats the counter twice and heads back down Main Street to put a sign in the window.

"Word of mouth seems to be working," Holly says to Calista. "When a tough old crow like Cap Duncan is ready to strip down and put himself in your capable hands, you know you're winning people over. Good work."

Calista smiles knowingly. "Just wait and see, Mayor. After tomorrow, you'll be a regular here, too."

"Maybe we can schedule a standing massage appointment for one evening a week so you can catch a breather from your mother-in-law," Holly says, looking at the hand that Millie's just finished polishing.

"Aaaggghhhh," Calista says in a strangled voice, throwing her head back and putting both hands in the air. "My mother-in-law...*don't remind me!*"

TRUE TO HER WORD, CALISTA GIVES HOLLY A MASSAGE THE NEXT evening that leaves her feeling like a bowl of jello—a very happy, very mellow bowl of jello.

She drives back to her house in the dark, and brushes past the saw palmetto with the side of her cart as she pulls into her driveway. Buckhunter's house is dark and his golf cart is gone; Jack Frosty's is still open for a few hours, so Holly will be alone on the property for a while. The fear she'd felt the night she saw the man foraging around in her bushes has dissipated, and being home alone feels comforting again.

Holly lets herself in through the front door of the house, flipping on the light in the entryway. She kicks off her flip-flops and tosses her purse onto a rustic-looking white wooden bench next to the door. Pucci rushes to greet her, so she grabs his furry face in both hands and bends down to nuzzle the top of his head.

"Are you hungry, boy?" she asks him, scratching between his ears. "Let's get dinner. I'm starving."

In the kitchen, she turns on the light and pulls the bag of dog food from under the sink. She pours some into Pucci's bowl before dumping and refilling his water dish. For her own late dinner, she pulls a box of pasta from the cupboard and puts a big pot of water on the stove to boil. Her phone lights up on the counter where she's left it plugged in during the massage.

There's a text from River: *How are things?* It's simple. To the point. *Things are good. Just got a massage from our new island masseuse.* She sets the phone on the counter and digs through the fridge for the cube of parmesan in her cheese drawer. From the cupboard she pulls a jar of extra virgin olive oil and the salt and pepper. It's going to be a simple dinner, but with a glass of red wine, it'll work.

Is he hunky and ripped?

SHE'S petite and waif-like, but surprisingly strong.

Sounds like change is afoot.

Holly stares at the message as she breaks the long spaghetti noodles over the boiling water on her stove. When she's done, she wipes her hands on a dishtowel. *I'm cooking dinner...talking would be easier. Can I call?*

I'll Facetime you.

In a panic, Holly runs to the mirror in her entryway, yanking her hair out of the messy bun she'd worn during her massage. She smoothes the lines on her forehead from being facedown on the table at Scissors & Ribbons, and wipes at the stray smears of mascara under both eyes. *Of course he wants to Facetime*, she thinks. The timer goes off on the stove at the same time her phone starts to ring, and Holly hurries back to the kitchen.

"Hey," she says, taking the call and propping the phone up on the windowsill so that River can see her as she moves around the kitchen. "Sorry, I need to drain my pasta."

"By all means, drain the pasta." River is sitting in the cab of what looks like a pick-up truck. It's only 5:30 on the west coast, and through the windows of the truck the skies are gray and heavy. Drops of rain run down the glass behind him.

"Wait," Holly pauses with the pot of steaming water and pasta in her hands. "Do you drive a truck?"

River laughs. "Yeah, I do. But that looks hot—you should dump it."

"Right. Hold on." Holly stands in front of the window over the sink and pours the water and noodles into a strainer. A cloud of steam rises up between her and the phone.

"Are you going with marinara or alfredo?" River asks, zipping up the front of his dark green jacket so that the collar fits snugly under his chin.

"Olive oil and parmesan. There isn't much food in the house, and I don't feel like going over to Jack Frosty's for a burger."

"You're out of food? I'm shocked," he says, clearly not shocked at all. "Not even a frozen pizza to burn, or a box of cereal to douse with half and half?"

"Funny, funny, funny, you are." Holly dumps the strained noodles into a large metal bowl. "I have a couple of things around—I'm getting better at feeding myself."

"Hey, you're only thirty. Don't rush into adulthood, kid."

Holly takes in his rugged face and the spill of blonde hair that falls onto his forehead as he sits in the cab of his truck over three thousand miles from her. "This is nice," she says, glancing at him shyly and then looking away. She unscrews the lid on the bottle of olive oil and pours some over the pasta. "I mean, us talking again."

River is quiet for so long that Holly finally looks at the screen to see if he's still there. He's staring off into the distance. "Yeah," he says. "It is."

It isn't flowery prose, by any means, but the simple acknowledgment makes them both smile.

"So why are you sitting in your truck in the rain? Where are you?" Holly picks up the block of parmesan and digs through the utensil drawer for a grater.

"Outside the grocery store. I was about to go in and find something for dinner, and it made me realize how much it sucks to be a single dude all the time. People always give you 'the look' when you go through their line with three bananas, a half gallon of milk, one chicken breast, and a single baked potato."

"Maybe 'the look' is actually the girl at the cash register checking you out—did you ever think of that?"

"The 'girl' at the cash register is named Steve. He has a thick mustache and went to high school with my older brother."

"Oh, so Steve is on to your single guy lifestyle, huh?"

"Steve is definitely on to me. In fact, he tried to set me up with his cousin Sheryl once."

"That sounds promising," Holly says, grating a heavy layer of parmesan onto the pasta as she talks.

"Sheryl also has a thick mustache and went to high school with my brother, so...she doesn't really ring my bell."

Holly laughs and drops the grater into the sink. "Sounds like you have about as many options in all of Oregon as I have on Christmas Key."

"I think you have one more option than I do," River says seriously. When Holly looks up from grinding the pepper mill over the bowl, he's staring at her intently through the camera lens. She sets down the pepper.

"River," she says, walking over to the phone on the window sill. "That isn't even an option." And as she says it, she knows it's true—finally, completely true. "Bridget is still here."

"And if she wasn't?" He looks away from her. There's a rough, unshaven shadow to his strong face in the evening light.

It's a valid question, and one that Holly knows she needs to answer. When River left on Christmas Eve, the palpable distance between them had been filled with her feelings for Jake.

"There's a lot of history there, and it would be easy to fall back into the same pattern and spend our lives disagreeing about the same things we always have," Holly says carefully. "But it's time for me to move on; the world is bigger than Christmas Key, whether I like to admit it or not."

A silence expands in the space of Holly's small kitchen. Steam coats the window over the sink as the pasta cools on the counter. An equal silence overtakes River's truck cab, and the rain runs down the window behind him.

"It's cold in here," he finally says, putting two red hands to his mouth and blowing into them. "I turned off the truck before I called you."

"You're freezing!" Holly says. "How cold is it there?"

"The high today was about forty degrees, and it's been raining since November." River gives her a half-smile. "I miss the sun."

"You could come visit," she offers with the slightest hesitation.

"Let's go somewhere else." River drops his hands. His eyes flash with possibility. "Let me take you someplace you've never been. Then we can see if there's something there without all the other distractions."

"Really?" Holly reaches over and plucks a long-handled wooden fork from the canister next to her stove. She jabs it into the cooling pasta and starts to twist the noodles, coating them in olive oil and cheese. "Like where?"

"Anywhere. You name it."

The possibilities are endless. The idea of escaping the too-quiet B&B office, Bridget and Jake's lost pregnancy, and her day-to-day chores is beyond enticing.

"Well," Holly says, letting the fork rest against the side of the bowl. She folds her arms across her chest. "I don't know."

"Come on, Hol. You know that place can survive without you. Someone else can take reservations at the B&B for a week or two, and we can go in-between village council meetings so you don't miss anything." Without her saying a word, River is checking the items off her list of objections like he's reading her mind.

"Well..." she says again.

"Think about it. Promise? We could pick a time and place, and just go." River's eyes are faraway, and he's obviously already left the cold, rainy Pacific Northwest far behind for a trip to somewhere more exotic in his mind.

Holly gazes longingly at the lips she'd loved to kiss. Her knees feel weak thinking of River's strong arms, of the way her fingers had traced the hard muscles of his abs in her darkened bedroom, of the way it had felt to wake up next to him in the morning. She's completely distracted by River as she reaches for the bowl of pasta. Her fingers miss the edge of the dish, and instead of grabbing it, she knocks into the bowl and sends it tumbling off the edge of the counter. The noodles plop onto the tile floor in a greasy pile.

"Yes," she says, looking at her dinner on the floor. "Yes. Let's go. We're doing this."

River gives a hoot. "Was that your pasta? And are you serious? You're not kidding?"

"It was my pasta, and I'm not kidding."

"We're going?"

"We're definitely going. I want to see you again. And you're right: it needs to be somewhere else—not here."

River laughs to himself and puts his chapped hands in front of his chin. He rubs them together like sandpaper. "Okay. But first you need to figure out what you're going to eat tonight, because I'm guessing Pucci will get to that pasta before you do."

Holly bends over and scoops up the noodles in big handfuls, tossing it all into the garbage can under the sink. "Oh, don't worry about me— I have Oreos. I won't starve."

"Oreos for dinner?" River makes a face.

"Absolutely. I've got high fructose corn syrup, chocolate," she reaches for the pack of cookies on the counter and scans the list of ingredients, "palm oil, cornstarch, and a glass of milk to wash it all down. I'm good." To show him she isn't kidding, she pulls a cookie from the package and shoves the whole thing into her mouth.

"Okay, feast on those Oreos tonight, but then start thinking about our trip. Let's make some plans."

"Got it. Cookies for dinner, then make plans for Europe," Holly says around the mouthful of Oreo. She pulls the carton of milk from her refrigerator and takes a swig. "But first I need to pry Bonnie out of the arms of a pirate and get her back to Christmas Key, and then I need to kick a racist off my island."

"Of course you do," River says indulgently. "All in a day's work."

CHAPTER 23

S omeone is playing Big Band music on a phone speaker when Holly walks to the podium at the front of the B&B's dining room the next morning. She searches the crowd to see who's blaring Glen Miller, but can't pinpoint exactly where it's coming from.

"I'd like to call the village council meeting for March fifteenth to order," Holly says into the microphone. All around the room, people ease into chairs and get comfortable. The music stops, and phones are switched off and put away. "We've got a few things to cover here and then I'll set you free to get on with your day." Holly consults the typed agenda in front of her. Heddie Lang-Mueller is sitting in a chair to her right, taking the meeting minutes as always. "First off, I'm excited to tell you that I got confirmation from the network and I know when *Wild Tropics* is going to air."

People shift in their seats, whispering. Wayne Coates, the producer of the reality show that filmed on the island from Halloween to Christmas, had finally emailed Holly the air-date for the premiere. The show had caused mixed feelings amongst neighbors, with some hating the exposure, others thinking it was fun, and a few wishing they'd gotten as much air-time as the reality show's competitors. But in the end, they'd all pulled together and helped to make the taping a success.

"Can we make it a big deal, like a Hollywood movie premiere?" Mrs. Agnelli asks loudly from her spot in the front row.

"I think we should." Holly says. "How about if we do it here at the B&B? We could set up a screen over there," she points at an empty wall with no windows, "and then we could do a red carpet entrance and serve something fun for dinner."

"Like a dress up event?" Millie asks.

"Sure, if you want." Holly nods. "That would be fun."

Millie cups her mouth like she's telling the whole crowd a secret. "I've got openings at the salon if anyone wants a wash-and-set or an up-do for the big event."

"Got it," Holly laughs. She's losing the crowd as they talk animatedly about what to wear and what type of food would befit a Hollywood premiere event.

The early spring sun is streaming in through the lobby and all the windows of the B&B. As her neighbors laugh and talk around her, Holly stops for a minute, a million thoughts flowing through her mind as goosebumps race up her arms and spine. Here she is, leading a village council meeting. She's successfully brought a reality show to the island, and they're planning a premiere at the B&B. She's been mayor now for a few years, and there's no place in the world she'd rather be. It's a good feeling.

"I think we should talk about the elephant in the room," Cap says from where he's sitting. His voice startles Holly out of her thoughts, and the bright sunlight that fills the room dims a few watts, like a cloud is passing over the sun.

"Right," Holly says, coming back from her reverie. With a light tap of her pink marble gavel, she gets the crowd's attention. "Cap has a valid point. I think we need to address a few issues."

The room settles again, and Holly glances down at her agenda. What she needs to talk about isn't officially scheduled for discussion, but they've always been able to work things out as a group, and she doesn't want to shy away from the difficult stuff now.

"As we grow and change, there are going to be moments of discomfort," Holly says carefully. Her eyes flick around the room. Hal Pillory is sitting near the door, a fading bruise and a long cut that's healing still visible on his forehead and temple. Vance and Calista are both at the meeting, as Holly has set up a movie on her laptop in the lobby for Mexi and Mori. Emily Cafferkey has agreed to watch the boys for an hour or so and make sure neither wanders off or gets into mischief. Jake and Bridget are sitting together near a window, and Holly notices the space between them. Jake has his arms folded across his firm chest, and there are several inches between their chairs. It's almost as if he knows what's coming and wants to distance himself.

"I'd like to welcome Vance and Calista Guy to their first Christmas Key village council meeting, and to let them know that we love having them on the island." Simplicity is best here, Holly reminds herself, thinking of the typed book full of wisdom that her grandfather had left for her. He'd called it his "island prospectus," and filled it with helpful tidbits about developing Christmas Key. *Stick to the facts, and don't sugarcoat the hard stuff*, it had said.

"My grandparents had a singular vision when they bought this island in the eighties," Holly says. Maria Agnelli is poised to add something, so Holly quickly shuts her down. "And yes, I know they had a teenage daughter with a baby, but their real dream was to create a paradise where people could escape the fast-paced world."

Heads nod around the room as the people who'd known Frank and Jeanie Baxter agree with Holly.

"They had a beautiful dream," Hal Pillory says in a scratchy, wavering voice. "And this place has always been paradise for me."

"Me, too," Maggie Sutter adds. "Everyone gets along here like peanut butter and jelly, and there's more love on this tiny island than you find in most families."

"Here, here!" Jimmy Cafferkey holds a finger in the air. Next to him, his wife Iris nods.

"I'm glad you all feel that way," Holly says. "I think one of the things I prize most about this little community is the way we all accept one another with open arms."

"I can vouch for that," Cap Duncan offers. His own hidden past had been pulled to center stage during the taping of the reality show, and he'd been surprised to find that the secret he'd been keeping for years had done nothing to change his neighbors' unwavering affection for him.

"We can't go on like this. It's unacceptable." Millie Bradford stands up in the center of the room, her eyes wide. She's impassioned and ready to let her thoughts fly, but her husband reaches out a hand and touches her arm gently.

"Honey," Ray Bradford whispers. "Let Holly say what she needs to say."

"I'm sorry, Holly," Millie says soberly, sinking back into her chair.

There's a part of Holly that wishes Millie would have just said the words for her, but she knows that—as mayor—settling uncomfortable situations and disputes falls squarely in her lap.

"Well," she says, clearing her throat. "It's come to my attention recently—and I hadn't really noticed it before—but we have a bit of a...uhh...well, we're not very...I mean, we don't—"

"We're as white as a polar bear's ass," Maria Agnelli offers at full volume.

"We don't have much diversity here, is what I was *going* to say." Holly can feel the heat crawling up her chest and neck towards her face. "But essentially, yes. We're white and we're pretty long in the tooth when it comes right down to it." She clears her throat again. "Man, this is awkward. This conversation is *so hard* to start." With apology in her eyes, she looks at Calista and Vance. They're sitting together on the left side of the room, heads held high, jaws set to hold back whatever they might be thinking or wanting to say.

"Anyway," Holly goes on. "We'll never make progress if we don't do the hard work, and I'm willing to be the one to say this: Christmas Key is a loving, welcoming place. We don't discriminate against any particular religion." Her eyes sweep the room. "We don't decide who we accept based on their nationality," Holly says, looking directly at Cap Duncan and remembering his nervous admission at this very podium, "and we desperately need some young people here, which we now have."

Calista gives Holly a tight smile; Vance's face remains impassive. A cell phone chirps somewhere in the crowd and is quickly silenced.

"Most importantly, determining someone's value or worth based on the color of their skin is something that's unacceptable on this island. *My* paradise will never be a place where that happens." It takes all of Holly's willpower not to look directly at Bridget or Jake. Instead, she looks down at her hands, which are laced together on the podium. "And if anyone takes issue with that, there's a boat leaving the dock around four o'clock today after it delivers the groceries and mail. Feel free to be on it."

There are a few small items on the agenda that Holly knows she should cover, but they'll hold for the next meeting. As she picks up her gavel, the crowd breaks into applause, some standing and beaming at her as they show their support for the hard stance she's taking. Holly finally lets her eyes sweep the left side of the room and she meets Bridget's gaze.

The gavel hits the sound block with a loud tap. "Meeting adjourned."

CHAPTER 24

T he sun is on Holly's bare shoulders as she walks down Main Street and stops in front of Mistletoe Morning Brew. She looks out at the dock and the vast expanse of blue water before her. They're just days from the official start of spring, and the island is responding to nature's prompts exactly as it should, giving forth trees full of pink hibiscus, and bounties of dwarf pineapple plants, passion fruits, and sea grapes. The air is filled with salt and citrus; Holly is sure this must be what heaven smells like.

The gossip about Bridget's outburst at Jack Frosty's had instantly lit up the wires connecting everyone on Christmas Key, and because Millie Bradford had overheard the whole exchange with her own ears, it hadn't taken long for Calista to hear that not everyone was excited to have her family on the island. Holly had left the village council meeting on Wednesday feeling strong and content, certain that her grandparents were looking down on her with pride for upholding their vision of paradise. After the meeting, Calista and Vance had called Holly to thank her for not pretending that everything was fine when it really wasn't.

It feels good to deal with an issue—particularly one as sensitive as this—up front and without delay, and Holly is in high spirits as she admires the new pane of glass on the front of the coffee shop. Inside, Carrie-Anne and Ellen are bustling around wearing white lace aprons and woven crowns of fake flowers. They've decorated the tables with vases full of real orange and key lime flowers from their own garden, and long garlands of yellow, white, and purple silk love-in-idleness flowers hang from the white trellis that the women have set up from floor to ceiling. A sliver of moon made of *papier mâché* hangs from the ceiling, and white fairy lights twinkle in the tall Norfolk Island Pine trees that Carrie-Anne has potted and placed in the corners of the shop.

"Coffee, milady?" Ellen asks Holly, setting down the mugs in her hands and wiping her palms on the front of her apron.

"Yes, please." Holly looks at the hand-drawn sign that's propped up on an easel next to the front counter. In chalk, Ellen has artfully written out her quote of the day from Shakespeare's *A Midsummer Night's Dream: "The juice of it on sleeping eyelids laid/will make man or woman madly dote/upon the next live creature that it sees,"* Holly reads. "Better not put any of that love-in-idleness juice in my coffee—or on my eyelids," she says, digging in her purse for her wallet. "I'd hate to fall madly in love with the next person who walks in here."

The bells on the door jingle behind her. Holly turns to see Jake.

"Could be tragic," Ellen agrees with a smile. She busies herself with pouring Holly's coffee.

Jake sighs loudly and pulls off his sunglasses. "Good. I wanted to talk to you."

"To me?" Holly asks, pointing at the center of her chest.

"Yeah, you." Jake doesn't come in any further than the door.

"Get you a coffee, Officer Zavaroni?" Carrie-Anne asks as she bustles by in her crown of flowers.

"I'll swing back through for one later," he says to Carrie-Anne. "And, Ellen—you'd better make hers to go." He nods at Holly and she does a double-take.

"Excuse me? You're changing my drink order?" She's completely taken aback by Jake's assertiveness, and even more put off by the look in his eyes. "Fine, to go, please," she says to Ellen, who has paused mid-pour and is openly staring at Holly and Jake.

"You got it," Ellen says quietly, pouring the hot coffee from the mug into a paper cup and slipping it into a sleeve. She snaps a lid into place and passes Holly the coffee. "Two bucks."

Without another word, Holly leaves two crumpled bills on the counter, takes her coffee, and follows Jake back out into the sun.

"What's going on?" she asks, sipping her coffee through the opening in the lid. "You look...I don't know. Peeved?" Holly follows him to the end of the sidewalk and down to where the dock starts.

"Peeved isn't even the half of it," Jake says, stopping abruptly. He shoots her a hard look before sliding his sunglasses back on. "That stunt you pulled at the meeting the other day was a lot, even for you."

"What stunt?" Holly is about to take another drink of her coffee, but instead she pauses, holding the cup near her chin. It hasn't even occurred to her that someone might have been displeased with the way she'd handled things. "I didn't pull any stunts, Jake. And what does that mean, 'even for you'?" She narrows her eyes at him.

Jake makes a disbelieving face. "Trying to turn people against Bridget because of one dumb thing she said when she was grieving and not in her right mind."

"I wouldn't do that," Holly protests. "It wasn't the first time she said it, and I brought it up at the meeting because we're talking about something serious that needs to be addressed."

"Right," Jake says, obviously getting ramped up. "So there's no way that you'd use it against her to, oh, I don't know, get her to leave Christmas Key?" He shoots a glare of ice at Holly from behind his sunglasses. "There's no part of you that thinks we might be able to patch things up and get back together if Bridget is gone?"

Holly pulls her head back and lowers her chin. Of course she *has* thought this—many times—but not recently.

"Should we keep tiptoeing around this, Hol? Maybe we can drive out to Hal Pillory's and argue on his front lawn again? Or get into it on December Drive while we haggle over who has to fill the holes in the road?"

Holly wants to defend herself and toss something back at Jake that will shut him down, but she can't. She knows he's right.

"You've been on my ass since your boyfriend took off at Christmas, and I see that look in your eyes." His tone is accusing, and his face is hard and unyielding. "I know that look, because it's the same one I saw every time I looked in the mirror last summer and wondered whether there was anything I could do to get you back." Holly picks at the tab on the coffee's lid, not meeting Jake's gaze. "I would have done anything to patch things up last summer, but you made it clear that that wasn't happening."

"You're right," she whispers, still not looking at him. The palm trees near the dock move in the breeze and their fronds send up a shimmer of noise.

"And now I've got someone else, and we're dealing with some heavy stuff. I need a little space to figure things out, and you think it's a great idea to basically call Bridget out in front of *the entire island*. You even told her to get on the next boat and leave!" he almost shouts, unfolding his arms and pointing at the water. "Would you have handled things the same way if it had been your baseball player boyfriend voicing an opinion that you don't share?"

Holly shrugs, but she knows he's got her over a barrel here. Of course she wouldn't have dragged River to a village council meeting and shamed him—she would have simply had the conversation with him in private and made a decision about whether they could go on seeing one another. But rather than give Jake the chance to do the same thing, she'd taken matters into her own hands.

"Listen," Jake says, putting both hands on the sides of his head and squeezing like he's got a headache he can't shake. "You and I are always on different pages. We can't agree, we argue, we want different things." He runs his palms over his hair and lets go of his head, holding his arms wide. "I'm not even sure this island is big enough for both of us anymore."

"No," Holly says without thinking. "Jake. Don't say that." She reaches out with the hand that isn't holding her coffee cup with the intention of touching him. Jake takes a step back.

"I don't know. But you and I aren't getting back together. We need to just admit that and move on." Jake takes two more steps away from Holly. "Maybe if you accept that, you can give Bridget the same chance you give everyone else who sets foot on this island."

Holly inhales deeply again—just like she'd done before walking into Mistletoe Morning Brew—only this time she doesn't smell spring in the air, only the rancid scent of misunderstanding, regret, and defeat.

"Oh, and I forgot to mention," Jake says, both hands shoved into the deep pockets of the black shorts he wears while on duty. He stops walking backward and stares at her. "There's a new hole on Holly Lane, and it's about three times the size of the other ones. Have fun with that."

Holly simmers and stews as she watches Jake walk back to the coffee shop, but she knows it isn't worth it to rebut his accusations. Some of what he's saying is right, and some of it is just his anger talking, so she bites her tongue and lets him go.

A new hole on Holly Lane? It's been weeks since the last one, and while it still bugs her that she has no idea how or why the holes came to be, it's a mystery she's been happy to forget about, so long as no new ones have shown up. But now she's got to get her shovel and go fill this hole, knowing full well that it isn't pirates or gophers or aliens leaving pock marks on her little rock in the sea.

The coffee she normally loves is suddenly cold and bitter tasting to Holly as she walks back up to the sidewalk. Without looking in the window of Mistletoe Morning Brew at the Shakespearian floral paradise, Holly pauses at the trash can and tosses her nearly full coffee into its gaping mouth. She knows Jake is still inside, so with a proud, undefeated toss of her head, she strides towards the B&B, ready to get her shovel and golf cart and go fix this damn hole.

CHAPTER 25

Holly rolls over in bed on Sunday morning. She pushes her eye mask up onto her forehead as she slides her finger across the screen of her buzzing cell phone.

"Hello?" she rasps, holding it in the general vicinity of her ear.

"He is too much, sugar, just *way too much*," Bonnie says in a rush. "That damn Sinker McBludgeon wants me to…well, he wants me to—I just can't," she says with anguish.

"What, Bon? He wants you to what?" Holly sits up in bed, leaning against her pillows. The spaghetti strap of her turquoise nightgown slips off one tanned shoulder. "He wants you to have dinner on the table every night at six? He wants you to get matching tattoos? He wants you to start watching *Sons of Anarchy* with him?" She rubs her forehead and yawns. It isn't lost on Holly that Bonnie has called Doug "Sinker McBludgeon" for the first time since their fling officially started.

"He wants me to—good lord, honey, I can't even say it."

"Well, you're gonna have to say it, because I'm out of guesses." Holly's hand flops down on top of the cool duvet cover. She looks at the clock on her bedside table: it's only seven.

"Okay, here I go. I'm just going to rip this off like a band-aid," Bonnie says.

"I'm ready."

"He wants me to go on a date." Bonnie says this and then sits there, letting her words drop like a stone in a pond.

"But you two have already been dating," Holly reminds her.

"Not on a date with *him*, sugar. He wants me to go on a date with someone else."

"Oh," Holly says. "With someone else. Like who?"

"Like another couple. He wants to date a couple. He wants *me* to go on a date with *him* and some strange people he met on Craigslist." The pitch of Bonnie's voice is creeping up to the point where Holly can sense an imminent wail. "I think he wants me to—oh, God, sugar—I think he wants me to—"

"I have a pretty good idea what he wants you to do, Bon." Holly throws off the covers and stands up slowly with the sleep mask pushed up on top of her head. She needs coffee. "But how did you get to this point? Did he like, I don't know, warm you up? Ask if you'd be in to this kind of thing?"

Pucci follows close behind Holly, his body swaying as he lumbers over to the front door and sits down in front of it. He stares at the door knob patiently.

"No! He's been at work every day, then he comes home, drinks a lot, and complains about his boss. I've been trying so hard to see the same sexy, strong man I saw when he was on the island, but it just feels all wrong. And now there's *this*."

Holly unlocks the door and turns the knob to let Pucci out. "Yeah, there's this," she agrees, putting one arm across her midsection as the early morning air hits her bare skin. She pulls the strap of her nightgown up and takes the eye mask off her head. "So what are you going to do?"

"Sugar," Bonnie says, sounding direct and determined. "I tried. I know some people are going to think I'm a fool and they won't be shy about saying so, but this just ain't right. I made a huge mistake."

"Come home." The words are simple and to the point, but the emotion behind them is intense and complicated. Of course Holly wants Bonnie to come back for her own happiness and peace of mind, but there's a part of her that wants her friend back by her side as she grapples with everything that's been going on.

"You think I can?" Bonnie's voice sounds small and hopeful.

"Are you kidding me? Everyone will be *thrilled*. We miss you like crazy!" Holly pats her thigh as Pucci noses around in the bushes at the bottom of her porch steps. He bounds up to her and brushes past her bare calf. "How soon can you be here?"

"This double-couple date thingy is scheduled for tonight, and I don't plan to be here for it."

Holly laughs and closes the front door. "So you're going to be packed and on the boat from Tampa this afternoon?"

"Girl, you'd better believe it."

Holly can't stop grinning. She does a little dance in the middle of her kitchen, one fist in the air. Through the window over her sink she spots Buckhunter, filling his coffee pot with water in his kitchen; he gives her a thumbs-up and an amused smile.

"I can't wait. I'm so happy, Bon. I mean, I'm not happy that you're not happy, but I'm happy you're going to be home, and everyone else is going to be happy—"

"Sugar, that's a helluva lotta happy right there," Bonnie laughs. "But I can't wait to see you. I'll text you when I know for sure what time I'll be there. And, um, would you do me a favor?"

"Anything," Holly promises without hesitation.

"Would you tell people I'm coming back, but maybe leave out the part about why? Just tell them Clearwater didn't suit me, or I missed Christmas Key too much?"

"So, wait—you *don't* want me to tell them that you went from a pirate's wench to a full-fledged swinger after less than a month on the mainland?"

"Oh, shoot! You're just gonna be a little sassy britches about this now, aren't you?" Bonnie scoffs.

"I might."

"That's fine. I guess I deserve that," Bonnie says. "Just as long as you promise not to say *I told you so*."

Holly flips on her electric kettle and dumps a few scoops of coffee into the French press. "Bon, you have my word. I just want you back."

Bonnie is quiet on the other end of the line. "We have a lot to catch up on, sugar. I'll see you soon."

Holly hangs up and stands there in her kitchen. She thinks of all that's happened while Bonnie's been gone. The tile is cold under her feet, and she lifts one foot, flexing her toes. "Bonnie's coming home," she says out loud, smiling to herself. "Hey, Pucci—did you hear that?" She turns and looks at her dog, who's found a comfortable spot near the door that leads to the lanai. "Bonnie's coming home!"

TRUE TO HER WORD, HOLLY SPREADS THE GOOD NEWS AROUND THE island with as little information as possible.

"Yep, she's supposed to be on the boat this afternoon," she says to Cap as they slow their respective golf carts at the intersection of Cinnamon Lane and Holly Way. Cap is about to turn left onto Holly Way and head over to Christmas Key Chapel, where he's started running a nondenominational church service one Sunday a month. Holly's heard from some of the other islanders that it's a reflective, peaceful event, and that his humor adds a nice touch to the gathering.

Cap looks out over his steering wheel, eyes narrowed into the distance. "Glad to hear that. She belongs here with us," he says definitively. "And Wyatt's been a real pisser since she's been gone." Cap holds up one hand. "Pardon my language, Mayor. I'm trying to keep it clean."

"At least on Sundays," Holly says with a wink.

"Seems like the best day for it." Cap's face folds into lines and crevices as he smiles at Holly. "Why don't you join us for the service this morning? I'll throw in a prayer for Bonnie's safe return, and we can spread the good news that she's coming home."

It's on the tip of Holly's tongue to bow out politely when she realizes that Cap is right: this is the perfect opportunity to let a whole group of her neighbors in on the news that Bonnie's coming back. She's already had two cups of coffee, showered, and is even wearing a summer dress that's appropriate for church, so she really has no good excuse to say no.

"You know what," Holly says, putting her cart in reverse so she can let Cap turn in front of her onto Holly Lane. "I think I will join you. Lead the way, Minister."

Cap waves a hand to indicate that she should follow. He turns his cart and smiles broadly. "I don't like to put on any airs, mind you," he says over his shoulder as they drive under the low-hanging branches of the Jamaican dogwood trees. "I'm only ordained through an organization I found on the internet, but I did get a card in the mail to prove that it's real."

"It's real enough for me, Cap," Holly calls, keeping a few feet between their golf carts. The morning is clear and warming up quickly, and the sun breaking through the branches makes a lacy pattern on Holly's thighs as she passes under the trees.

They park in a sandy clearing with several other carts and walk the short distance to the tiny chapel. The doors are already open. Ray Bradford is standing on the front steps, greeting the few people who trickle into the building.

"Morning, Mayor," he says, holding out a hand to take Holly's. "Glad you could join us."

"Me too," Holly says, meaning it. Inside, Maria Agnelli is already seated in the front pew. Millie Bradford is next to her, leaning in close to listen to what Maria is saying. Fiona is on one side of the chapel, head bowed, the light of the stained glass windows playing over her strawberry blonde hair. At the back are Vance and Calista with Mexi and Mori between them; they wave at Holly as she enters.

"Sit anywhere," Cap says, making his way to the pulpit to prepare. Holly stands there, taking it all in. It didn't even occur to her to join this gathering when Cap started it a few months back. Her church time has been limited to Easter and Christmas since her grandparents passed, but she has fond memories of Sundays spent in these very pews as a girl. She takes a few steps in Fiona's direction, sliding in quietly next to her.

"Hey," Fiona says with surprise, looking up from the open book of hymns in her lap. "I wouldn't have expected to see you here."

"I'm kind of surprised myself," Holly says.

Fiona glances over her shoulder at the open doors. "Any chance you convinced your heathen of an uncle to join you?"

"I didn't even know I was coming until I turned my cart onto Holly Lane and parked outside," Holly admits. "Otherwise I would have tried to get him off his porch and asked him to join us."

"Good luck with that."

"Oh, I forgot to tell you two things." Holly picks up a hymn book of her own from the pocket in front of her. "One, I had to come over here the other day and fill another hole."

"What?" Fiona hisses. "I thought we were done with that."

"I thought so too, but apparently we're not, so the mystery continues."

Fiona shakes her head and flips a tissue-paper-thin page in her book.

"And the other thing is actually good news: Bonnie is coming home!"

Fiona slams the book shut. "What?" she says in her full, non-church voice. "Are you kidding me?"

"Nope. Not kidding. She missed us too much and she'll be home today."

"Wow," Fiona says, turning back to the pulpit as Cap straightens his papers and clears his throat. "That is *great* news. Between that and you throwing Bridget out of here on her ear, this is shaping up to be a pretty good week, huh?"

Holly's stomach turns at the mention of Bridget getting thrown out on her ear. She's given some thought to Jake's accusations, and she's examined her own motivations more closely than she ever wanted to. A lot of what Jake said rings uncomfortably true, and she isn't sure how she'll make things right with him again.

"It's been a decent week," Holly says with reluctance. A loud tapping starts at the back of the church and Holly turns to see Calista and Vance shushing Mexi and Mori and patting their legs to get them to stop kicking the pew in front of them. "But I'm kind of second-guessing myself and how I handled Bridget."

"Why? You were straightforward, honest, and to-the-point. You didn't mince words, but you also didn't call her out by name."

"Still," Holly says, looking around at the triplets and their husbands as they walk up the aisle and duck into a pew. "Would I have done the same thing to anyone else? Like, what if River had said those things— would I have dragged him through the mud in front of the whole island at a village council meeting?"

Fiona digests this. "Maybe not, but it wasn't exactly the Salem Witch Trials. No one was threatening to burn her at the stake, you were just being clear about what is and isn't acceptable around here."

"I guess." Holly faces the front of the church as Cap holds both hands in the air to indicate that he's about to begin speaking. She still isn't convinced that Jake is wrong, but what's done is done, and she stands behind her message regardless of its delivery.

Cap leads the small group through a lovely service, inviting people to make song requests and to add anything that might touch the hearts of their neighbors in attendance. Maria Agnelli requests that they sing "Bridge Over Troubled Water" by Simon and Garfunkel, Holly stands up and tells the group about Bonnie's impending return, and Vance gives a moving reading of a poem by W.H. Auden. Through it all, Holly lets the service wash over her, taking in the quiet pleasure of being amongst friends.

"Thanks for inviting me this morning," Holly says to Cap at the door to the chapel when the service is over. He takes her hand in both of his.

"Of course. The offer stands for you to join us anytime you like. I'm hoping that we'll start meeting more frequently, but for now, any Sunday morning we can spend in reflection together is good enough for me."

Holly smiles up at him as he clasps her hand in his. It's the old Cap she knows and loves looking down at her, and she takes a moment to appreciate the ups and downs they've had over the past year. From Cap falling off the wagon while the reality show was on the island, to his challenging her seat as mayor, it's been a rocky road. But Cap has always been (even when he's a thorn in her side) one of Holly's favorite people, and his formidable presence at the helm of something as personal as a church service feels peaceful and right to her.

Outside, Holly slides behind the wheel of her cart and flips the switch to turn on the power. The small crowd of islanders will surely spread the word about Bonnie coming home, but she turns right onto Main Street off of Holly Way, ready to make a few more stops just in case. At Jack Frosty's, she drops in to tell Buckhunter the good news as he turns over chairs and sets things up for lunch. She waves at Millie and Calista as they open up the salon, then heads over to Mistletoe Morning Brew to spread the word to anyone who might have opted for coffee over fellowship that morning.

By noon, she's satisfied that most of the island knows the basics: Bonnie'll be on the afternoon boat. She's coming back because she missed everyone, and Clearwater was far too busy for her liking. Holly is giddy as she checks her watch for the fortieth time since Bonnie's phone call. By late afternoon the island will have its resident spitfire back. Everyone will be coated with the Southern sass they've come to know and love, and Holly's world will be right again.

All she has to do now is wait.

CHAPTER 26

A ll talk of pirates (and Sinker McBludgeon in particular) has been banned from the B&B office. In a matter of days, Bonnie is back in her chair across the desk from Holly, and they've got their morning routine up and running like clockwork: iced coffees from Mistletoe Morning Brew; morning gossip and chatter; email rundown and plans for the day.

Bonnie had marched off the boat on Sunday with a suitcase in each hand and a determined look on her face. When Holly raced down to the dock to greet her, she'd dropped both bags and opened her arms wide.

"Sugar!" she'd screamed, holding Holly tightly and rocking back and forth. "As I live and breathe," she whispered into Holly's ear. "I've missed you so much—don't ever let me do something this stupid again, you hear?"

Holly had stepped back, her face flushed with joy and relief. "I hear you, Bon. I won't." Without further discussion, she'd loaded Bonnie's bags onto the back of her golf cart and driven her home.

"You get this message about the potholes?" Bonnie asks now, holding up her cell phone and turning the screen to Holly so she can read it from across the desk. It's a text from Jake. Holly looks down at her own phone.

"No, it looks like he just sent it to you." Holly unlocks her phone to double-check. No messages.

"He says the end of his driveway is all dug up," Bonnie reads the message aloud. "And he also wants me to tell you that he caught the little munchkins out alone on White Christmas Way and—"

There's a loud knock at the B&B's office door; it's Jake. He's got one hand on the top of Mexi's dark, curly head, and the other on top of Mori's. He looks perturbed, and the boys look chagrined.

"These two," he says, putting his hands on the back of the boys' necks. "These two were out roaming the streets with a wagon full of coconuts."

"Coconuts?" Bonnie says, standing up and walking over to the boys. She bends forward, both hands on her knees. "What are you two rabble-rousers doing with a wagon load of coconuts?"

"Mek-thee wanted to use them for bowling," Mori explains, turning his head to look at his brother.

"Nuh-uh!" Mexi says, shoving Mori so that his shoulder hits the doorjamb. "You wanted to see if we could break that window again!"

"Whoooooaaaa." Holly jumps to her feet. "Nobody is breaking *any* more windows—understood?" The impishness of their coconut hoarding has suddenly gotten a whole lot less cute. "Where are your parents?" she asks the boys. They shrug in unison. "Jake?" Holly looks up at him. "Do you know where they are?"

"Calista just started a massage and Millie won't interrupt her, and Vance is nowhere to be found."

"He's jogging," Mexi finally admits. "He told us to eat cereal and stay inside."

"But here you are." Holly puts both hands on her hips and looks at Bonnie. "Can you watch them for a few minutes?"

"Coupla rapscallions like this?" Bonnie puckers her lips and shakes her head at the boys. "I raised three of 'em. This job is right up my alley." Her face breaks into a wide smile as she waves the boys in. "Sit. You—there. And you," she motions to the other boy, "there. I'll get you paper and pens, and I want you both to start writing a letter to Santa Claus."

"But why?" Mori wails. "It's only March."

"You think Santa stops watching kids just because it isn't December?" Bonnie asks him, a look of shock on her face. "No sir, he does not. And you'd better start writing him an apology right now for the nonsense y'all are trying to pull. No way is he going to be pleased to hear about you wanting to break windows with coconuts." She thrusts a piece of paper and a pen at each boy. "Now get crackin'."

Holly and Jake exchange an amused look as the boys bend over their papers and start writing in big, blocky, six-year-old handwriting.

"Be back in a few," Holly says to Bonnie as she and Jake duck out of the office.

Jake's cart is parked at the curb and they slide into it without a word. "Let's run over to their house," he says. "I'm guessing Vance is back from running and he's going to wonder where his kids are."

They drive the short distance in silence. Holly holds on to the edge of her seat as Jake bumps over the sandy road, taking curves at full speed.

Sure enough, when they get to the pink bungalow on White Christmas Way, a sweaty, confused Vance is standing in the driveway.

"Have you seen the boys?" he asks frantically, jogging up to the passenger side of the cart. He puts both hands on the edge of the roof and peers in at Holly and Jake. "I went for a run, and when I got back they were gone."

"They're at the B&B," Holly says, swinging her legs around and forcing Vance to take a step back. Jake puts the cart in park and gets out of the driver's side. "Bonnie's watching them for a few minutes."

"I'm so sorry," Vance says. He's standing in the grass, and sweat rings the underarms of his dark t-shirt. "They weren't supposed to leave the house, and I...I don't know." He looks up at the blue sky and then closes his eyes for a minute. "Calista is going to kill me," he says when he opens his eyes again. "She really is."

"Let's just talk about what happens next," Jake says. "Because when I picked them up they had a wagon full of coconuts they'd collected, and their plan was to throw them at windows or use them to bowl in people's lawns. I think they had their eyes on Maggie Sutter's plastic flamingo collection for their first strike."

Holly wants to find the whole thing funny, but she can't. Not yet anyway. "Listen, Vance. We need to figure something out to occupy these guys. Do we know if your mom is coming down?"

Vance gives a fast nod. "Yep, yep. She's coming—at least for a visit. She says it's a lot to ask of her to give up her life in Toronto and just move down here, but she's willing to come and check things out."

"So that's a start," Holly says. "But even if she does stay, we need to —" Holly stops, remembering how defensive the Guys had been when they'd discussed the boys before. "It would be a good idea if we talked about ways we can better accommodate a young family," she says, taking a different tack. "With some structured activities or something." Holly has no idea what this will look like, but she does know that if the boys get anywhere near Ellen and Carrie-Anne's shop with a coconut and the intent to hurl it, the whole island is going to quickly jump ship from Holly's idealistic "we accept everyone" mentality and become decidedly anti-kid.

Vance claps his big hands together and holds the palms in front of his chest like he's praying. "Yes. Let's do this. We need to," he agrees. "This is turning out to be way harder than I thought it would be."

"I'm going to do a little thinking," Holly promises. She reaches out a hand and puts it on Vance's forearm reassuringly. "And you and Calista do the same. Let's see if we can't put our heads together and come up with a plan to make sure these boys are busy and accounted for, huh?"

"You got it," Vance says, smiling at them both gratefully. "I'll go to the B&B now and get the boys," he says, tipping his head in the direction of the spare cart he and Calista had bought from Hal Pillory, who'd finally been ready to let his late wife's golf cart go. "Thank you—both of you," Vance says, holding up a hand in farewell as he jogs over to the cart and hops into it.

"SO YOU JUST PUT IT ALL OUT THERE, RIGHT IN FRONT OF EVERYONE at the village council meeting?" Bonnie takes the umbrella out of her drink and lays it on the bar at the Ho Ho Hideaway. "How did that go?"

"About the way you'd expect," Holly says, elbows spread wide as she leans forward on the bar, nose just inches from the shot glass that Joe Sacamano's placed in front of her. "Everyone thought it was bold and brave—except for Jake, who thought it was shallow and manipulative."

"Oh, pshaw, honey," Bonnie says, lifting her drink to her red-painted lips. "Of course he thinks that. You turned up the heat underneath his bigoted girlfriend, and now he has to make a move."

"The mayor was ballsy—that's what she was," Joe Sacamano says. "And don't let her tell you any differently." He passes through the middle of their conversation as he pours Jimmy Cafferkey a drink and then walks it over to his table.

"Yeah, well..." Holly trails off. She runs a finger around the rim of her shot glass. "We've argued on and off for the past couple months." She thinks of the various disagreements they've batted back and forth all over the island lately. "But the weird thing is that whenever something comes up where we need to pull together as mayor and police officer, we immediately put it all aside and work as a team."

"Because you're both adults," Bonnie says, nodding at Holly wisely. "You know that your relationship shouldn't stand in the way of the needs of everyone on this island, and they never will." She sets her glass on the bar with a clink.

"I don't know." Holly looks around. The Wednesday night crowd at the Ho Ho is thin, but the women have agreed on a celebratory drink to mark Bonnie's return to the island, and after the near miss with the twins and the coconuts that afternoon, Holly's in no mood to turn down alcohol.

"Well, well, well. Look what the cat dragged in." Wyatt Bender saunters over to the bar in his Wranglers and a crisp shirt with pearl buttons. He takes off his cowboy hat and holds it over his heart. "Miss Bonnie Lane, back on Christmas Key with her tail between her legs."

Bonnie sits up straight on her bar stool and holds the stem of her glass between her polished fingers the way a proper British lady might hold the handle of a tea cup. "There's no tail between this girl's legs," she says to Wyatt, looking him up and down with an impervious gaze.

"And yet you show up at my favorite watering hole on a Wednesday night when you *know* Joe will play our favorite song at some point. I can only imagine it's because you've missed being in these arms." Wyatt wraps his arms around his own shoulders and sways like he's on the dance floor.

"You need to get your wits about you, cowboy. I think the only time I was ever in those arms," Bonnie nods at Wyatt's thin, muscular appendages, "was one cold night at Christmas time when we both drank too much and stumbled onto the dance floor." She turns back to the bar and takes another drink.

"The lady cuts into my soul like a hot knife through butter," Wyatt says, turning to Holly like he's imploring someone to see his side of things. Holly shrugs and picks up her shot glass.

"There'll be no knives in anyone's butter tonight, Wyatt Bender," Bonnie says, looking more tired than usual. "I'm just happy to be home. Clearwater didn't suit me in the least. And even though a real lady never goes into the details of her romantic life, I will say that I learned a lesson about not running off with a man who spends his weekends in breeches and an eyepatch."

"Noted." Wyatt winks at Bonnie. "No men in breeches and eyepatches."

"But I am glad you missed me," Bonnie says. She tilts her head, giving Wyatt a glance out of the corner of her eye. "I'm sure there was no one around to put up with your bellyaching and nonsense while I was gone."

"Just Cap." Wyatt pats the bar top to get Joe's attention. "Budweiser, if you don't mind, Joe. And Miss Lane has already requested the pleasure of my company on the dance floor whenever you get around to playing some Steely Dan."

"The hell I have," Bonnie laughs. Her words are fierce, but her tone is teasing.

The lights are low inside the open-air bar, and it's still early enough for the sun's last rays to bounce off the sand and sea and burn brightly inside the Ho Ho. Holly turns on her bar stool and squints out at the water. A few more of her neighbors have joined them, and she lifts her shot glass at Ray and Millie and then knocks back the vanilla rum in one go.

It won't be long before Joe gets everyone served and takes out his guitar. If Bonnie and Wyatt want Steely Dan, he'll play Steely Dan. And if he does, Holly knows they'll dance—no matter what Bonnie says now, they always do.

Hell, if Joe gives her one more shot of vanilla rum, maybe she'll even join them.

CHAPTER 27

H olly's got a stale donut clamped between her lips as she walks around the B&B office. It's after eight o'clock on a warm, early April evening, and she's long since sent Bonnie home. But there are emails to answer and Facebook posts to respond to, so she's turned up the satellite radio on her computer, found a station that's playing R.E.M. all evening, and dug half a donut out of a waxy white bag from Mistletoe Morning Brew that she'd brought into the office the day before.

Pucci is passed out on his bed in the corner. He's making jerky running motions like he's dreaming about an epic jog on the beach. With the sun completely set, the giant window that looks out onto Main Street is dark. Holly can see her own reflection in the window as she dances around the office, singing the words to "Losing My Religion" around the donut she's still got wedged in her mouth.

The window rattles loudly as a fist pounds against it from outside. Startled, Holly spits out the donut. It hits the floor and rolls over to Pucci, where it comes to a stop next to his nose. At the same time that Holly spits out the donut, she accidentally inhales a bite, and the chunk lodges in her windpipe.

The front door of the B&B flies open and footsteps come

pounding down the hall. It's Jake. "Hey, are you okay? Are you choking?"

Holly nods and thumps her own chest.

"Come here," Jake says. He turns her around and holds her arms out to the sides so he can put his hands under her sternum. With a smooth pull of his fists, he dislodges the donut that's blocking Holly's windpipe. She spits it onto the floor.

"What the hell is wrong with you?" Holly coughs. She's bent at the waist, trying to catch her breath. "You almost killed me!"

"Don't think I haven't been tempted lately," Jake says. "But I probably fantasized about something sexier than death by donut."

Holly pats her chest as her breathing returns to normal. "There are sexy and unsexy ways to kill someone?"

Jake rolls his eyes. "Whatever. You're welcome."

"Anyway," she says sternly. "You're knocking on my window at night because...?"

"Because I saw you in here and it's after eight. Because we haven't talked since that day a couple of weeks ago when I caught the twins hoarding coconuts for an ambush."

Holly makes a face as she reaches down to pick up the soggy, choked-on donut chunk off the floor; Pucci's already woken up and eaten the bigger piece that landed near his bed.

"Okay, I'm listening," she says, brushing her hands together and sitting in her chair. She puts her feet up on the edge of her desk and reaches over to turn down the music with a click of her mouse.

Jake throws both hands up in the air and makes an exasperated sound. "Well," he says. "You win."

"I win what?"

"Bridget's leaving."

"Why does that mean I've won?"

"Because you got what you wanted."

"I guess I did." Holly leans back and laces her fingers together, resting them on her stomach. "But I want to be clear: I wanted her off the island because she's narrow-minded, not because she's your girlfriend."

"Was. She *was* my girlfriend."

Holly lets this sink in. "I'm sorry."

"Right." Jake is watching her face, waiting for her to look away first. "I'm sure you are."

Holly sits up straight again and puts her feet on the floor. "You being unhappy doesn't bring me any joy. I am sorry for that. But I'm *not* sorry for trying to keep this island free of the kind of nonsense that floats around out there," she says, flinging an arm out to indicate the mainland and the rest of the world. "And I'm not sorry about bringing new people here and changing things up."

Jake rolls his head around on his neck like the conversation is making him tense. "I get it, Holly. Again—you win. But I have to go back to what I said last time we talked: I don't think this island is big enough for both of us." Jake looks her straight in the eye again. "I think I should leave. At least for a while."

The office is silent. Pucci gives a satisfied huff in the corner, and the chime of Holly's email inbox bleeps in the quiet room. "Don't go," she says softly. "I mean it."

"How are we going to be on this island together after everything that's happened in the past year?"

Holly stands up and reaches for Jake's hand. He pulls back. "Jake. We'll figure it out," she pleads. "This place wouldn't be the same without you." They stare at one another wordlessly. "I mean that."

Jake is about to say something when a movement and some noise on the sidewalk outside the B&B's office window gets their attention. They squint at the darkened glass. Beams of light flash around, illuminating the sidewalk and the faces of their neighbors.

"What's going on out there?" Jake makes a beeline for the door as he's talking. Holly follows him, her hair flying behind her as they rush through the lobby and out onto the sidewalk.

Outside, Vance is frantically waving a flashlight around. The Bradfords, the Cafferkeys, and Cap Duncan are aiming their own beams of light at the darkened storefronts and toward the dock at the end of the street. The stars aren't as bright as they usually are, and the air feels still and unyielding.

"What's up?" Jake asks, putting himself in the middle of the fray.

Holly hangs back, wishing she'd grabbed her shoes from under her desk.

"It's Mori," Vance says in a panic. "We put the boys to bed early, and when Calista went to check on them, he was gone. Mexi said he climbed out the window."

"Out the window?" Jake frowns. "Man, these kids are daredevils." He looks up and down the dark street. The only sounds are of shuffling feet as Ray and Cap look around for the missing boy. Buckhunter comes out the front of Jack Frosty's, a spatula still in his hand from the grill.

"Let me get my shoes and a flashlight," Holly says, ready to join in. "Then we can split up and canvass the island."

"I think that's a good idea," Jake agrees. He takes the few steps over to his parked golf cart and opens the metal box on the back. From it, he pulls a long-handled flashlight, two walkie-talkies, and an electric megaphone. "Cap, take the other walkie-talkie," Jake orders, switching it on and handing it over. "I've got this one. Ray, use the megaphone like this," he says, pushing a button and showing Ray how to shout into it. "And Holly, keep your cell on you. Go with Vance, okay?"

Holly nods. "I'll be right back," she promises, her breath catching in her throat. In under two minutes, she's got her Converse on her feet, her Yankees cap on her head, and her cell phone in the back pocket of her cargo pants. "I'm ready," she says to Vance, rushing down the front steps of the B&B and catching up to the boys' dad. "Let's take the west side of the island—I know the forested area like the back of my hand."

Without arguing, Vance follows Holly to her pink golf cart in the B&B's small lot. They climb in and peel out, taking a sharp right onto Main Street and barreling up the road as fast as the cart will take them.

They bump off the paved road of Main Street and onto Cinnamon Way. Holly swerves around the snaking arms of a Gumbo Limbo tree, and narrowly misses the wide fans of a Silver Palm as Vance hangs out the side of the cart with his flashlight trained into the brush.

"Mori!" he shouts, his voice strained. "Mori! Where are you?"

Holly slows near an opening into the trees so that Vance can jump out of the cart and illuminate the area. There's a rustling in the trees and he chases it into the brush, pushing limbs and branches out of his way blindly.

"Mori—are you in there?" he calls out.

Vance is flicking through branches, and his flashlight beam momentarily blinds Holly as he runs back to the cart.

"He's not in there," Vance says breathlessly. He's super-charged with adrenaline, and his eyes are wild with fear. "Let's go."

The tires spin on the sandy lane as they bounce over pits and dips in the road. Vance scans the area around them with his light.

"We're going to hit my property in another minute or two," Holly says, pointing off to the left, "and then beyond that is the beach." She scratches her head, not wanting to think what it would mean if Mori had reached the beach on his own. December Drive is long and winding, and it wraps all the way around the island. There's a lot of sand to cover, multiple dunes and mini-coves that a little boy could hide in and fall asleep, and more dark, commanding ocean than she wants to think about.

"Can we scan your property to see if he might have seen a house and wandered that way?"

"Of course," Holly says, swinging into her driveway. The headlights catch the eyes of a small animal in the trees next to Buckhunter's bungalow, and after a minute of wide-eyed surprise, the little marsh rabbit bounds away from the glare of the headlights. Holly puts the cart in park. "Let's have a look."

They jump out and run around the darkened yard. Holly crosses the lawn that separates her house from Buckhunter's and checks his porch for signs of Mori. She trains her flashlight under his rocking chair and over the side of the porch. No sign of the little boy.

"See anything?" she calls out, running back to her own yard. Vance is looping around the back of the bungalow, and through the windows of her dark house Holly can see the light he's flashing as it flickers across her lanai and through her kitchen and side windows.

"Nothing!" Vance shouts back. He and Holly meet at the bottom of the stairs that lead up to her front door. "Mori!" Vance yells again, turning in a circle. His anguished voice filters up through the treetops and echoes in the night sky. "Answer me!" he bellows. Nothing.

"Let me try calling Jake," Holly says, crossing her yard and snatching the cell phone off the seat of her cart.

Jake answers on the first ring. "Any sign of him?" he says without preamble.

"No. We're out at my house, and we're going to drive over to the beach. We'll turn right and go towards the Ho Ho to see if he went that way. The lights and the music might have caught his attention."

"Okay, call me with news." Jake hangs up abruptly.

"Let's go." Holly puts the cart in reverse and starts backing up as Vance is still climbing in. He swings onto the seat and points his flashlight out into the yard and the trees beyond.

"Beach?" Vance asks.

Holly glances at his profile as she drives. "I think we have to," she says carefully.

"Okay," Vance says in a calm, resigned voice. "Let's do it."

OVER THE CRASHING OF THE WAVES, HOLLY AND VANCE SCREAM Mori's name repeatedly. They search behind palm trees and fallen logs, waving their flashlights like lighthouse beacons to get the attention of a lost little boy. They split up briefly, each scouring a different area from the water back to the trees, but when they meet up again at Holly's parked cart, they're both empty-handed.

"Nothing," Holly says, taking off her baseball cap and readjusting it on her head. "And it feels like there's no moon tonight."

"No sign of him that direction, either." Vance stands next to the cart, shoulders slumped forward like he's about to give in to despair.

"Let's take December Drive up past the Ho Ho Hideaway," Holly says. She flicks off her flashlight and gets in behind the steering wheel again.

Vance stays rooted to the spot, staring into the distance. "What have I done?" he rasps, running a hand over his tired face. "I thought I was giving my boys this chance to live an unconventional, adventurous life, and instead I brought them to a place that's too wild for them."

He finally meets Holly's eye. "Or maybe everyone here is right, and they're the ones who are too wild for this island."

A loud wave crashes violently on the shore.

"No one can fault you for wanting to give your kids a life away from a big city, Vance," she says, leaning across the bench seat so she can look up at him from under the roof of the cart as he stands beside it. "And please don't forget, you're talking to someone who grew up on this wild island—when it was much wilder than it is now."

"You're right. It's not impossible to be a kid here, but we've been on the island for a little over a month and already done serious damage."

"Vance," Holly says. "Get in. You're hysterical and talking nonsense. Your son is still missing, and we need to find him."

As if he's waking up from a dream, Vance comes back around, his eyes clearing and his attitude changing. "Oh my God. What am I doing?" He falls into the passenger seat. "Go! Go!"

Holly hits the gas pedal again and takes off, tearing along December Drive with her headlamps on to light the way. Vance uses his flashlight to shine it into the dunes, shouting Mori's name as they drive. Every so often, Holly slows to a stop and they wait, listening to hear a cry or a response. After about ten minutes, Vance moves to the back of the golf cart where he stands on the low step that allows passengers to climb up to the back seat. He holds on to the roof with one hand to steady himself, propping the flashlight up on his other shoulder and aiming it at the sand dunes.

"I'm ready," he says to Holly, patting the roof to let her know he's holding on tight. She pulls out again, driving steadily so Vance can see ahead and around them.

At the turnoff for the Ho Ho, Holly slows and makes a left into the sandy clearing that the islanders use as a parking lot.

"Let's check out this area, and I can ask Joe if he's seen Mori tonight. Why don't you head over there," she points at the palm trees wrapped in twinkling Christmas lights, "and I'll stop inside the bar. Be right back."

Joe is alone in the bar except for two people sitting out on the sand with cans of beer, and he stops wiping off clean glasses to listen to

Holly and to assure her that he hasn't seen Mori anywhere at all for several days. He offers to close up the bar and help with the search, but Holly asks him to stay put and to call her or Jake if a stray six-year-old wanders up the steps of the Ho Ho.

"No sign of him here," Holly says, jogging down the steps and across the sand to where Vance is searching in the trees around the bar.

"Moving on," Vance says, climbing back into the cart. They take December Drive slowly, wrapping around the north side of the island and passing the spot where the crew of *Wild Tropics* had set up camp and done most of its filming. They're about to turn right onto Pine Cone Boulevard and wind back down to where the road meets Main Street when a shadowy figure catches Vance's eye.

"Over there!" he shouts, pointing at someone on their knees. "I see him!"

Holly swings the cart to the left and off the road. She slows considerably as her wheels try to move across the soft, unpacked sand. As her headlights capture the crouching figure, the person looks in their direction and stands. Holly's cart has almost come to a standstill, so she stops where she is and gets out.

"Hey!" she calls, running across the loose sand in her tennis shoes. "Mori!"

Vance grabs his light and follows Holly as they run in that direction. The figure stands in the pitch darkness and pauses for a second like a deer in headlights, then breaks into a slow, wide-legged run across the sand.

"Where are you going?" Vance shouts into the sound of crashing waves. "Stop running—you aren't in trouble!"

But he keeps running, ducking behind a sand dune and disappearing from Holly and Vance's view in the darkness.

"Moritz Leonard Guy!" Vance shouts. He trips over something and falls to one knee. "Get back here, or you *will* be in trouble!" He pulls himself up quickly and keeps running, but Holly's stopped. She's reached the spot where the shadowy figure had been kneeling, and she's staring at an abandoned shovel and the start of a small hole.

"What the hell?" she mutters, sticking the toe of her shoe into the hole and digging around. Sand falls onto her foot as she does. She picks up the shovel and turns it over in her hands. The handle is smooth wood, and it's about four feet long. The metal looks well-worn in the light from the cart's headlamps, and Holly turns the shovel on its end, looking at its sharp point. It's clearly been used in someone's yard or garden, though it's currently covered in wet sand.

She's still standing there when Vance comes back, frustrated and empty-handed. "He kept running," Vance pants, bending over at the waist and putting his hands on his knees as he catches his breath. "We need to get moving—I think we can catch him if we keep driv—" He stops talking and looks at the shovel in Holly's hands. "Where did that come from?"

Holly nods at the hole in the ground. "Whoever that was running away from you," she says, nodding in the direction the person had gone, "is the person who's been digging holes all over this island for the past couple of months." She almost forgets about the reason why they're out on the beach at night as she takes the pieces of the puzzle and tries to fit them together in her head. "The same person who digs holes in people's lawns and in the middle of our streets is now out here on the sand, digging up our beach. I'm so confused," she says, looking past her cart at the inky blue night.

"So you're saying that's not my son we just chased?" Vance asks, pointing into the darkness in the direction Holly's looking.

"Not unless he has a shovel and a plan to dig to China." Holly takes the garden tool and marches back over to her golf cart. She feels around on the dashboard for her cell phone and unlocks it, dialing Jake's number with a few taps on the screen.

"What? What did you find?" Jake asks.

"Not Mori, but we found the hole bandit."

"Huh?" Jake is completely focused on the task at hand, and it takes him a second to shift gears. "Oh, the holes—right. Okay. Where?"

"We're almost to Candy Cane Beach, and we caught him digging in the sand. He took off running and left the shovel behind."

"Who was it?"

"I don't know. It's too dark out here to see."

"Then how do you know it was a 'he'?" Jake asks, covering the mouthpiece of his phone and mumbling something on the other end that Holly can't quite hear.

"Can you think of any woman you know who'd be out here in the dark, digging in the sand like a maniac and then running away when someone else shows up?"

"You make a solid point," Jake says. "Which way did he go?"

"He ran down Pine Cone in the direction of Main Street. We're headed that way, too."

"Okay, I'll meet you at the corner of...hold on," Jake covers the mouth piece again. "Holly," he says into the phone. "Get back here. Now." He shouts something at the other people on his end. "Get to the B&B as quickly as you can. We found Mori."

"THEY FOUND MORI," HOLLY SAYS TO VANCE AS THEY SCAMPER TO get into the cart and get it out of the soft sand. "Jake says he's at the B&B."

"Thank God," Vance sighs, putting his elbows on his knees and burying his hands in his face as they roll over a sand drift and end up with their wheels on firmer ground. "I need to call Calista."

Vance pulls his cell phone out of the pocket of his shorts and dials his wife. They're talking in relieved tones as Holly navigates the dark end of Pine Cone Boulevard. Once they reach the first houses they'll have a light source other than her headlamps, and the houses along the street will lead the way down to Main.

As they reach the edge of Turtle Dove Estates and pass by Bonnie's well-lit house, Holly peers in the windows. She's overwhelmed by a sense of completion when she sees Bonnie walk through the kitchen in her reading glasses; just that glimpse of her friend reminds her how happy she is to have Bonnie back.

They pass by the entrance to the tiny grouping of houses that makes up Turtle Dove Estates, and Holly steps on the gas to try and get them to the B&B faster. There's a streetlight ahead, and she races towards it, eyes focused ahead on the place where Pine Cone and Main intersect. She'll turn right there and pass Mistletoe Morning Brew, and then they'll be at the B&B.

Vance is still talking to Calista on the other end of the line, who—to Holly's ears—sounds a little hysterical with joy and relief. Holly is smiling and mentally calculating the seconds it'll take to reunite Vance with his son when Cap Duncan whips around the corner out of Turtle Dove Estates, nearly broadsiding Holly and Vance.

"Whoa!" Holly shouts, swerving expertly. The nose of Cap's cart narrowly misses the passenger side of Holly's cart, and Vance drops his phone as he flails around, steadying himself on the dash. They come to a stop. "Cap, are you okay?" Holly puts the cart in park. Her headlights are pointed at the small, wooden Turtle Dove Estates sign as she rushes over to make sure he's alright.

"Where's Fiona?" Cap growls. "We need her."

Holly scans Cap; he looks fine, and they hadn't even bumped into each other. That's when she sees Heddie Lang-Mueller is in the back-seat of Cap's cart, her arms around Hal Pillory's shoulders to steady him.

"We need to get Hal to Fiona," Heddie says, her voice low and steady. "He's been hurt."

"Again? What happened?" Holly goes over to the cart and reaches out a hand to touch him.

"Holly, I'm going to run the rest of the way," Vance shouts, getting out of her cart and taking off without his flashlight or the cell phone that slipped from his hands and landed on the floor of Holly's cart as they'd swerved.

"She's at the B&B," Holly says to Cap and Heddie. "Hal, what happened? How did you get hurt?"

Hal moans in response. He's facing Heddie, and Holly can't tell whether he's bleeding or not.

"We were leaving Heddie's to go over to Jack Frosty's," Cap says, lifting one hand off the steering wheel. "Didn't see him walking through the grass and crossing the driveway, and I hit the old bastard with the cart."

Holly's hands go to the sides of her face. "No."

"Yep." Cap bangs the heel of his palm against the steering wheel. "Gotta get him to see the doc."

"We're all headed that direction," Holly says. Without another word, she gets back into her cart and leads the way to Main Street. They both park carelessly at the curb, leaving the keys in the ignitions of their carts.

Holly leaves Hal with Heddie and Cap and she races through the open side gate of the B&B and onto the pool deck, where she hears a loud commotion and several voices. The gate swings wide and bangs against the wooden fence as she unlatches it and rushes in. The scene playing out on the smooth concrete around the aquamarine pool stops her dead in her tracks. The lights from under the water are distorted by the small waves rippling through the pool. Buckhunter, Jake, and Jimmy Cafferkey all have their flashlight beams trained at Fiona in her yellow one-piece bathing suit. She's kneeling on the ground, barefoot and frantic as she performs CPR on Mori.

Vance is standing apart from the group, completely stricken and inert when his wife rushes through the open gate with a sleepy-looking Mexi in tow. She stops short next to Holly and drops Mexi's hand; a guttural wail escapes from her throat and she falls to her knees, reaching for the plastic mesh of a pool chair to support her as she sobs.

"Come here, buddy," Holly says to Mexi, scooping him up without hesitation. She holds his small, surprisingly light body next to hers, cupping the back of his curly head with one palm so that he's forced to look away from the sight of his twin brother, drenched and unmoving in a pool of water on the concrete.

As she turns to take him back out to the sidewalk, she nearly runs into Cap and Heddie, who are each holding one of Hal's arms to support him. Now that he's upright, Holly can see that one of his legs is scraped and bleeding, and his eyes are unfocused.

"Jesus," Cap says, dropping Hal's elbow momentarily. His first instinct is to rush in and help, but Holly blocks his way.

"Fiona's got this," she says with intensity, tightening her grip on Mexi. "Let's go inside the B&B."

With Mexi in her arms, she leads the small group through the front door of the inn, pausing as Heddie and Cap help Hal up the handful of stairs and into the lobby.

"Where should we go?" Heddie asks, out of breath from the exertion and excitement.

"I'll get the keys," Holly says, supporting Mexi under his body with her strong forearm. She grabs a ring of keys out of the drawer by the computer. "The Sea Turtle Suite is closest," she says, leading them hurriedly down the carpeted hallway. The shell-shaped sconce on the wall next to the door burns at a low wattage, but it's enough to help her guide the key into the lock. "Help Hal get comfortable on that bed, and if you don't mind," she says, setting Mexi on the other queen sized bed, "turn on the Disney channel for this little guy while I check to see what's going on."

Holly rushes back through the lobby and out the front door, approaching the pool deck via the gate again rather than barging into the middle of the scene by exiting through the building's side door that leads to the pool.

As Holly carefully approaches Calista, Fiona gives a final chest compression that seems to jolt Mori to life. He turns his head, coughing out water and gagging hoarsely. Fiona rolls him onto his side, placing her hand between his head and the concrete. After expelling what looks like a half-gallon of chlorinated water, he immediately throws up and starts crying.

"Oh my God!" Calista screams, trying to stand. Instead, she ends up doing an animal-like crawl over to where her little boy is curled on the wet ground. Vance meets her there and they surround Mori, covering him with their parental love and concern; this forces everyone else to take several steps back.

Fiona walks in a big circle, hands on her hips as she blows out a breath and pulls in another one. She does this a few times as water drips from her body and hair. The soles of her feet leave wet prints on the concrete.

"What happened?" Holly whispers, pulling her best friend into a hug when she finally stops pacing.

Fiona hugs Holly back and then turns to look at Mori and his parents. "I came down here to swim some laps, and when I got here,

I found this little guy in the pool. He was facedown and not breathing."

Jimmy brings Fiona a towel. He holds it open to her, wrapping it around her shoulders. "Nice work, doc," he says, giving her a single nod before walking out the gate and away from the scene. The other people on the pool deck discreetly disappear as well, leaving the family together. Holly and Fiona stand off to the side.

"I hate to dump on you, Fee, but it seems like tragedy keeps happening in twos around here," Holly says, putting her hand on Fiona's back and steering her out onto the sidewalk.

"I really need to make sure Mori is okay and check his vitals—" Fiona clutches the towel around her shoulders with one hand like it's a superhero's cape.

"Heddie and Cap ran into Hal Pillory with Cap's cart."

"What?" Fiona drops the towel and starts to cross the street in just her yellow bathing suit. "Where is he? I'll open up the office and get my stuff."

"Fee, you don't have your keys," Holly points out. Fiona stops in the middle of the street and looks down at herself. She's cast in a pool of pale, golden light from the old-fashioned street lamp that stands in front of Poinsettia Plaza. Her freckled chest heaves as the adrenaline pumps through her system, and her strong, toned legs are naked and still dotted with water. Fiona's red-painted toes stare up at her from the center of the paved street.

"I don't have anything," she says, sounding lost. "I have no idea what I'm doing." She looks around like she's just realizing where she is.

Holly watches as Fiona rides the crest of emotion that all doctors must feel when they're in crisis mode. She's obviously got her medical faculties about her, but her focus is so laser-sharp that the rest of the world has faded out around her.

"Hey, wait here. I'll get my keys from the B&B office," Holly says, remembering the set of master keys she keeps in her desk so that she can open up any building on the island in case of an emergency. "And I'll grab you a robe."

She rushes through the lobby again at full-speed, pausing in the doorway of the Sea Turtle Suite. "Hey," Holly says, bracing herself against the frame of the open door. Mexi is inside, sitting criss-cross-applesauce on the edge of the bed as he stares, open-mouthed, at a Disney cartoon. Hal lies prone on the other bed with Heddie next to him, holding his hand. He's moaning and staring at the ceiling.

"What, Holly? What is it?" Cap is across the room in three long strides to meet her at the door. He talks in low tones, obviously expecting the worst.

"Mori is fine—he's with his parents," she says, looking up into Cap's concerned face. For the first time all evening, Holly feels something release inside of her. The fear and adrenaline that have pushed her forward sink back like a retreating wave, and the gate that's been holding her emotions in check is unlatched. Hot, salty tears run down her cheeks. "How is Hal?" she asks on a quiet sob.

"Not making any sense," Cap says, putting both of his large, rough hands on Holly's shoulders and guiding her out into the quiet hallway. He reaches back and closes the door to the room behind them so they can speak. "He's asking about Sadie and telling Heddie that he's lost her again, and I...he's confused, Holly," Cap says carefully, his hands still on both of her shoulders as he looks down the hallway with sad eyes. "I know this is my fault, but I didn't *see* him."

"It's not your fault, Cap," she says. He looks down at her. "It isn't," Holly says with conviction. "Vance and I were out looking for Mori at Candy Cane Beach, and we found someone out there on the sand in the dark, digging holes."

"What for?" Cap takes his hands off Holly's shoulders.

"For the same reason they've been digging holes around the island since January, I suppose," Holly says, raising both shoulders and turning her palms up. "Your guess is as good as mine. Anyway, I think it was Hal."

"You think what was Hal—the holes?" Cap pulls his bushy, white eyebrows together in a deep frown. "Why on earth would Hal Pillory be digging holes?"

"He'd have to tell us that, but Vance and I thought it was Mori and we chased him. He ran away in the dark, and my guess is that he ducked into Turtle Dove Estates and got nicked with your cart as he cut across Heddie's property."

"Noooo," Cap says, pulling back in disbelief. "Do you think?"

"He left a shovel behind when he ran." Holly examines the giant banana leaves on the wallpaper behind Cap as she remembers the scene on the beach. "But before we solve that mystery, we need to make sure he's okay."

"We do," Cap agrees.

"I'm getting my keys for Fiona so she can open up her office. If we bring one of those flat board stretcher things over here, can you help us get Hal onto it and carry him across the street?"

"Of course." Cap opens the door and steps back inside to let Heddie and Hal know what they're about to do, and Holly goes to her office to grab the keys. She makes a pit stop in the laundry room and pulls a clean, white hotel robe off its hanger on the rack for Fiona.

It takes about ten minutes to get Hal rolled onto a stretcher, secured with velcro straps, and carried over to Poinsettia Plaza (in the end, Cap and Jimmy do the heavy-lifting, with Fiona directing everyone in her white bathrobe and stethoscope). Fiona spends an hour behind the closed door of her exam room, giving Hal X-rays and a thorough physical to check for broken bones and internal bleeding while the word spreads across the island that tragedy has narrowly been avoided. By the time she gets Hal settled into the only hospital bed she has and gives him enough pain medicine to keep him comfortable, the islanders are starting to gather over in the B&B's dining room.

Bonnie is the first person Holly calls, and she comes over right away wearing a velvety black sweatsuit and clean white Keds. Her reading glasses dangle from a chain around her neck as she bustles around the dining room, asking whether people want coffee, tea, or sparkling water. Iris Cafferkey has enlisted Maggie Sutter to help her in the kitchen, and they're sifting through the refrigerator and the cupboards, trying to piece together enough food to put out so that people can nibble nervously while they wait for news.

Fiona strides across the paved street in a pair of flip-flops and the robe, hands shoved into the deep pockets like it's a lab coat. "Is my other patient handy?" she asks Holly, black bag in hand.

"I'll take you to him." Holly gets up from behind the front desk and leads the way to the Sea Turtle Suite. She knocks softly on the door and Vance opens it a crack. He pulls it open all the way when he sees that it's Holly and Fiona.

With Hal transported over to Fiona's office, Vance and Calista have moved into the room with Mori, who is on the bed next to his brother. They've bathed Mori and wrapped him in clean towels, but neither parent wanted to leave his side to drive home for new clothes, so they've simply tucked him into bed with Mexi. Holly watches the boys in awe as they curl around one another in a deep, untroubled sleep, their hot breath warming one another's cheeks.

Calista stands up and crosses the room. Without a word, she throws her arms around Fiona and buries her face in the fuzzy shoulder of her white robe. The women are both petite and of similar size, and Holly and Vance stand there while they clutch one another like sisters. Calista cries with relief.

"Thank you," she whispers. "Thank you for finding my baby. Thank you for saving him." Calista pulls back and wipes under both of her eyes.

"It was lucky I was there," Fiona says, swiping at her own eyes. "I just came for a late night swim, and I happened to walk in at the right time."

"Some might say luck, some would say divine intervention," Vance says in his rumbling voice, putting his hands together and holding his fingertips in front of his mouth in gratitude and prayer. His tall frame fills the room.

"Either way, Mori is a lucky little boy," Fiona says, smiling at both of them. "Things could have ended differently."

"Is he going to be okay—I mean, long-term?" Calista asks. Her eyes brim with hope and trepidation.

Fiona levels her gaze at Vance and Calista. "I don't know how long he was in the water." It's an honest answer, but one that doesn't necessarily give the Guys what they want to hear. "We should let him sleep tonight. Tomorrow we'll make arrangements to get him to Key West. They'll want to run more tests at the hospital and then go from there."

"He was talking while we had him in the bathtub," Calista says, nodding at Vance. "Right, honey?"

"He said he was sorry for running away, and that he just wanted to show us that he could swim." Vance looks at his wife. "Calista told the boys yesterday that they weren't allowed to go near the pool or the beach without us, but he thought that because he watched the Olympics, he knew how to swim."

"How did he get into the pool area?" Holly finally asks the question that's been weighing on her since the moment she arrived on the scene. The safety of anyone visiting the B&B is her responsibility, and she's been combing through her mind, trying to figure out how he might have gotten in. "I feel responsible for him having access to it in the first place, but all of my fences and locks are up to code, so..."

"No, Holly," Calista says, holding up a hand. "Don't even go there. Jimmy said they found an outdoor table that Mori must have dragged over from the coffee shop and used to climb over the fence. He was determined to get in that pool, no matter how many things you did right."

Relief and horror wash over Holly in equal parts as she accepts that her own negligence hadn't played any part in Mori's ending up in the pool.

"I need you guys to stay awake tonight—you might want to do it in shifts," Fiona instructs, bending over Mori as he sleeps. She watches as his eyes flicker beneath his lids. The long, dark fringe of lashes that rim his hazel eyes brushes against his soft cheek. "Just stay here in this room for the night. Keep an eye on him, make sure he's breathing normally, and if he wakes up and wants anything then you should be right there to comfort him."

"Of course," Calista says.

"If anything at all happens—if he throws up, feels dizzy, or seems disoriented—call me on my cell phone, okay? Doesn't matter what time." Fiona picks up the pad and pen on the nightstand between the beds and scribbles her phone number on it.

"We will. Thank you." Vance takes the sheet of paper from Fiona's hand as she and Holly walk to the door. "If nothing happens tonight, then we'll talk to you in the morning, right?" he asks.

"I'll make arrangements for transport to Key West first thing in the morning," Fiona promises. She and Holly step into the hallway. They wait until the door clicks shut and Vance locks it. "I've been here for, what, two years? And all I've seen so far are hemorrhoids and bunions. Now all of a sudden we've got traffic accidents, near-drownings, miscarriages…" Fiona leans her back against the banana leaf wallpaper. Her wild strawberry waves are nearly dry after jumping into the pool to save Mori, and the frizz of her long hair frames her tired face.

"You okay, Fee?" Holly puts her back against the wall so that she's standing shoulder-to-shoulder with Fiona. "What can I do for you?"

"I need to run back to the office to make sure Hal's sleeping comfortably. I also need to call Lower Keys Medical to let them know that Mori will be headed their way tomorrow. But then I want a burger," she looks down at the robe, gesturing at it with one hand, "some underwear, and dry clothes."

Holly nods at each request. "I can arrange all of those things."

Fiona pushes herself away from the wall, straightening the stethoscope around her neck. She's partway down the hall, flip-flops slapping against the carpet, when she turns to Holly. "Oh, and if you're going to delegate duties, then send Bonnie to dig through the underwear drawer in my house, not one of the men, okay?"

Holly laughs. "Got it."

"And one more thing: see if you can't get Buckhunter to mix me up a strong screwdriver and send it over here with the burger."

"In a to-go cup with a straw?" Holly jokes.

"That'll work," Fiona says. "See you in twenty."

CHAPTER 28

"Here's what we know," Holly says, presiding over the informal gathering at the Jingle Bell Bistro two nights after Mori was found in the pool. "Vance's mom has agreed to come down here and give them a hand with the boys for a while, just to see how it goes."

"Amen!" Mrs. Agnelli says, putting both arthritic hands in the air.

"It might not be a permanent solution," Holly warns, "but it will at least allow the family to get used to island life, and it will allow us the time to put some things in place."

The crowd has gathered after dark at Iris and Jimmy Cafferkey's restaurant, and while the invitations were passed furtively from ear to ear and phone to phone, they've intentionally chosen not to extend an invite to Jake and Bridget, to Hal Pillory, or to Vance and Calista. This semi-secret meeting allows the islanders the opportunity to discuss things off the record—something they can't do at a normal village council meeting.

"To that end," Bonnie says, standing up and sliding her reading glasses up her nose, "Holly and I have come up with some ideas."

"We won't get anywhere without some good ideas," Wyatt Bender says, tapping the table in front of him with two weathered fingers as he waits for whatever Bonnie has to say.

"As luck would have it," Bonnie shifts her gaze to Wyatt, "you're on my list of people to impose upon, Mr. Bender."

"Please, Miss Lane, impose upon me to your heart's content." Wyatt raises an eyebrow at Bonnie and elicits laughter from the crowd.

"Oh, you mind your manners, you dirty cowboy." Bonnie leans forward and swats Wyatt on the knee with the stack of white papers in her hand.

Holly reaches for the papers and Bonnie passes them to her. "I'll hand them out," she says, walking through the crowd and giving a sheet to each person. "What we've come up with is a fairly comprehensive—if not official in the eyes of the state's Board of Education—curriculum of activities for the kids," Holly explains. "Even with Vance's mother here on the island, we need to consider ways to contribute to the growth of our youngest Christmas Key residents."

People around the room pull reading glasses from shirt pockets and hold the sheets out in front of them at a distance in order to see the words.

"Now," Holly says, coming back to stand next to Bonnie. "Several of you have reservations about little ones roaming our island, but I think there's strong a possibility that Mexi and Mori won't always be the only kids on Christmas Key."

"Are Jake and Bridget going to give it another go?" Cap frowns.

"Maybe they'll get married first this time." Mrs. Agnelli gives a disapproving shake of her head.

"No," Holly assures them. "I don't think so. I just meant that we might have other people wanting to move here at some point, and those people might have kids. I mean—maybe. I don't know." She feels flustered at the thought of Jake and Bridget trying for another baby. In fact, it brings her to the next topic of conversation. "Actually, my understanding is that Bridget and Jake are splitting up."

Holly watches her neighbors' faces to see if any of them register shock at this news; most don't.

"When is she leaving?" Buckhunter asks, as succinct and to-the-point as always.

"Well," Holly stalls. "I'm not sure. All I know is that they broke up and she's leaving at some point."

"Now you and Jake can get back together!" Mrs. Agnelli says, snapping her fingers like she's just come up with a fabulous idea.

"That is—*wow*," Holly laughs nervously. "That's not even a discussion point."

"Maybe it should be," Maria Agnelli says.

Holly claps her hands together and pretends not to hear this last comment. "Okay, the next thing we need to discuss is Hal."

"Oh, sweet Hal," Millie Bradford says, putting one hand over her heart and looking around at the people sitting closest to her. "That poor dear."

"He's had a rough go of it," Holly agrees. "But Fiona got him all patched up."

"Again," Fiona points out.

"Yes, again—and we called his daughter in Ohio to talk about what happened."

"What *did* happen?" Jimmy Cafferkey is standing at the back of the crowd near the window that opens onto his kitchen. He's still wearing a stained apron over his red t-shirt and khaki shorts, and he's got a snug, white skull cap covering his gray hair.

"We all know that Hal is the one who's been digging all the holes around here, but now we know why." Holly leans against the edge of the table behind her. The bistro has been re-set for breakfast the next morning, and Iris and Emily look tired as they sit in a booth in the back near Jimmy. Running the bistro keeps them busy, and they work incredibly hard. Holly smiles at the Cafferkey women and goes on. "So, the night we found out that he was the one behind the holes, he ran away from me and Vance and disappeared. Not long after that he was hit by Cap and Heddie's golf cart in Turtle Dove Estates."

Cap looks sheepish, and Holly knows he still feels guilty, though everyone has assured him that he doesn't need to.

Fiona stands up next to Buckhunter in the crowd. "If I may?" she asks Holly.

"Of course," Holly says, holding out a hand.

"I've had the chance to assess Hal's mental state as well as to oversee his physical recovery," Fiona says. "I know we're all like family here, so I feel comfortable sharing with you that he's got some very clear deficits in memory. However, he *did* seem to know why he's been digging the holes."

The faces around the bistro are sympathetic and concerned, and as she looks around at them, Holly knows with certainty that this won't be the last time they have to gather to discuss the future and well-being of one of their own.

"Apparently he panicked last summer when the tropical storm was headed our way," Fiona says. "He thought that his house might be destroyed, and with it, Sadie's ashes."

"Oh, Sadie!" Glen says, the ache in her heart for her late friend etched all over her face. "He misses her so much."

"He does." Fiona nods. "In fact, he was so worried that he decided to bury the urn and come back for it after the storm had passed, only—"

"*He forgot where it was*," a chorus of voices says, the words coming out at slightly different paces as realization dawns over the crowd.

"That's my understanding." Fiona smiles sadly. "And he didn't want anyone to know that he'd forgotten, so he's been out digging for months, trying to find the urn so he can bring Sadie home."

"What about the holes in his own driveway?" Maria Agnelli asks. "He made a big ruckus about putting up video cameras and finding out who did it, but you mean to tell us it was just him digging those holes all along?"

"I guess he either forgot that he'd dug in his own yard, or he was trying to cover up for not remembering where Sadie's ashes were. It's kind of hard to say what he might have been thinking at that point," Fiona says. "The aging mind can play cruel tricks."

Tongues cluck and heads shake as people think about all the holes that have popped up around the island these past few months. To think poor Hal Pillory had been skulking around in the dark with a shovel, trying to remember where he'd buried his late wife's ashes...a wave of pity and concern spreads through the crowd as they imagine it.

"His daughter is flying down here as soon as possible to be with him and to figure out what her next steps will be in terms of his care."

Fiona sits down next to Buckhunter again and puts her hands between her knees. Holly knows this is news that Fiona hadn't wanted to share —after all, it opens up a conversation in the minds of many about what will happen to *them* when the time comes for someone to step in and start making decisions about their care—and there's always the chance that people might shoot the messenger. Being the bearer of bad news isn't new for Fiona, but she's keenly aware that the islanders might point fingers at her as the person who ordered Hal's daughter to come down and retrieve him.

Cap puts a hand in the air; Holly points to him and he stands. "This is one of those things in life that none of us look forward to," he says, eyes flashing with emotion as he pulls himself to his full height. "And I just want to say I'm grateful I don't have any kids to step in and boss me around, but it means you all are stuck with me until the bitter end. Sorry." He pretends to sit down again as people chuckle politely. "All kidding aside," Cap says, standing straight again. "Hal is a valued member of our community. What happens to him is his family's decision, but how we help him is ours. So I'd like to suggest that we find Sadie for him and bring her home."

Heads nod all over the room. Holly looks around and sees set faces —grim and accepting—as well as a few tears.

"I think that's a great idea, Cap, but how will we know where to look if he doesn't even remember where he buried her?" Holly asks.

"The urn is a tin box," Cap says simply. "How about a metal detector?"

The group goes wild as people spring to action. The hands of those who own metal detectors go up all over the room (these are, after all, Florida retirees, Holly reminds herself), and everyone seems to have a shovel to offer.

"Okay, okay," Holly says loudly, holding up both hands to silence them. "This is a great idea, and I think it takes precedence for now over the plan Bonnie and I originally came here to pitch to you tonight. But I just want to say that filling these holes has been a huge pain in the butt, so if you're going to dig, make sure you fill, okay?"

The talking and plan-making kick into high gear again the minute the words are out of Holly's mouth, so she goes over to the table where

Bonnie's talking to the triplets and pulls out a chair. "Got room for one more?"

"Sit down, sugar." Bonnie pats the table. "We've always got room for you."

THE HUNT FOR SADIE PILLORY'S ASHES STARTS THE NEXT MORNING after a surprise pre-dawn rainfall. Water drips from the palm fronds and evaporates almost instantly when it hits the warm, dry ground. Holly scratches her upper arm as a bug lands and nips at her skin. She scuffs the hard-packed sand at the dock with her tennis shoe and readjusts her Yankees cap.

"Now, the island is divided into sections," Cap says, hands on his hips. "Jake is here to show us a map and to assign us locations." He steps aside so Jake can open the map of Christmas Key that he uses to identify locations on the island. Wyatt Bender takes one end of the rolled poster and holds it as Jake unspools the rest.

Holly had stopped in at Mistletoe Morning Brew as soon as it opened, knowing that Jake would be there getting his coffee. She'd wrestled with how to let him in on the plan to help Hal without giving away that there had been a meeting he hadn't been invited to, but in the end it was much easier than she'd imagined.

"Hal told Fiona he's been digging the holes because he buried Sadie's ashes before the big storm last summer, and now he can't remember where they are," she'd blurted, stepping up behind him at the counter.

Jake turned around slowly. "I'll be damned," he'd said coolly. "That's not what I expected."

"Me either. A bunch of us are going to meet up at the dock at seven and spread out to see if we can find Sadie's ashes."

"More holes?" He cocked an eyebrow as he picked up the coffee Ellen had set on the counter in front of him.

"Not just random ones: we're using metal detectors this time."

"Ah, of course. Because this is Florida, and probably two-thirds of the island has one tucked into a closet or forgotten in a garage."

"See? Now you're getting it." Holly clapped him on the shoulder before she remembered the animosity in his eyes the night they'd spoken in the B&B office. Her hand fell to her side.

Jake stared at her for a minute with a gaze that burned like hot coals. "Anyway," he said, "I'd be glad to help out. Hal's a good guy."

"I know. His daughter is coming down to figure out what the next steps are, but we'd really like to be able to give Sadie back to him," Holly had said, remembering her former teacher. Sadie was a gentle woman with a reading voice that had almost lulled Holly to sleep on warm afternoons. She'd learned to love *Anne of Green Gables* and *Little House on the Prairie* because of Sadie Pillory, and she was hoping to give that same gift to Mexi and Mori now by warming up the other islanders to the idea of pitching in when it came to the boys.

Jake walked over to the counter on the side of the shop to add a little cream and sugar to his black coffee. Holly had followed.

"So what do you need from me? I don't have a metal detector," Jake said, tearing open a little pink envelope and dumping the sugar into his cup.

"Your map of the island. You know, the one where you divided Christmas Key up into quadrants or whatever."

"It's more than just quadrants—it's a grid. And it would definitely help you." He threw the sugar packet into the silver trash can under the counter and grabbed a plastic stirring stick from a jar. "You want me to bring it to the dock at seven?"

"Yes, please," Holly said, smiling at him.

Jake snapped the lid onto his coffee and strode to the door with purpose. "Fine. I'll be there. Oh, hey, Ellen?" he'd called out, pausing with one hand on the doorknob. Ellen stopped what she was doing behind the counter and looked at him. "No donuts for this one," he'd said, pointing at Holly, "unless you know the Heimlich." A hint of Jake's good humor passed over his face and Holly had almost been able to imagine that nothing was amiss between them. Almost.

She stands at the dock now, his teasing words from the coffee shop ringing in her head as Jake points out squares and locations on the grid. Her neighbors raise hands and offer to take certain areas, and as they peel off and head to golf carts laden with shovels and

STEPHANIE TAYLOR

metal detectors, the gray clouds part over the water, revealing a sky of muted pinks and yellows. It's going to be a gorgeous day. Holly inhales as she watches the morning sky turn into a watercolor palette. Hopefully it will be the day they bring Sadie back home for Hal.

❄

VANCE AND CALISTA'S TRIP TO KEY WEST WITH THE BOYS TO HAVE Mori checked out at the hospital is a quick one. They're back on the island within twenty-four hours, and Calista is behind the counter of the salon when Holly drops in to see Millie in the middle of the hunt for Sadie's ashes.

"How's the search going?" Calista asks, leaning her forearms on the front counter. She's been there since morning ordering inventory and setting up a calendar for the summer on Millie's computer. Within the first couple of weeks of her being there, Millie had started to count on Calista for duties beyond her job as a massage therapist, and the new role had morphed into a sort of office manager/massage therapist/front desk woman. Calista seems to like the extended work load, and she can't be too upset about the chance to make more money, given that Vance is still at home with the boys and hers is the only source of income at the moment.

Holly looks at her watch. It's already one-thirty. "The search is hard. There's a ton of sand and a huge patch of forest out by my place, so this could take much longer than we'd originally planned."

"Do you think he made it out as far as the trees back by your house?"

"I *know* he did," Holly says, thinking of the night when she'd caught someone prowling around on her property. "I just don't know how far into the wooded area he actually went."

"How's Hal doing?"

"He's home. His daughter got in late last night and she's taken over his care, which frees us all up to hunt for Sadie."

"It's so sad and beautiful," Calista says, her eyes dreamy as she looks out the window and onto Main Street. "To think that he was so

208

worried about her ashes during a storm that he buried them. It's kind of poetic."

It is sad, but for more reasons than Calista knows. Seeing her neighbors become feeble and forgetful is yet another reminder to Holly of the passage of time, and also another cattle prod to the rear end that reminds her of the need to keep expanding. To keep bringing new life to the island. To keep growing and changing—even when it isn't easy.

"Anyhow," Holly says, patting the front counter twice with both hands like she's waking someone up from a hypnotic state. "How's Mori?"

Calista pulls her arms off the counter and stands upright. She picks up a few stray pens and puts them in the cup next to the computer. "He's good. The doctor who treated him in Key West said the whole thing was the best case scenario. If Fiona hadn't found him when she did, then..." She stops, her eyes tearing up. "I'm sorry," Calista says, looking at the ceiling as she puts both ring fingers to the corner of her eyes to stop the flow.

"Oh my God, don't be sorry," Holly says, reaching across the counter and putting a hand on Calista's arm. "He's your baby."

"That was the scariest moment of my life, seeing him like that."

"But he's fine, and I've talked to everyone on Main Street about pulling in bistro tables and chairs at night—anything that might serve as a ladder to get over the pool fence—so there's no way it'll happen again. I can't help you much with the ocean, but I can promise you that the pool will be safe."

"Thank you, Holly. I hate that my family is making everyone change the way they do things, but—"

"Stop. Seriously—it's nothing. We need to think of the future, too. Mexi and Mori aren't the only kids who'll ever visit Christmas Key, and I want things to be safe for everyone."

Calista looks at the shiny black countertop. "Well, thanks again. It means a lot to us."

Holly goes around behind the counter and opens her arms, pulling the shorter woman into a tight hug. "I've said it before," she says, Calista's head tucking neatly beneath her chin, "but we're glad you're here, and we want to help. The happiness and well-being of anyone who lives on this island is important to me."

Calista squeezes Holly back before letting go. "I guess you'd better get back out there and keep looking for Sadie."

"You're right. Oh," Holly says, remembering why she'd stopped into the salon in the first place. "Is Millie out?"

"Yeah, she left with Iris and Emily about an hour ago. Said they were going to search around Snowflake Banks and that they'd be back to the B&B at five, unless someone radios or calls to say they've found anything before then."

"Perfect. Thanks, Calista!"

Holly is back in her cart and driving toward home to make a sandwich and grab Pucci when a thought hits her: if Hal had been that worried about something happening to Sadie during the storm, then it makes sense that he wouldn't have wanted her to be alone as the wind and rain whipped across the island, howled up Main Street, and knocked over branches and trees. He would have wanted her to have some peace and solace until he could come back for her. She rolls to a stop in the middle of Cinnamon Lane and picks up her cell phone to text Jake.

Meet me at the chapel. Bring a shovel and a metal detector.

Holly turns her cart around. Pucci and the sandwich will have to wait; she knows where Hal left Sadie.

CHAPTER 29

"What are we doing here?" Jake screeches to a stop in the sand next to Holly's cart. "Did Hal remember where he buried her?" He gets out and walks over to where Holly is kneeling.

"He wouldn't have wanted her to be alone," Holly says, looking up at Jake's handsome face as she crouches in front of a single headstone behind the chapel. She runs her hands over the weathered surface, tracing the carved letters with her fingers: *Christmas Key's original settlers will always be here in spirit, if not in body. But beware: just like Santa, they'll know when you've been naughty!*

"But no one is actually buried here," Jake says, pointing at the headstone that Frank Baxter had commissioned to make his dying wife laugh one more time. He'd promised her that he would erect it behind the chapel, but because the island's soft sand shifted too easily, it wouldn't really be a final resting place for anyone.

"That's true," Holly says, standing. "But you have to admit, there's a certain humor and a light to this area that makes you feel like you're not alone." She looks up into the tall trees. Almost impossibly, a slight wind picks up, shifting the branches above enough that a beam of sunlight breaks through. It falls directly over the grave stone. Chills run up and down Holly's body and she rubs her bare arms in spite of the fact that it's a warm April afternoon.

"I'm not gonna lie—that was kind of creepy." Jake's eyes are cast heavenward. "Do you really think she's around here somewhere?"

"I do. In fact," she says, looking at Jake's profile, "I think there's a peace to this particular spot that attracts all of the good things that come and go from Christmas Key."

Jake looks at her wordlessly.

"I mean," she pauses, not sure how she wants to say this, "I think this is where I'd find my grandparents, if I wanted to feel their presence. And when Pucci goes—" she stops, unable to finish the thought. "Well, you know. And even an unborn baby might find its way to this spot to be surrounded by—" Jake holds up a hand to stop her.

He looks at the headstone in the sunlight that hasn't stopped shining. Holly isn't sure if he's going to yell at her and tell her to mind her own business, or whether he might break into quiet sobs. She has no idea where he stands with Bridget's miscarriage, or if he's even processed any of it yet. It's hard not being able to reach out to him and offer comfort, but the things that have happened between them feel as heavy and solid as the gravestone before them.

"Yeah," he says, looking around the small clearing. "This might be the spot."

Instead of hugging him, Holly returns to the golf cart and leaves him with his thoughts for a moment. With her back to Jake, she lifts the tools they'll need off the back of his cart and waits.

After a minute or two, Jake walks over to her. "Let's do this," he says, holding out a hand. Without another word, Holly passes him the shovel and switches on the metal detector.

"You headed to the Ho Ho tonight?" Jake and Holly are riding out to Hal Pillory's together after finding Sadie's ashes behind the chapel.

She looks out at the sandy road as Jake drives them across the island at top speed in his official police golf cart. The seats are tan-colored leather bucket seats up front with a drink holder between them, and the back is a wide bench. Holly's got the tin container that holds Sadie's ashes resting in her lap.

"Why—are you making sure it's safe for you and Bridget to show? I can stay home if you guys want to go tonight," Holly says without any hint of sarcasm or bad feelings.

"Don't be like that." Jake switches hands impatiently, holding the wheel first with his left, then with his right. "Bridget is leaving on Tuesday, and she wants to say good-bye to everyone."

"Oh." Holly brushes at the damp box, swiping sand from its slightly dented top. She'd known that Bridget would leave at some point, but this end to Jake's relationship doesn't make her feel victorious, it just makes her feel sad for him. In spite of all they've been through and all the mixed emotions between them, ultimately Holly wants to see him happy.

"Yeah, it's time. We've tried to talk things through, but she's pretty convinced that her views on the world are right."

"People usually are," Holly says, watching the houses as they pass by.

"I finally had to ask myself what my mother would think if I brought a girl home who felt that way, and I realized I had to end it."

Holly just listens. Neither of them mention the fact that he was nearly tied to Bridget permanently, but the thought that his life almost went a completely different direction hangs between them.

"Anyway, I want to part on good terms. I need to let her say her good-byes to everyone and then help her pack up her stuff and head back to L.A."

"She's going to miss the *Wild Tropics* premiere we have planned," Holly notes, sliding out of the cart as Jake comes to a stop in Hal's driveway.

Jake gives a faint smile. "Yeah, I guess she will."

They walk together up the stone path to Hal's bungalow. Holly cradles Sadie's ashes in her hands. Inside is a frail widower who's been waiting to be reunited with his wife's cremains, and a middle-aged daughter with the decision about what to do with her dad still ahead of her. Holly prepares herself for the sad scene.

"You ready?" Jake asks, hand poised to knock. Holly nods.

Paula Pillory opens the door with a smile. "Holly!" She pops the screen door and reaches out to pull Holly into a one-armed hug. "How are you? Come in."

Holly makes the introductions and follows Paula into the sitting room. There's a loveseat and a reclining chair with a small coffee table, all facing an older box television in one corner. Everything is neat and dusted, and a stack of magazines is lined up on the coffee table.

"Can I get you anything?"

"No, thank you. We just wanted to return something to your dad that we know he's been missing."

Paula's eyes fill with tears. "Ohhhh," she says. "My mom." She reaches out for the box and takes it from Holly gingerly, placing it on the table. "I can't believe you found her—where was she?"

Jake looks at the lines in the freshly vacuumed carpet. His hands are clasped behind his back politely.

Holly tears her eyes from Jake and turns her attention back to Paula. "Hal buried her behind the chapel, and I had a hunch about it that turned out to be right."

"Thank you—both of you. This will bring so much peace to his heart. He's napping right now, but I'll show him as soon as he wakes up." Paula sits on the edge of the recliner and motions for them to take the loveseat. She's a thick-legged woman of fifty-nine with a head of tightly permed gray curls, and she's dressed in a knee-length shift dress and Birkenstock sandals. Her upper arms are soft and freckled.

"What do you think now that you've spent some time with him?" Holly asks.

"Well," Paula says, slapping her knees and leaning back in the chair. "I think he's been better. It's hard to see your own parents decline, and it's definitely a situation where you aren't always the most objective person. I've talked to Dr. Potts quite a bit, and she's made some recommendations. I know Dad doesn't want to leave the island, but I also know he isn't your responsibility at this point. I'm still working out the details here because I need to get back to Ohio."

"We all love Hal," Holly assures her.

"I know you do," Paula says, her eyes crinkling. "And I can't tell you how grateful I am for the way your grandparents took in my folks and made them a part of this community. It was a blessing for them."

"Your mom was an amazing woman." Holly glances at the framed black-and-white photos of Hal and Sadie on the small end table next to her side of the couch. In the pictures, Sadie is a young bride with a smooth, unlined face and bow-shaped lips. "She would read to me for hours and hours when she was my teacher."

Paula nods, her eyes full of fondness and memory. "She did the same for me. And when I was in veterinary school she'd stay up all night, helping me cram for tests and memorize the parts of a cat's intestinal tract the way some moms teach their little girls how to apply make-up or choose matching shoes and purses. She was quite a gal." Holly and Jake laugh appreciatively. "Anyhow, I need to get back to my practice. I've got three more years until I can retire, and I have another doctor seeing my patients while I'm down here for a week or so."

"Of course," Holly says.

"So my options are either to take Dad up to Ohio and find a facility for him, which—in my opinion—will do nothing but age him and speed up his decline, or I can find a way for him to stay put."

"We've been pitching in here to look after him the best we can," Jake says, clearing his throat. "And no one wants to see him out wandering the beach at night with a shovel or putting himself in harm's way."

"Oh, I know that, honey," Paula assures him, leaning forward and stretching a hand out in Jake's direction. "It's not on you all to look after him. My daughter, Katelynn, is willing to come down and give it a shot. She's a freelance journalist, and her son, Connor, is sixteen." Paula turns to Holly. "Much like your own mother, she entered parenthood before she'd exited her teens, and she's been a single mom to my grandson ever since. Having them come down here is one option."

Holly and Jake exchange a fast glance; a teenager on the island? It's something to be discussed at a later date.

"That sounds like a real possibility," Holly says.

"It is. And it'll need to happen fast if it's going to happen." Paula stands up and straightens her linen dress. "I'll keep you posted and let you know as soon as I have everything worked out." Holly and Jake stand, following her lead. Paula walks them to the door. "Thank you again," she says, reaching out to give Holly a hug and offering Jake a hand to shake. "This means more to my dad than you know."

Holly and Jake wave to Paula as they climb back into Jake's cart. The holes that Hal had complained about that day in his front yard have long been filled, and the patches of brown dirt dot the grass like crop circles left by unknown beings. Holly watches his house as it disappears behind them.

"Well, that was depressing," she says, thinking of Hal and Sadie as they used to be.

"No, *that*," Jake says solemnly, "was life."

CHAPTER 30

The morning of the premiere is a busy one. Holly and Bonnie are putting the finishing touches on the B&B's dining room to make sure it looks worthy of a Hollywood bash, and the triplets have volunteered to iron the white tablecloths and napkins for the tables. Buckhunter has a bar set up in the corner of the dining room with a variety of bottles and clean glasses lined up on a cart, and Fiona is on her knees next to the bar, fixing a string of lights to it so that it looks like a marquee when it's all lit up. She's done the same thing to the overhang of the B&B with strings of white bulbs, and the red carpet they've rented from a prop shop in Tampa had arrived by boat the day before and is now waiting to be rolled out.

"Do we have enough candles?" Holly shouts to Bonnie as she hurries through the dining room holding a stack of the programs that they've put together on the B&B's computer. "I want to be able to turn off all the lights in the dining room during the show and still have it bright enough for people to keep eating and drinking while we watch."

"We have two hundred tea lights and a hundred tall pillars, sugar. I feel like we've got it covered, but I can go and hunt in the storage room for more if you like."

"Would you, Bon?" Holly wipes at her brow and fishes her cell phone out of the back pocket of her shorts. April is coming to a close, and the heat of summer is pressing up against the island like an insistent Avon lady ringing a doorbell.

"You got it." Bonnie sashays out of the dining room through the French doors. She brushes past Wyatt and Cap as they wheel in potted ficus plants on dollies. Wyatt pauses and glances over his shoulder at Bonnie as she goes.

"Those can go all around the room, guys," Holly instructs, pointing at the spots along the wall where she's planning on filling in with the trees. Fiona has more white twinkle lights in a box on a table in the middle of the room, and the triplets are going to wind all of the ficus plants with lights to give the room even more of a glow at night.

"Hol?" Fiona calls, standing up. "Does this look right?" She plugs in the lights that she's just put around the bar.

Holly looks at it. "Yeah. I like that." She jabs a pen through the loose bun she's made on top of her head and strides over to the open doorway to meet Jake.

"You wanted help pressure-washing the sidewalk?" he asks. He's still wearing his sunglasses, and his black police t-shirt is clinging to his torso with sweat after driving around all morning in the humidity.

"If you have time. If not, it can probably stay as is." Holly tries to keep her tone as neutral as possible. She'd forced herself to go to the Ho Ho the night Bridget had been there to say good-bye to everyone, and things had been cool but cordial between her and Jake for several weeks since.

"No, it's fine. It'll only take about fifteen minutes. Your red carpet won't look good on a dirty porch and sidewalk. Where's the pressure washer?"

"Jimmy brought it over from the bistro and left it in the B&B's parking lot," Holly says, pointing east.

"Okay. I'm on it." As Jake turns and walks through the lobby and out into the bright sunlight, Holly watches his strong back. With luck, things will be normal between them again someday. Or maybe just normal-ish.

Holly's cell phone rings and she pulls it from her pocket again. It's a Facetime call from River.

"Hey," she says as his face pops up on her screen. "What's new?"

"Just checking in to see how the movie premiere is shaping up."

"Hollywood has come to Christmas Key," Holly says, turning the view of the screen around so she can show him the dining room. "It actually doesn't look like much yet, but it's going to be awesome. We even rented a projector and a giant screen from the same prop store we got the red carpet from."

"You never cease to amaze me," River marvels. Holly turns the view around so that he's looking at her face again. "How's everything else?"

Holly takes her phone and wanders down the hall toward the B&B's kitchen. "Well, Hal's son is here temporarily to take care of him while his granddaughter gets her life in order to move down. She'll be bringing her teenage son with her, so...that's going to take some getting used to."

River laughs. "A teenage boy on Christmas Key? He's going to be miserable."

"You think?"

"I know. What is there for him to do but get into trouble? No girls, no excitement, no friends. You thought six-year-old boys were a handful—just wait." River glances around and the camera jostles on his end.

"Where are you?" Holly pushes open the door to the kitchen and peeks in at the activity. She's got six women plus Jimmy Cafferkey in there cooking, and it smells like chicken marsala and heaven. She takes a deep breath and lets the door swing shut again so that she won't disturb them.

"The store," River says. "I'm waiting in line."

"Whatcha buying? Pudding cups and paper clips? Dog bones and denture cream? Balloons and buckwheat?"

"Denture cream and buckwheat?" River makes a face. "You need to spend less time with old people."

"You're right," Holly glances around to make sure she's alone in the B&B hallway, "and to that end, we're finally about to get out of Dodge."

"I feel like we've been planning this trip forever," River says, leaning forward and disappearing from view. "And now it's almost here."

Holly sighs. She still has a lot to do to get ready for their trip. And beyond that, she still has a lot to do to get ready for the premiere in five hours. "Hey, can I call you later? I need to keep setting up here."

"Sure. Call me whenever." The relaxed look on River's face reminds Holly of how things had been when they'd first met the summer before. Gone was the strained distance that had divided them during his visit at Christmas, and back was the playful, trusting River she'd first been attracted to. Jake hadn't been a part of their conversation in weeks, and if things went well, he wouldn't come up at all on their trip.

Holly is out on the front steps of the B&B observing the activity on Main Street when Mexi and Mori come running up the sidewalk with Carrie-Anne and Ellen close behind.

"Holly!" Mexi calls, nearly tripping as he skids to a stop in front of the B&B. "Guess what we saw?"

Holly walks down the stairs and sits on the bottom step so that she's closer to eye level with the boys. "What did you see?"

"We saw a tow-key give boith!" Mori shouts, stealing his brother's thunder.

"You saw a turkey give birth?" Holly looks up at Ellen, who is standing behind the boys with both hands on her hips.

"We've been waiting for it," Ellen confirms. "Even got a video of it if you want to see."

"Maybe later," Holly says. The thought of birth and all its inherent gore leaves her feeling squeamish. "But you didn't tell me we were going to have turkey babies on the island."

"Well, doll, you give us ten turkeys and then just guess what's bound to happen!" Carrie-Anne looks at the top of the twins' heads fondly. "We have Mexi and Mori out to our place once a week for an hour to help take care of the animals. We've been waiting and waiting for these eggs to hatch, and today we got lucky and had one of the babies finally make her appearance."

"It's a boy," Mexi says. "We're naming him Thor." Over their heads, Carrie-Anne cups her face with both hands and mouths the word 'girl' to Holly.

"Thor, huh?" Holly says with enthusiasm. "Who's his mommy?"

"Godiva." Mexi turns to his brother. "Right?"

"No, it's Twik-thee," Mori says.

"Nuh-uh. Trixie is the *grandma*," Mexi argues.

"They're all family." Ellen puts a hand on top of each of the boys' heads to stop the bickering. "And we need to finish picking grass for Madonkey to eat and take it back to her before she starves." The boys drop all discussion of the turkeys and instead tilt their heads to look up at Ellen with concern. "I'm kidding, guys—she won't really starve."

Holly laughs and waves at the foursome as they continue up Main Street to pick grass in the wooded area that starts at Cinnamon Lane. Her neighbors have held up their end of the bargain like champs: as soon as they'd found Sadie's ashes and put the mystery of the holes behind them, they'd all signed on to donate their time and expertise to help round out the schooling that Vance and Calista are doing online with the boys.

Aside from the weekly lessons on animal care from Ellen and Carrie-Anne, Cap has taken Mexi and Mori out on his boat a few times already, instructing them about water safety, tides, and how to catch fish. Fiona has pitched in by teaching the boys how to swim in the B&B pool, and she's also had them come by the office twice to study the posters on her walls as they learn about bones and muscles. The boys spend one hour a week on Monday mornings at The Jingle Bell Bistro, where Jimmy Cafferkey has given them basic lessons on how to be careful in the kitchen and how to measure things. Heddie Lang-Mueller sits with them at the tables outside Mistletoe Morning Brew on Thursday afternoons to teach them a little German, and Jake and Holly take turns showing them what the civic duties of a police officer and a mayor look like.

It's all working out so far, and the rotating cast of "teachers" has freed up Calista to work more at the salon, and Vance to write his novel and start thinking again about opening up the bookstore next to Mistletoe Morning Brew. And whether they'll admit it or not, the islanders get a lot of joy out of teaching something they know about to the little guys. It's helped to smooth over all the bumps and snags they've hit since the beginning of the year, including the animosity towards Bridget that ultimately sent her away, the various mishaps and accidents, and Bonnie's leaving and returning.

"Unless you want to end up looking like an extra in a Warrant video, then you might want to move," Jake says, hefting the pressure washer into place on the sidewalk. Holly looks down at her white t-shirt and then back at Jake's hose.

"Christmas Key has never hosted a wet t-shirt contest," she says. "Let me see if I can get Mrs. Agnelli on board." Holly stands up from where she's been sitting on the bottom step. "Maybe Heddie and Millie will want to get in on it."

"Let's not permanently scar my mind's eye, huh?" Jake plugs the extension cord into an outlet on the outside of the B&B.

"Thanks again for doing this," Holly says. She takes off her Yankees cap and wipes at the sweat on her forehead before putting the hat back on again. "I'd better go in and finish up in the dining room. See you tonight?"

"I'll be the dashing gent in the tux and tails," Jake deadpans.

"Really? You'll be in a tux?" Holly pauses on the top step of the B&B, hand on the doorframe.

"No, but I promise to wear something nicer than my sweaty uniform."

"That works."

Jake switches on the pressure washer and a loud, repetitive blast fills the air as he starts to hose down the sidewalk. Holly shuts the door to keep the water out.

CHAPTER 31

The stars are out that night as people pull up to the curb in their golf carts. Holly and Bonnie stand on the top step of the B&B holding cameras and snapping photos like paparazzi as the islanders step onto the sidewalk.

"Hi, Holly!" Emily Cafferkey climbs out of the back of her parents' golf cart in a pink knee-length satin dress. Her blonde hair is twisted up and clipped on top of her head, and Iris has applied a swipe of pink lipstick and some mascara to her daughter's face.

Holly holds up her camera and snaps a photo of Emily standing next to her mom. "Hi, ladies. You look beautiful!" She and Bonnie hug both Iris and Emily as they ascend the stairs, holding hands for support in their dress shoes. Jimmy Cafferkey gives a wave and then pulls the cart forward to park it up the street.

Bonnie is dressed in a silver top with sequins and a long black skirt, and her red hair has been curled and coiffed by Millie just that afternoon. After spending the day hanging spray-painted gold stars that look like the ones on the Hollywood Walk of Fame around the dining room, Holly had raced home to change. She'd spent fifteen minutes scrubbing under her nails to get rid of the paint while a conditioner sat in her hair, and she'd quickly applied two coats of red polish to her nails as she sat on the lanai to let her hair dry. Without a closet full of dressy clothes to choose from, she'd settled on a knee-length black sheath that she'd worn on a weekend trip to Miami with Jake one time, and she'd accessorized with bare legs, black high-heeled sandals, and her grandmother's diamond earrings.

"This is a real bang-up event, Mayor," Wyatt Bender says, holding her hand in his and leaning in to place a kiss on her cheek.

"Thanks, Wyatt. It's not every day that Christmas Key is on the verge of becoming a household name, you know?"

"Indeed." Wyatt lets go of Holly's hand and turns to Bonnie. "Miss Lane," he says, bowing slightly at the waist. "You take my breath away. No goddess of the silver screen has ever been so lovely."

Bonnie flushes hotly under the B&B's porch lights. "Well, you do have a way with words, Wyatt Bender," she allows, watching him as he takes her hand and kisses the top of it. "If you play your cards right, I might sit with you during dinner."

"I would be honored, ma'am," he says in his thick Southern accent.

Once Wyatt has disappeared inside the B&B, Holly leans over to Bonnie and whispers in her ear. "Shouldn't Wyatt have gone back to Texas by now?"

Bonnie's blush deepens. "I suppose he usually leaves around April first."

"And yet here we are at nearly May first, and old Wyatt is still kicking around the island..." Holly lifts her eyebrows. Wyatt is one of a handful of islanders who still spends summers somewhere other than Christmas Key, but if Holly were to place bets, she'd be willing to wager that he's more than a little worried that leaving the island—even for a season—might mean he comes back in the fall to find Bonnie shacked up with a pirate or hitched to a fisherman who's just passing through.

After everyone has arrived and the guests have filtered through the dimmed lobby and passed through a doorway ringed in twinkling lights, Holly and Bonnie close the front door and head into the dining room. It looks amazing with the white tablecloths, gold stars, and hundreds of flickering candles. The happy chit-chat of the islanders fills the room as they visit and sip cocktails.

Everyone who pitched in to prepare the meal has changed into their own fancy clothes, and a buffet table along one wall is laden with plates and silver serving dishes full of chicken marsala, garlic mashed potatoes, and green beans florentine. Buckhunter nods at Holly from behind the bar in the corner as he tips a bottle of rum over a glass and adds a splash to the drink he's mixing.

"Are you nervous?" Jake asks, materializing at Holly's side.

"Not really. Are you?"

He shrugs. He's wearing a black blazer and a collared white shirt. Holly can smell his aftershave.

"I feel pretty confident that I won't embarrass myself," Jake says. "But it is kind of weird to think that strangers all over America are about to watch me on TV."

"Yeah. And it's weird to think that people will be seeing our beaches—*our island*—for the first time. I wonder what they'll think." Holly folds her arms. Her eyes fall to her own cleavage, and she realizes how low-cut her black dress is. When she looks back up at Jake, he's staring at the giant screen that they'll project the show onto.

"They'll probably think it's paradise," Jake says. People get up from the tables, leaving their drinks behind as they trickle over to the buffet to start serving themselves dinner. "They won't see it as the lonely place it really is."

Holly frowns. "Jake," she says, putting her red-tipped hand on his arm. "I don't want you to be lonely."

He smiles and a quiet laugh that sounds like a sharp exhale escapes him. "Well, Hol, sometimes I am. I can't win for trying here. And you and I go back-and-forth on a daily basis: are we angry today, or are we joking? Are we friends? Are there still feelings? I never know which way is up with you."

Holly smiles at the triplets as they walk past with full plates in their hands. "We're friends, of course," she says, pressing her lips together. "Always."

"But?"

"But what?"

"But you weren't sad at all when things didn't work out with me and Bridget, and you're still talking to River, right?" His left eyebrow lifts a fraction of an inch, but in this small movement, she senses a challenge.

Holly's been trying to keep her face neutral so their conversation will look like nothing more than friendly cocktail chatter to anyone who passes by.

"Right?" he presses.

"Yes. I am still talking to River."

Jake nods. "I decided that I'm going to take a leave of absence," he says. "Maybe if I disappear for a few weeks, I can clear my head and come back here with a different outlook on things."

"Jake, you don't have to go..."

"No, I do. I feel like if you and I don't spend some time apart, I'm going to have to leave for good."

Holly bites her lower lip. She hasn't been looking forward to this moment. "I mean, you don't have to leave," she pauses, "because I am."

Wyatt turns on the projector and an Olive Garden commercial fills the screen. They're just minutes from the start of *Wild Tropics*, and everyone is taking their seats.

"Where are you going?" Jake lowers his chin, looking at her intently.

"Europe. For three weeks. I'm leaving on May eleventh."

Understanding registers on his face. "With River." It's not a question.

Holly looks down at the criss-crossing straps of the sandals on her feet. "With River," she confirms.

"I guess that will give me time, won't it?" When Holly looks up at him again, his Adam's apple is bobbing in his throat. He swallows repeatedly. "We should get dinner." Without looking at her again, Jake walks over to the buffet and serves himself a plate.

"Mayor," Wyatt whispers loudly to get Holly's attention. "I can put this on mute if you want to say a few words." He points at the projector.

Holly takes one last glance at the back of Jake's dark head from across the room before heading up to the podium that she uses for the village council meetings.

"Hi, good evening," she says into her microphone. The candles on the table closest to her make her earrings sparkle. "Welcome to the world premiere of *Wild Tropics*," she says. "I hope you all think this Hollywood-worthy evening is as much fun as I do." Applause breaks out around the room. "Thank you. We've been through so much together, and this reality show is the next step on our journey. I don't know anything more than you do at this point—no one has sent me a sneak preview of the pilot episode, and nobody from the network has given me a heads-up about how it was received by test audiences—so I'm going into this as blindly and as hopefully as the rest of you."

Holly looks around at the faces of her neighbors, so different when they're lit from beneath by candlelight in her dining room as compared to when they fill the chairs in broad daylight to discuss the basic operations of the island.

"It's always an honor and a privilege to live amongst people who care about each other the way you all do, and I hope the rest of the world sees this beautiful place for what it is." On the screen behind her, the commercials end and the opening credits of the show begin. The islanders whoop with joy, holding their drinks in the air in a toast. Holly glances over her shoulder. "Here we are! So, without further ado..."

She ducks away from the podium and takes a spot at the round table in the center of the room where Fiona and Buckhunter have saved her a seat.

Everyone cheers when Jake appears for the first time, and there are jolts of excitement as people recognize island landmarks and familiar spots.

Fiona leans her shoulder into Holly's to get her attention. "What's with Jake?" she whispers, lifting her chin in his direction.

"I told him I was leaving for three weeks," Holly whispers back. The candles on the table flicker hotly, blurring her view of Jake as he sits in his chair with a drink in one hand.

"Ohhhh," Fiona says. "Poor guy."

"Why? My trip has nothing to do with him," Holly says, feeling defensive.

Fiona puts her hand on top of Holly's on the white tablecloth. "Of course not," she says. "It's about you and River." There isn't a hint of sarcasm in Fiona's words, but Holly knows her well enough to know that she isn't totally convinced.

Arguing the point will just make it sound like she's in some sort of denial, so Holly stays silent all throughout *Wild Tropics.* It's pretty amazing to see the show come to life. Even when Bridget and Jake interact on screen and their interest in each other is evident, Holly is impressed with the way the island looks. It's clearly an undeveloped paradise, and the network has already laid out the premise for the viewers, which means that this first episode sets up the fact that the competitors are actually on a Christmas-themed island without knowing it.

"What time do you leave tomorrow?" Holly asks Fiona when the show goes to commercial break.

"We're taking the boat to Miami at three o'clock." The swim to Cuba that she's been prepping for all spring is this weekend, and she and Buckhunter are heading over on Friday afternoon to stay on South Beach and enjoy a weekend away. It will be the first time Holly can remember that Buckhunter hasn't been around to open Jack Frosty's on a weekend, but she's happy for them; they deserve to get off the island as much as she does.

"Make sure Buckhunter takes lots of pictures of you swimming and sends them to me so I can put them on our Instagram," Holly says, fishing her silenced phone out of the black clutch purse in her lap. As she'd suspected and hoped, her phone is full of notifications from all of the island's social media accounts: people have already looked up Christmas Key and started following them on Facebook, Twitter, and Instagram. "Wow," she says under her breath, using one finger to scroll through all the notifications.

Fiona leans over to see the screen. "Holy cow," she says in shock. "Are all those new followers?"

"Yep," Holly says, distracted. "All new." There's a moment of confusion inside her that feels like a storm brewing; it's exciting to have people be so curious about the island, but it's also surreal. Strangers are now following Christmas Key on Instagram and looking at photos of Cap holding up a giant marlin on the dock, Millie standing in front of Scissors & Ribbons with her arms spread wide on opening day, and

Ellen and Carrie-Anne smiling behind the counter of Mistletoe Morning Brew as the sun shines through their brand new front window. Holly realizes for the first time that viewers will have opinions about Jake and Bridget's relationship on the show, and that people she might never meet will comment on her photos and posts.

Holly swallows hard and locks her phone, putting it back inside her purse. She reminds herself that she's invited these changes, she's waited for this day, and she welcomes the potential influx of tourism and interest. It's all going to be fine.

When the pilot episode of *Wild Tropics* ends, the islanders sit in the dim room and talk by candlelight, dissecting the first show. Holly makes the rounds, stopping at the various tables to hear what everyone thinks. The comments are overwhelmingly positive, and there's a general feeling of excitement, even from those who were most reticent about the initial idea of a reality show.

By ten o'clock, Holly's sent the last stragglers home, and even Bonnie is looking beat. They've gathered all the dinner plates, silverware, glasses, and serving dishes, and Holly kicks off her heels on the carpet of the dining room as she pulls the tablecloths off the tables and collects napkins from chairs.

"Here, hon, let me start that load," Bonnie says, holding out her arms and taking a huge pile of linens from Holly. It'll probably take two loads to get everything washed, but Holly will be happy if they get just one done tonight.

"Bon," she says, lifting up her right foot and examining the blister that's formed where her sandal bit into her skin all evening. "Why don't you throw that in the wash, and then we can just call it a night. I'd rather come back in the morning and do the dishes."

"Are you sure?" Bonnie calls over her shoulder on her way to the laundry room. She sounds tired and Holly can tell that it won't take much convincing to send her home.

"I'm positive," she says, picking up her sandals and purse from the floor. She takes a look around the dining room. It'll be just as easy to rearrange the tables and chairs and run the vacuum in the morning; this room can wait.

Holly tosses her shoes and purse onto a chair in the small lobby and bends over to pick up the end of the red carpet. She drags it toward her, rolling it on the ground like a snowball and gathering more carpet as she goes.

"Are we sending everything back tomorrow?" Bonnie walks into the lobby, unfastening the earrings on her lobes as she does. She tosses them into her handbag.

"Monday. The carpet, projector, and screen should all leave on the boat heading for Tampa at noon."

"Perfect. And you're sure about leaving the dishes for morning, sugar?" Bonnie wrinkles her brow.

"Of course. Thank you for all your help, Bon," Holly kicks the rug with her bare foot and it rolls to the side. She opens her arms and pulls Bonnie in for a quick hug. They hold each other for just a moment longer than is necessary. "I'm so glad you're home," Holly says in Bonnie's ear.

Bonnie squeezes back with so much force that it feels like Holly's ribs might snap. "Honey, I'm so glad to be home. I never should have left—it won't happen again."

The women pull away and look into one each other's eyes. "But don't ever stop looking for love and adventure, you promise?" Holly searches Bonnie's gaze intently. "I want you to be happy."

Tears fill Bonnie's eyes and she blinks fast. "Sugar," she says, taking Holly's hands in her own. "I've never been more happy."

Holly watches as Bonnie walks out of the B&B and onto Main Street. Her cart is parked within view, so Holly locks the front door behind her and switches off the lights in the lobby. With no guests on the island, she's the only person left inside the B&B. It's rare to have an empty inn and to be there totally alone, and Holly basks in the silence for a minute, looking out at the darkened storefronts on Main Street from her own unlit lobby.

After Bonnie switches on her headlamps and pulls away, Holly wanders the hallways. She's still shoeless, and her footsteps are muffled on the floors of the carpeted hallway. The wall sconces light her way to the kitchen, where Holly switches on the little silver radio that sits on a shelf. She messes with the dial until she gets a fuzzy station all the way from New Orleans. Prince's "Raspberry Beret" is playing.

The counters are stacked high with dirty plates, and the glasses are filled with food-caked utensils. The pans that the evening's chefs had used to prepare everything have already been run through the industrial-sized dishwasher. Holly pulls the door open and steam puffs out and fills the air. It takes her about ten minutes to get everything from the dishwasher hand-dried and put away, and then she spends the next hour rinsing the dishes from the dining room with the hand-held hose in the deep, stainless steel sink. She washes off the remnants of dinner, and stacks the plates and cups and silverware in the huge dishwasher.

The announcer on the radio station comes on to let his listeners know that someone has called in to request Milli Vanilli.

"Y'all think I'm joking here," says the deejay in a husky voice, "but I take my music seriously. So Benjamin Carl, if you were only playing around with this request, then you're now being punished. Crank it up good, my friends—we've got "Blame it on the Rain" by the unforgettable Rob and Fab."

Holly wipes her brow with her wrist and dances around a little as the opening beats of the song fill the kitchen. She knew when she sent Bonnie home that she wasn't going to leave until the kitchen was clean, and there's something cathartic and right about doing the job herself.

By eleven-thirty the dishwasher is humming again, and the counters have been wiped until they shine. Holly's swept the kitchen floor and run the steam mop over it, and everything—the olive oil, pepper grinder, bottle opener, and even the can of cornstarch—is back in its rightful place, tucked into cupboards or drawers like sleeping soldiers.

She switches off the kitchen lights and heads to the lobby to grab her shoes and purse. The night has been a success, and it's invigorating to think about where *Wild Tropics* might take the island. It's still amazing to Holly to think of people all over the country watching a show that takes place on Christmas Key, but this moment has been inevitable since the second that she officially signed on with the network. Still...the reality of it is going to take some getting used to.

The night is warm and the scent of orange blossoms follows Holly as she putters up Cinnamon Lane with her high-heeled sandals on the seat next to her. The moon is full and bright, and her mind wanders to her upcoming trip. She's never been to Europe. The idea that the Eiffel Tower and Big Ben are real, and that she'll see them with her own eyes, feels as foreign to her as Christmas Key must feel to the people seeing it on their television screens for the first time.

Holly's tires crunch over shells and sand as she turns left into her driveway. The property is illuminated by moonlight. Buckhunter's cart is already parked next to his house, and Holly pulls up to her own porch and drags the cord away from the wall of her house to plug into her golf cart so that it will charge while she sleeps.

Glancing around her yard, Holly listens to the unseen night animals chattering and chirping to one another. This place is her heaven, her home—no trip abroad will change that. And yet, she still wants to know what's out there, and to see how things are between her and River when they're not on Christmas Key. There's so much change afoot that she can hardly process it all in one go. Instead, she sits on the back of her golf cart under the moon, watching her red toenails catch the light as her feet dangle off the ground. She thinks about Jake being on television, about people who call in to a radio station to request Milli Vanilli, and about chicken marsala and rum drinks.

Finally, when the sounds of the cicadas and the crickets and the beating of dragonfly wings turn into one steady, calming hum in her ears, Holly slides off the back of her cart and walks up the steps of her front porch, sandals dangling from one hand, purse clutched in the other.

She takes one last look at the full moon, then shuts her door behind her and switches off the porch light.

You just finished book three of the Christmas Key Series! Download Book four, *More Than This*, to find out what happens next!

READY FOR THE NEXT BOOK
IN THE CHRISTMAS KEY
SERIES?

Christmas Key will have to function without its beloved mayor, Holly Baxter, while she embarks on a European adventure with her long-distance love...Join Holly and River on their journey across the pond!

ABOUT THE AUTHOR

Stephanie Taylor is a high-school teacher who loves sushi, "The Golden Girls," Depeche Mode, orchids, and coffee. Together with her teenage daughter she writes the *American Dream* series—books for young girls about other young girls who move to America. On her own, Stephanie is the author of the *Christmas Key* books, a romantic comedy series about a fictional island off the coast of Florida.

https://redbirdsandrabbits.com
redbirdsandrabbits@gmail.com

ALSO BY STEPHANIE TAYLOR

To see a complete list of the Christmas Key series along with all of Stephanie's other books, please visit:

Stephanie Taylor's Books

To hear about any new releases, sign up here and you'll be the first to know!